I0659827

Interesting Times

The Richard Jackson Saga, Volume 11

Ed Nelson

Published by Eastern Shore Publishing, 2024.

Table of Contents

Other books by Ed Nelson

The Richard Jackson Saga

Book 1 The Beginning

Book 2 Schooldays

Book 3 Hollywood

Book 4 In the Movies

Book 5 Star to Deckhand

Book 6 Surfing Dude

Book 7 Third Time is a Charm

Book 8 Oxford University

Book 9 Cold War

Book 10 Taking Care of Business

Book 11 Interesting Times

Book 12 Escape from Siberia

Book 13 Regicide

Book 14 What's Under, Down Under?

Book 15 The Lunar Kingdom

Book 16 First Steps

In the Richard Jackson World

Mary, Mary

Stand-Alone Story

Ever and Always

Cast in Time Series

Book 1: Baron

Book 2: Baron of the Middle Counties

Book 3: Count

Book 4: Earl

Book 5: Earl of the Marches

Dedication

This is dedicated to my wife Carol for her support and help as my first reader and editor.

Thanks to my Editors, Ernest Bywater, Lonelydad57, Old Rotorhead, Lon, and Antti.

Also, the Bellefontaine High School Class of 1962 just because.

Professionally edited by Janet E. Rupert

Quotation

That's the way it happened, give or take a lie or two."

James Garner as Wyatt Earp, describing the gunfight at the OK Corral in the movie *Sunset*.

Copyright © 2021

Chapter 1

On Tuesday, January 2nd, I flew back to London on my jet. Nina was staying an extra week with her parents. Her school wasn't back in session until the following Monday. It is just as well; things had been heating up with us, and I don't know what would have happened with the two of us alone for many hours and a bed right there.

We both agreed that was where we wanted to go but that it was too soon; we had some living to do before we settled down. Neither of us was the type to casually have sex; by our upbringing, it would result in a lifelong commitment.

I had picked up copies of the *LA Times* and *Variety* to read on the flight.

I found it interesting that the US Navy created a group called SEALs, formed from World War II groups known as the Scouts and Raiders. There would be two teams. There was SEAL Team 1 stationed on the Pacific and Team 2 on the Atlantic.

The article told how they traced their origins to the Scouts and Raiders, Naval Combat Demolition Units, Office of Strategic Services, Operational Swimmers, Underwater Demolition Teams, and Motor Torpedo Boat Squadrons of World War II. It seemed to me like they were just rearranging deck chairs.

In *Variety*, I learned that the Beatles auditioned with Decca Records and were turned down. I think someone at Decca will live to regret that decision.

I also read about the NBC Laramie Peacock, which debuted last night. It was used to highlight their shows in color. The black-and-white programs were disappearing.

Dad had bought two color sets for Jackson House, one for the entertainment room and one for his and Mum's bedroom. How decadent!

I had a good night's sleep flying over the North Pole. They called it the polar route; I don't know how close we got. I didn't care enough to go up front and ask.

When I first obtained this aircraft, I had all sorts of intentions of riding up front and getting hours in. Somehow, that wasn't happening. I needed to decide and stick to it.

We landed in Oxford, where the plane was based, but I immediately went over to flight operations and filed a flight plan to London in my Cessna.

It was early morning here, and I had a noon lunch meeting with Mr. Norman about my Queen's Messenger's duties. I would be staying in London overnight—no rest for the wicked.

Harold packed me an overnight bag, and I had plenty of clothes at the Plaza. It is a wonder he didn't have a full wardrobe there. I wasn't going to mention it. I could afford it, but it seemed silly.

Lunch had been those little watercress sandwiches with the crust trimmed off that I hate. I would have to get a snack to tide me over until dinner.

Some ham or beef on them would have helped, and maybe a slice of cheese with a little mustard and lose the watercress and keep the crust.

I didn't say anything as he seemed to enjoy them. You can pick up a lot of bad habits over time.

The subject of my meeting was my trip. He wanted the highlights, not of my business but the political part. Mao's death had come as a shocking surprise to the world.

A full-blown civil war was underway, with Deng Xiaoping's following winning. They had support and weapons from some unknown source. They knew where the weapons were coming from, Russia, but they didn't know who supplied the money.

I was in a quandary as I realized who was backing this revolution. Me! It didn't take me long to decide to come clean. They would find out in the long run.

"I have guaranteed a one hundred-million-dollar loan through a bank in Switzerland for food and weapons. I did it to prevent mass starvation. I didn't think at the time it would have much impact on the fighting."

"You are telling me that you, as a private citizen, without the backing of Her Majesty's government, have financed a revolution?"

I responded with a hangdog-sounding yes, thinking I was about to get my head handed to me.

"Sir Richard, this is great. The government has deniability, but when Deng wins, we can take credit."

I didn't think it would be that simple, but I kept my mouth shut.

"What was used to secure the loan? Where is the paperwork?"

"There isn't any."

"What, paperwork or something to secure the loan?"

"Neither, I sealed the deal with a handshake with Lady Ping."

At this, his mouth worked momentarily as he tried to get some words out that wouldn't form.

"You're telling me that you know the empress-in-exile of China well enough to hand her a hundred million dollars on a handshake?"

"Yes, I like her and think she will be honest with me."

"How long have you known her, and how did you meet?"

"She has always been my contact at those dry-cleaning pickups."

"We never suspected."

I think Mr. Norman gave something away there; he was more connected with MI6 than he let on. My name is Norman, John Norman. Nah, it doesn't have the ring to it.

"My head is spinning from the possible ramifications of this. Do you think Deng will take political power but put the empress back on the throne?"

"I have no idea, though I would support that; she is good for China."

"We have to discuss this with the Queen. She may want to recognize Lady Ping in the title in advance. It would open a lot of doors in China."

"I can see that. Please let me know how that comes out."

"Nonsense, you are coming with me."

At that, he called the Queen's private secretary and made us an appointment just before dinner. This bummed me out as I wouldn't be able to work in a snack before dinner.

We spent the rest of the afternoon reviewing possible scenarios to present to the Queen. I asked if the prime minister would be involved and was told that this was a chance for the Crown to be ahead of the politicians, so no.

They would be told, just not upfront. They would try to take over this opportunity to normalize relations with China and bungle it as usual.

At long last, we were escorted into Her Majesty's presence. My stomach told me starvation was setting in. I knew better, but tell that to my stomach.

The Queen listened calmly as though she heard about civil wars, enormous loans, weapon deals, and starving populations as if she heard about them all the time. I guess maybe she had.

"The best outcome would be that Deng takes political power while putting the empress back on the throne. The Communist Party would continue in power, but the old guard members who are the true believers are dying out, if not outright being killed in the unpleasantness.

"The newer younger members will be looking for changes where they can come into the modern world and make money and obtain power. The current Chinese economy has been stagnant. There is no room for growth."

"That sounds plausible, Sir Richard. How would you proceed?" asked the Queen.

"I would keep as close of contact as I can with Lady Ping. At the same time, I can shift my finances around so that I could free up another one hundred million to support the Deng group."

"That is an awful risk you are taking. We cannot back your finances in any way."

"I understand, but this is a rare opportunity to help half a billion people better their lives. Besides, I'm only seventeen. I don't need that sort of money. If I were still in Ohio, I would be doing good to have twenty dollars a week.

"As it is, I could end up down to my last fifty million until I made more."

"You poor boy; you go with our best wishes. Mr. Norman, stay for a word."

I backed out of the small room, thinking of food. Just outside the doorway, I had to stop for a footman carrying a heavy load.

I accidentally heard part of a conversation, well, a few words; one of them was dukedom. Nah.

I couldn't get to Arthur Treacher's place for fish and chips fast enough. I didn't inhale them, but I ate them quickly. They were so good I had a second order.

From my hotel room, I placed a call to my parents, updating them on my conversations of the afternoon with both Mr. Norman and the Queen.

I was urged to play this close to my vest. There was a good chance I would lose all my money, and so be it. There was also a chance to do some real good in the world.

Chapter 2

Friday morning, I flew back to Oxford and returned to The Meadows. I had big plans for Friday night. I was to meet up with my friends from school and have a pub night.

I had the house to myself as Grandmum and Mr. Hamilton were still in California enjoying the weather. I hadn't seen their forecast, but it had to be better than England's cold and rain.

As to having the house to myself, the staff was still there. The cook made a wonderful Yorkshire pudding for dinner, so I was ready for a night out.

Bill, Tom, Steve, and I met at the Dog and Crown, our favorite hangout. It had been a while since we had seen each other, so we had a lot of updating to do over a pint or two.

Bill was doing well in school and was going to get a first.

Tom was hanging in there with his current girlfriend. He was a little nervous because she was making wedding hints. He wanted it and didn't want it. I didn't try to give any advice on this.

Steve told us he was considering dropping out of school and joining the army. We had a go at him to find out what was causing this. It turned out his dad's business was in trouble, and money was short.

That is one I could talk about.

"Steve, would a loan help your father get back on his feet?"

"I think so; he says it was just a bad drop-off in business that caught him short. He went to his bank, but they refused him."

I wrote my bank's name and the officer to contact and asked him to give it to his father.

"Rick, I can't ask you to do this."

"You didn't, I volunteered. Do you know how much he needs?"

"He told me ten thousand pounds would do it."

I pulled out my ever-present pocket notebook and wrote a reminder to call the bank early on Monday.

"I'm serious; do it; it is what friends do when they can. Besides, you would be the sloppiest-looking soldier in the history of soldiering."

That last remark worked as intended as the other two piled on about what sort of soldier Steve would make. It relieved the tension and allowed us to return to the serious drinking business.

Since we had last met, I had been involved in that rescue in the creek, broke an arm, been made a baron, killed a robber, and been wounded by him. Then, I made a business trip around the world.

In other words, the usual. They didn't see it that way, but I had come to accept my life.

When I told them about my new jet, they wanted to go somewhere. When they heard about the interior Tom had to ask, "Have you and Nina joined the the-mile-high club?"

"I'm not that sort of boy, but more realistically, she isn't that sort of girl."

That impressed them, not about me but that Nina appeared to be playing a long game. According to them, I was done for.

That wasn't a fate worse than death, so I didn't react to their teasing.

They asked, since I was in Hong Kong, did I have any inside information on Chairman Mao's death.

"Only what is in the papers and what Lady Ping told me." Oops, I shouldn't have said that.

"Who is Lady Ping?"

"The empress-in-exile of China."

"Of course, you would know her. Next, we will hear you are helping her regain her throne."

I tried not to react, but something gave me away. They jumped all over me, "You are! What are you doing, financing their civil war?"

"Guys, I've said too much. We are now in official secrets territory. The Queen could have my head."

When will I learn to keep my big fat mouth shut?

Fortunately, they let it go; it might have been helped by the two young ladies who came up looking for dart partners.

Bill and Steve jumped at the chance; by the look I got from one of the girls, she had missed her target.

The evening wore on, and the stout flowed. I had left my car at my in-town garage. I managed to semi-stagger back there and spend the night.

In the morning, I had a raging headache. I had some aspirins, but they didn't seem to help. I managed to get back to The Meadows where I took a long shower and had the cook fix me a large breakfast.

From the way she rattled her pans, she knew my problem and had no sympathy. I took my coffee and told her I would be in the library. I had to get away from the racket.

I managed to eat my breakfast. At least I didn't have digestive problems at either end. Why did I drink so much? Never again!

I went back to my room and lay down. I ended up sleeping until lunch. I was feeling better by then. At least the anvil chorus had stopped, and it was now the occasional trip hammer.

I hadn't had anything to drink for months, and I wouldn't drink alcohol in the foreseeable future. I wondered how the men in my family managed to become alcoholics.

I hoped that those blighters who had made me drink all that were suffering as bad as I was. Well, maybe they didn't force me, but I didn't mind the thought of them suffering along with me.

Saturday was a lost day. Staff showed their approval of my actions by hoovering any room I was in while playing the wireless loud.

I finally went for a long walk around the grounds. As it was Saturday, work on the ruins and the amusement park was down for the weekend. The fact that it was cold and misting might have had something to do with it.

I kicked around the ruins wondering if I could find more treasure but didn't even find a hobnail. I must say the walk did me a world of good.

Returning to the house, I settled in with a newspaper, *The Telegraph*. The only story of note was that Pope John XXIII had excommunicated Fidel Castro.

The fact that Castro was excommunicated meant little, as he had the guns. What impressed me was Pope John XXIII. Twenty-two previous Popes named John. That had to be a track record. I looked it up in the encyclopedia, and it was.

The funny thing was there was never a Pope John XX. I wondered if there would be a Pope John XXX. Probably not; the church has to watch its image. Though some of the stories the Catholic boys in Bellefontaine told made me wonder if they cared.

Sunday was a quiet day, though it wasn't lost. I spent the day on horseback and then drove into town for dinner. I was getting tired of cook banging around. She certainly didn't approve of drinking.

At the restaurant, I was given a quiet table in the corner as it was a slow night. That didn't deter a man from approaching my table and sitting down without an invitation.

He was a little older than me. He dressed like an Oxford student, carelessly. His accent marked him as a longtime resident.

"Lord Blackhoof, please excuse my rudeness. This appears to be the only way I can talk to you. Since he was polite, I decided to hear him out and signaled the approaching manager that it was okay.

"How can I help you?"

"You already have. I'm here to tell you that Deng is in power now and that Lady Ping will be ascending the throne."

"Any date on her ascension?"

"We think February 1st by your calendar, which is our January 8th. Neither of them are Dragons, so there is no clash. The ceremony will be facing south, the opposite of north, which is evil that day.

"Lady Ping and Chairman Deng have requested your presence to represent the British Crown and an ambassador from the British government."

"I can commit to being there as a private individual. I will have to get the Crown's permission to represent the Queen. As far as an ambassador, that is up to the prime minister and his cabinet, but I suspect they will be happy to send someone."

I could see that Monday would be a terribly busy day. The gentleman gave me a telephone number to call when I could answer the invitations. He gave his name, Hsian-Tsung. He had to be a relative of Lady Ping.

After passing me that information, he got up abruptly and left. I wonder what that was about. I was finished with my meal, so I threw more than enough to pay for the meal and tip on the table and followed him.

I stopped and looked out the restaurant's front window when he went outside. I was glad I did. He seemed to have a security detail that didn't appear to be happy with him. He had dodged them long enough to talk to me.

Not wanting to ruin his risk-taking, I walked to the kitchen door. The manager joined me as he had been watching the curious doings.

"May I leave out the back?"

"Follow me, Lord Blackhoof."

Sometimes notoriety has its advantages. I went down the alley several blocks and came out near my garage, where I had parked my car.

As no one was in sight, I got into the Aston Martin and drove sedately out of town. I may have stepped on it a little when I was outside Oxford limits, but no panda chased me down.

Chapter 3

The first thing I did Monday morning was to call my bank. I explained to my account manager that he would get a call from the father of my friend Steve, who is applying for a loan.

I would guarantee the loan, and even though he would ask for ten thousand pounds, he was to extend a line of credit of twenty-five thousand. Things always cost more than you thought.

I no sooner hung up the phone than I had an incoming call from my movie agent, Clark Miller. It had been a long time since we had communicated. I had instructed him not to send me any scripts until told otherwise.

The last time we talked was commiserating on being snubbed by the Oscar committee. It seems *Over the Ohio* had too much commercial success for their taste. If the common public liked it, it couldn't be highbrow enough for an Oscar.

I will take the money over their silly little statue any day. Granted, it is a true honor for those who earned it, but there was as much politics as worthiness involved.

I learned about this at Warner Brothers. It still didn't mean it didn't sting a little. I thought it was well done, especially since I didn't have many scenes.

Clark wanted to let me know that the Wayne people had contacted him about the script John Wayne had shown me. I apologized for not contacting him. So much else had been going on, feeding a country for one.

Anyway, they were sending him a copy. I still had the one John had given me, and I promised to give it a serious read to see if I was interested, and I would get back to him no matter what. I had some time on my hands now since Oxford didn't seem interested in educating me.

I knew this because when I got back to The Meadows, a letter was waiting for me. I had put off telling my parents or even thinking about it. I was in denial.

Oxford was making my expulsion permanent. They felt I was a bad influence on the student body and traditions of the university. Oh, by the way, my financial contributions were appreciated. Would I keep sending them?

My support for the archaeological dig was in a contract, so I couldn't change that. I wouldn't, anyway. I loved the work and discoveries going on. As far as financial contributions, they must be kidding me!

I will continue to support the military students but not the university's endowment fund. They can go pound salt...up somewhere.

I wonder if a 707 can be used for low-level bombing.

I had to have something to do; maybe a movie would be just the ticket. It would get me out of England, the scene of my disgrace.

After hanging up, I went to get a bottle of Coke, and the phone rang again for me. It was Mr. Norman.

"Rick, I have been expecting a conversation with you about your expulsion from Oxford. Since you haven't called, I thought I would reach out to you."

"To tell the truth, I've had the letter for several days but have been ignoring it."

"Dear boy, you know it won't go away."

"I know. It does hurt. I didn't think hitting the Chancellor in the face with purple dye rated expulsion. I understood being sent down for a term but kicked out for good!"

"It does seem harsh; I made some inquiries. It seems you have riled up some of the senior dons."

"What have I done?"

"Been successful."

"They feel that your success has little to do with them. Since it doesn't reflect well on them, they don't want you overshadowing them."

"How do I overshadow them?"

"They are used to being pointed out when they walk across campus; now all eyes are on you."

"I can't fix their jealousy. It's not that I tried to get in these situations."

"If you had only waited until graduation, they could have taken credit for your successes."

"How inconsiderate of me. Hey, do you know if a 707 can be retrofitted for low-level bombing?"

"Let's not be hasty."

"I won't, but I wouldn't care if they got word I was looking at the option."

"Settle down, or I will call the countess."

"That's another thing I haven't done. I have to tell Mum and Dad."

"Before that, the Queen has asked if you want her to bring her pressure on Oxford."

I had to think about that. I was quiet on my end of the line for a few moments.

"No, it would be a waste for the Crown to use its influence. I don't want to be associated with them going forward, even if they would voluntarily reinstate me."

"All right, I will tell Her Majesty. In the meantime, you should call your parents."

"I'll do that as soon as the time zones let me."

Yeah, wake them in the middle of the night to tell them I've been kicked out of school; not on your life.

Before I hung up, I filled him in on my meeting last night. He told me he would inquire and give me a course of action. It would probably take several days.

I went to the library with my Coke and picked up the script Mr. Wayne had given me. He wanted me to call him John, and I would sometimes, but he would always be Mr. Wayne.

The script was good. I was a perfect fit. A young Englishman, newly arrived in America to study at Yale, accidentally gets involved with the CIA.

His not knowing Americanisms leads to some low comedy. As a counterpoint, there is some heavy action, especially a chase scene in which he is left dangling from the Statue of Liberty.

There were pretty girls involved but no real love interest.

I decided that I would like to do the movie. I called Clark and told him I had gone through the script and wanted to do the part.

He was to open negotiations with the Wayne group. A low salary was okay, but points in the movie an absolute.

He wanted to know how many points.

"As many as you can get. If John Wayne doesn't call me to complain, you haven't tried hard enough."

"I thought you two were friends."

"We are. This is how friends play; I will give in but want to have some fun along the way. Oh yes, and demand a bit part for Nina Monroe."

"Is her father the head of Warner Brothers? That Monroe?"

"Yes, and she is my girlfriend. Happy girlfriend, happy life, or something like that."

"Got it, points and bit part. I will take it from here."

"Thanks, Clark."

It was my day to be on the phone. I called Nina next, not to tell her about the movie; that would wait until it was a done deal. It was to tell her about being kicked out of school.

She already knew. It was in the tabloids. That meant my parents knew, also. Dang.

She was sympathetic, as one would expect from a girlfriend. They were unfair, mean, and nasty. What was I going to do?

I told her negotiations had just opened for a new movie being produced by John Wayne. She thought this would be great.

We would have been upset with the long distance between us at one time, but that wasn't a problem with a jet plane at our disposal.

I told her I couldn't talk long as I had to call my parents. She wished me luck.

I got through to Dad in his office. It so happened Mum was there. They put me on a speaker. These neat new devices were cropping up in a lot of offices.

It was a little awkward because you could speak or listen, but not both. We had to take turns. They did know about my expulsion and had made some phone calls.

I wasn't in any trouble because it was all political. We agreed that my time at Oxford was finished. I gave them an update on China and my invitation and seeing about the new Chinese being recognized by Great Britain. I was waiting for instructions from the palace.

There was also the matter of the new movie. They thought that was an excellent idea. It would give me something to do. They also wanted me to have another Hollywood success. I guess not being nominated for an Oscar bothered them more than me.

That was Monday, Tuesday, and Wednesday. I wanted to play golf, but the weather was bad; there was not even an inch of snow. Instead, I reread the movie script several times, getting a better feel for what they wanted to show.

Chapter 4

On Thursday morning, I received a phone call from Mr. Norman. Could I please attend a meeting at the palace at 2 p.m. today? I told him I could but would be driving down as the weather was too rotten to fly if you didn't have to.

He asked if I had considered taking the train to town. I hadn't, but that was a great idea. Mr. Hamilton kept a train schedule at the house, so I found out that by leaving at ten o'clock, I could have a nice lunch in London and still be at the palace on time for my meeting.

My nice lunch turned into a problem. An inattentive waiter serving the next table backed up, hitting me. I was taking a sip of coffee at the time and ended up with it all over my white shirt and tie.

Thank goodness I had taken off my coat jacket, and I didn't get any on my pants. They wanted to do a seltzer cleaning job on me, but I told them it wouldn't work and that I was due at the palace in an hour.

I left while hearing many apologies. I only hoped the guy didn't lose his job. Accidents happen, but I didn't have time to talk to the manager.

I was able to get a cab to Harrods. From there, buying a shirt and tie was a simple matter. Of course, I fumbled my cuff links, but it all worked out, and I got to the palace on time.

The meeting was about my invitation to China to see Lady Ping's coronation as empress. From what they had found out, she would be a constitutional monarchy like England's.

That seemed odd; I had never considered the Communists as working under a constitution, but they did. They consistently violated it to their benefit but had it as a fig leaf for their actions.

I thought Lady Ping may have some influence on their future actions. They may consider her a figurehead, but I think she would be more than that.

There was also the possibility that she was a figurehead, a figurehead for Deng as he changed China. That would be a best-case scenario.

I was told the Crown would be delighted for me to attend the coronation and that the government was to ask me if I would allow an official government representative to accompany me.

Talk about being a figurehead. I could recognize a power play when I saw it. The Queen was showing the government that she was still a power to be reckoned with.

Being from the US, I believed in the Republic's heart and soul. Being from the UK, I thought the Queen was doing simply fine and that the politicians had just mucked things up ever since Churchill.

The Queen and prime minister had one of their regular meetings at three o'clock. He would brief her on government actions and proceedings. Today, he would be in for a shock.

Later, as he was brought into a small parlor where I waited, he looked put out.

"Now hear here, Jackson, this is not how things are done. We will send an ambassador, and he will run the show."

"I'm sorry to hear that you won't be sending anyone."

"Didn't you hear me?"

"I heard your words, but you don't understand that the invitation is to me and those whom I choose to invite."

"You will invite us, and we will run the show."

"Or what?"

"I will run you out of England!"

"Okay, I can be wheels up from Heathrow in about three hours. It will take some time to ferry the plane down from Oxford."

That stopped him cold.

"I will have your departure denied."

"I thought I was being run out of England."

At that, the man stopped and collected himself.

"We have gotten off on the wrong foot."

"No, you have gotten off on the wrong foot."

All the time in the movies voicing the lines writers had given me taught me a good turn of phrase, especially from the Victorian Sir Nickalous.

He looked like he had swallowed a lemon but restarted.

"Would you please invite our ambassador along as we wish to establish relations with China? He will oversee diplomatic matters, and I hope he can guide you on proper etiquette in these situations."

"I would be delighted; I realize I'm not trained or competent for this situation. I intend to go and enjoy the show as a good guest."

At that, he gave a short laugh.

"You are just as hard-nosed as your mum."

"You know my mother?"

"The countess and I have a history going back to the war."

This was said in a neutral tone so that I couldn't read anything into it. He didn't seem inclined to elaborate, so I had to let it drop. What all had my mum done in the war? She certainly got around.

The PM said, "May I ask, has the same invitation been extended to the Americans?

"Not to my knowledge; nothing was said to make me think they will be part of this."

'Wonderful. Taking a world leadership victory from the Yanks will be nice. They are a good ally, but still, it is nice to one-up them occasionally."

"This one will be one for the history books. England opens up China."

"More along the line that Lord Blackhoof opens up China."

"I doubt that. You politicians are good at finding a way to take the credit."

He looked affronted for a moment, then gave an honest laugh.

"Got it in one. I will start the process when I return to Number 10."

"Is there a problem with letting the American government know what is happening?" I asked.

"As long as the Chinese don't object."

"I will ask them when I call my contact."

"Is your contact truly Lady Ping?"

"Yes."

"I was told that but wasn't certain I believed it."

"It is a long story, but I have had contact with her for several years now as a conduit between the Chinese government and MI6. Though now I wonder if the government in power even knew what was going on."

"What sort of security did you receive for that enormous loan?"

"It was sealed with a handshake."

"My God, I was told that but find it incredible. You could have and might still lose a fortune."

"Easy come, easy go."

At that, he bid me farewell, shaking his head as he went. Poor little politician, never able to trust anyone. What a sad life.

Before I left the palace, I returned to Mr. Norman's office and updated him on my conversation with the prime minister.

Mr. Norman had a good laugh about me being kicked out of England. The Queen would have dissolved the government first and called for new elections, making certain all knew what happened.

The average Englishman didn't pay that much attention to world affairs, but they understood fair play.

I decided to call Hsian-Tsung through the palace switchboard. I liked the thought of him picking up the phone and being told it was Buckingham Palace on the line. Would he please hold for Lord Blackhoof?

I got through to him, but he made no mention of my little power play. The games he played probably ended up in gunfire. My little trick would go unnoticed.

He was pleased to hear that I would be attending and that the British government was sending an ambassador. By the way, you can tell President Kennedy you have been invited, and the British are coming, but they will not be invited."

"May I ask why?"

"We remember Korea."

"UK forces were there."

"But we know the US wouldn't listen to Churchill or Atlee."

Then he let something slip.

"I hear the prime minister tried to have his ambassador take charge. That you put him in his place."

"How would you know that?"

"Both of you got rather loud. They heard it in Hong Kong.

I doubted that; it meant they had a spy in the palace. Now, why did he let me know that? To keep us honest. This was truly a puzzle.

I went back to Mr. Norman's office. He must be getting tired of me walking through his door. He did sit up straight when I relayed my conversation. He agreed it was puzzling that I was made aware of a spy in our midst.

Our best guess was that the spy was from the old regime and had reported back, but they wanted to get rid of the spy, so they let it slip. MI6 could do their dirty work for them.

Months later, I learned that everyone near that office had been investigated. They learned that one of the staff had sold the information to a reporter who had, in turn, sold it to the Chinese. It appeared that Hsian-Tsung wanted them to run in circles for a while.

Now, why would he do that unless it is to conceal someone or an ongoing operation? I hate the spy world.

Chapter 5

On Friday, I had a do-nothing day. I went over to the boarding stable and took a long ride on the horse that my parents had given me. I had been on it so infrequently that I never bothered to name it.

The kids from the orphanage sponsored by the Coram Foundation called him Big Red. Since I hardly ever gave him any exercise, we allowed them and several other horse owners to ride our horses.

I called ahead to make sure no children would be out today. Because he was ridden often by children, he had become very patient. He plodded along, not my idea of a ride. I think I will just deed him over; I will still pay his bills, vet, feed, and board, but I took no real pleasure in the ride.

I expect George was getting to be the same way at Jackson House.

Another decision I made about things that weren't doing me immediate good was that Ferrari I had won. All it did was sit in the garage in Oxford. Since I wasn't going there anymore, I didn't need the garage. I had meant to ship it to the US to torment Denny but never got around to it.

After thinking about what to do with it, I realized Valentine's Day was nearing. I called the dealer in London and arranged for it to be shipped to Switzerland. I hoped it would arrive on time.

After that, I told Mr. Hamilton to have the garage cleaned out and let it go. Mum had rented it for me and paid for it by the year. I had no idea who the landlord was, but he said he had the papers and would take care of them.

This year had been paid for, and I could legally stop them from using the garage for all of 1962.

I told Mr. Hamilton just to get me out and eat the loss. That was when it hit me hard that my days at Oxford were over. I started to tear up a little, then settled down. As they say, it was done and dusted.

I also called David Randel-MacIver and let him know that I would continue to fund the Roman dig and the amusement park. He had heard about my dismissal and was relieved to hear my promise to continue the funding.

I don't know why he was worried. It was only a couple of million pounds a year. Another loose end tidied up.

All caught up on the loose ends of my life, I wondered what to do next. I felt like playing golf but with this lousy weather and cold rain, there was no way I would play.

I did think that I had to contact John Jacobs as I hadn't talked to him in a while. About that time, I slapped my forehead. Why not go to dry, warm California to talk to John and play some golf?

Silly me sitting here in England with nothing to do, and I could go anywhere in the world. I picked up the phone and called the air leasing firm to see if my jet was ready to go. It was.

I asked them to set up a flight to California, leaving early tomorrow morning. I informed Harold of my intentions and that he was to accompany me. Grandmum and Mr. Hamilton were still at Jackson House.

I let the housekeeper know my plans. She told me she would take advantage of everyone being gone and let the staff take a week off. She would be heading to Corfu. It seems everyone was ready to flee this dreadful winter weather.

I wish I had thought of it earlier; I never gave it a thought that the only reason the servants were here was that I was in residence.

I called Nina and told her of my plans. She immediately declared she hated me. She had to stay in school. We talked for an hour, and she finally told me she didn't hate me but was jealous.

She wouldn't be getting any length of time off until spring break in May. She would model on the weekends and even in some lovely places, but it would be flying in, work, fly out.

I then called Jackson House to let them know I would be arriving tomorrow night and please have a room available for Harold. I assumed mine would be there.

Mum told me she wondered why I even bothered to return to England while the weather was bad. I pled, male, not thinking. She accepted that as normal.

My flight to LAX was getting to be old hat. I even sat up front with the flight crew. They let me log a few hours over the Arctic Ocean. I think they only did it because it was one of the most boring flights ever—nothing but white down below.

We arrived on time at LAX and spent the next hour circling as traffic was backed up. This was jet plane traffic, not cars. Though, from what I could see, the freeways had a major case of gridlock.

Finally, able to land, Harold and I took our limo, which Mum had sent for us, to Jackson House. He had more luggage than I did because of my duplicate sets of clothing. I told him to purchase and bill me duplicate sets of his own. It seemed dumb for me to be able to leave the plane quickly because I had no bags but then have to wait for him.

He told me he had been saving to do that very thing and would take me up on my generous offer.

At Jackson House, just in time for dinner, I was told there would be a treat for me after eating. I had no clue what it might be.

After the meal, the family retired to the TV room. There was a special documentary they wanted to watch. My shipping container documentary had been released.

I thought it was well done, but I couldn't stand my voice. Everyone assured me that it sounded fine. Even Mary gave me a pass. She must be up to something.

I had only been gone for a little while, so there wasn't much to catch up on. I did notice that Mr. Hamilton and Grandmum were sitting together on a loveseat.

No one else noticed or cared, so I let it go. Hey, if they are happy, so am I. Our resident gadabout, Mrs. Hernandez, appeared to have a night off from her frantic dating schedule.

I had the flight crew take a few days off. They were staying at my beach house. They complained to their home office about how hard their duty was—the nerve.

I even took the head stewardess to task over this. She told me it was incredibly stressful never knowing when their idiot client would take it in his mind to leave this paradise. The worry!

I called John Jacobs, and he was glad to hear from me. He didn't know if I had given up on golf. It wasn't the money. He was in high demand since he had caddied for a US Open winner.

He was looking forward to defending the title this year, and by the way, was I thinking of the Grand Slam? I hadn't been, but this was a good idea. I had the time now.

It would be the Masters in April. June was the US Open, then the PGA Championship in July, followed by the British Open the same month.

We talked about it. He volunteered to cancel all his caddie bookings if I wanted to get serious. I did. I would be playing or practicing every day that I could. I explained that I had to be in China the last week of January, but it would only be for a week, and then he had me full-time.

He had a few friends who worked at the Augusta National Golf Club. He would ask who on the board would most likely get me guest privileges.

He called back within the hour. If I had a way to contact him, President Eisenhower was a long-time member and carried heavy influence. I told him I would call Ike. John knew that Ike was my godfather and was pulling my leg.

Not letting any grass grow under my feet, and it still being early enough, I called the ex-president at his farm in Gettysburg. He was home and took my call.

I explained that I was going for a Grand Slam this year and needed to practice at Augusta. He immediately volunteered to get me guest privileges and that he would take me on my first round.

I suspect it was an excuse to get to Augusta and play a round or two.

He checked his calendar and said he could play next week. I offered to pick him up in Frederick, Maryland and take him with me to the Augusta airfield. I later learned we would have to fly into Atlanta and take a smaller plane to Augusta as the runways were not long enough at Daniel's field.

Chapter 6

I knew my golf was rusty, so I went to the Riviera County Club's practice range. I spent half a day and hit four buckets of balls. I took frequent breaks, so I didn't get sore or pull anything.

Starting with my 9 iron, I worked my way up. When I got to my driver, things had changed. I hadn't grown any taller but carried twenty more pounds. At six foot five inches and weighing two hundred and ten pounds, I was in the best shape of my life.

During the last six months, I have stepped up my running, weightlifting, and general exercising. I didn't make a big deal of it. I just did it.

I weighed fifteen pounds more than I did at the US Open. It showed when I hit my drives, I had gained about five yards. That doesn't sound like much, but at this level of golf, it could be a game-changer.

I might also add that the weight gain wasn't fat. I had what they called washboard abs. I felt good about myself, and it was evident that I was going to tear up the golf courses.

Then I went to the putting green, and my world collapsed around me. My speed and ability to read the lie were terrible; otherwise, all was well. It was trash!

I would have to spend hours getting my feel for the greens back. Not only was I bad, but I was also trying to putt on the practice greens of a busy golf course.

Groups were teeing off every ten minutes. Most groups hit the practice green while they waited. US Open winner or not, they wanted their share of the large green. I would never get the time I needed here. All the courses in the area would be the same.

I could go anywhere in the world. Where would I find a practice green that would be all mine? I was so desperate that I even mentioned it at dinner. Denny and Eddie shrugged; Mary thought I should buy a course of my own.

Dad didn't say anything. Mum was out at some charity event with Mrs. Hernandez. Those two made the local tabloids almost every day and the nationals once a week.

After dinner, Dad went to his office and came out a little while later.

"Rick, there is a golf course out by Ontario that is being torn down for residential development. The practice greens are still there, and I have rented them for you for the next month."

"Dad, you are awesome."

"You are paying for it, not me."

Have I ever said my dad can be a cheapskate at times? I think being raised in the Depression made him that way. It didn't matter; either of us could afford it; it was his tone of voice; he was serious.

No matter, I had my practice green.

In the morning, John and I drove out to Ontario to the golf course. The clubhouse was gone, and the first fairway was being bulldozed. The putting green and driving range were on the far side of where the clubhouse had been, so the equipment noise wasn't that bad.

One nice thing was that the green was still in good shape like someone was still tending it. We soon found out as a grumpy old man came out and demanded who we were and what we were doing there.

He didn't want to listen to us; he was calling the police. Before he did that, a guy in a construction truck pulled in. He was yelling as he came up to us. "Sam, wait a minute, it's okay."

The old guy turned and listened.

"These guys have rented the practice area for the next month. It means you have an extra three weeks."

A picture started to form.

The old guy named Sam had to be told twice before he understood. He started smiling.

"I knew the Lord would provide."

"Sam, it is only some more weeks; this area is coming down."

"I'm sure the Lord will provide."

He turned to me and asked, "Now, who is coming to my rescue?"

There was no way I could pass this one up. Using my most posh British accent, I said, "Lord Blackhoof."

Sam got all red in the face; I thought he might have a heart attack. I was worried when he started wheezing. He finally got settled down.

"I know the Lord moves in mysterious ways, but I didn't know he also has a sense of humor. So, you're the Richard Jackson who is the US Open Champion."

"I am."

"Nice to meet you. Now let me guess, you haven't played much recently and find your putting has gone out the window. Not only that, you need a green where you can spend many hours."

Sam is not as crazy as I thought.

"You understand my situation quite well."

The construction guy had headed back to his truck when he saw blood wasn't going to be shed."

"Sam, what's the story here?"

"I've tended this golf course for the last forty years. It's part of my life. I just can't seem to let it go. I know it is gone, but I want this last little piece to last as long as possible."

I could respect that. I didn't understand it, but I could respect it. I didn't have forty years invested in anything, so there was no way I could understand.

John had been standing silently the whole time. He now spoke up, asking technical questions about the large green: the foundation, sand, grass type, and a few other things.

Sam waxed enthusiastic, and I could see John forming a partnership with Sam.

I went right to work, lining up ten golf balls fifteen feet from one of the pins. I kept missing to the right. It was only inches, but the saying an inch is as good as a mile was correct in this case.

I lined them up again when Sam stopped me. He and John had been watching my poor display.

"May I call you Rick?"

"Yes, sir."

"Rick, stop what you are doing; you are only ingraining a bad habit."

"Do you know what I should be doing?"

"I think you are too tense. Try something for me."

I nodded, and he showed me a different grip.

"Try it this way."

I did, and the ball went in the hole. The second and third made it also. I missed the fourth, leaving it hanging on the edge. The point was it was headed towards the cup, not sliding away.

"You mean I have been gripping the club wrong all this time?"

"Not at all. When you changed your grip, you concentrated on that and forgot whatever was making it push."

I set up and stroked the other six balls towards the pin. I was sinking fifteen percent, good but not good enough to win a tournament.

I must have putted a thousand times that day. Towards the end, I was up to twenty percent. Better but not good enough. I needed to be above thirty percent at ten to fifteen feet.

Above fifteen feet, putting drops off dramatically. I didn't bother to practice any forty-five-footers. With the curves, hills, and dales used today, it would be almost impossible to read a green that well.

Sam proved to be a putting genius. I asked him why he wasn't a pro somewhere. He told me that his short irons were a mystery that he never solved and, as such, never made a name for himself, even locally.

As far as I was concerned, their loss was my gain. Further conversation revealed he is a widower with no children. He appeared to be all alone in the world.

I said something to that effect, and he laughed.

"I have my buddies at the VFW. We get together every week and tell lies."

It's still not the same.

I spent six hours putting and two hours on the range.

On the putting green, I would line ten balls up at three feet and put them in 98% of the time. I had to be 99%. Then, I would back off a foot and stroke ten more. The further back the lower the percentage in, but the more practice, and that percentage started to rise. Nothing spectacular, but anything I did was an improvement.

After working back to fifteen feet, I would move over to the driving range. I was using the range as a break from putting. At the range, I would start with the low clubs, hitting ten shots. Finally, the driver, using tees. I was booming them out.

We broke for lunch, my treat. At the end of the day, I felt like I had a real workout.

On the way back to my house, where John had left his car, he made a statement.

"It's a shame you don't have a putting green like that at Jackson House."

"Yes, it is, but putting one in and growing the grass would take a long time."

"Not if you transplanted."

"John, you are a genius!"

Chapter 7

I could hardly wait to get home and talk to Dad. I asked him who owned the golf course I had been practicing at. I wanted to buy the putting green and have it brought to Jackson House. He had no problems with that. We had the room.

We talked about the driving range; we had the room but didn't want to move that much grass. Dad made a phone call and talked for a while.

"Rick, I explained what you wanted. He is giving the green to you plus the driving range; all you must do is pay to move it and play one round of golf with him at a future date. He wants to brag he played with a US Open winner."

"That's great. I'll gladly play eighteen holes with him. Do you have any idea of the cost of moving?"

"None, but I bet a sod company could do it."

Dad made another call; he knew a guy who knew a guy. Anyway, he got through to a sod company.

My dad has become a wheeler-dealer, at least a better one. He had always made trades for interesting items, but this was on a larger scale.

The sod company would move the putting green for free in exchange for all the grass on the driving range. We could keep the driving range markers and other equipment. We could set up a driving range out back; it wouldn't have the nice grass for a few years, but I could still practice my irons.

My driver would clear the back fence. I don't think anyone walking along the trail near our back gate would appreciate that. That aggravated me to no end.

Then it dawned on me there was an area where I could hit the ball as far as I could with no danger—the US Forest Service airbase. I still had a Cessna in the hangar there.

John and I went over to the Forestry Service the next morning to see the chief ranger. He was in and when I explained that I wanted to put a driving range in he told me there was one condition. He and his people could use it.

I had no problem with that. He asked if I was going to put a putting green next to it. Having them together made sense, so I revised the backyard plan.

Then John and I went back to Ontario for my putting practice. Sam was there bright and early. I played it straight with him as this setup was near and dear to him. There is a time to be a jokester; this wasn't one of them.

"Sam, I have come up with a way to save the putting greens and use the driving range equipment on a new range."

He looked at me skeptically.

"We are moving the practice greens to a US Forest Service airbase near my house. We will set up a driving range using all this equipment. The grass out there is rough for a range, but I'm sure you can get it in shape."

From there, I gave him the whole story.

"Where do I fit into this?"

"I thought we would build you a small house next to the equipment shed we need, and you live there rent-free plus a salary. You will maintain it for the forest service people and my use."

I had to go over it several times until he understood. Then I got a hug. Sometimes, it is good to be rich.

The sod people were anxious to start. They had been told that they would be working with Sam. The move would start tomorrow, which worked well as I was flying to Augusta to play golf with Ike.

Then I got down to business. I went through the same practice routine I had the day before. Both John and Sam were watching my swing like hawks.

John suggested we might want to buy a camera so we could capture my swing. I told him to investigate that.

There were no dramatic improvements but no backsliding. Another ten thousand or so putts, and I might get it.

At home, I updated Dad on my plans for the practice setup. He told me he was glad it could be done that way. In our enthusiasm, we had forgotten that Mum used that area for her charity outdoor events. We had dodged a bullet.

The next morning, John's wife dropped him off at the house, and we took a limo to LAX. John had collected my clubs and other gear from Riviera.

I had thought about duplicate sets and had ordered a couple to be kept with me in case of a disaster, but I was reluctant to change them even if they were identical.

Our flight to pick up Ike was uneventful. I even picked up a couple of hours for my logbook. He was waiting with his secret service guard at the airport. He only had a small overnight bag. He kept clubs at Augusta, so we were good to go.

The flight down to Atlanta and then onto Augusta was smooth. John and I had our clothes with us. Harold had a small fit when he realized he wouldn't be traveling with us or that I wouldn't have my full wardrobe available.

I'm sure he will get over it.

Since I was traveling with Ike, I was invited to dinner with him. It was with other members of the Augusta National Golf Course. They were a stuffy group to me, though they were very polite.

John had to stay at our hotel and go out for a cheeseburger. Lucky John.

It appears I was made of the right stuff. After dinner, it was mentioned that if I had a sponsor and some thousands of dollars, I was welcome to join the club as an associate member. Since Ike was smiling as this was mentioned, I thought I had at least one sponsor.

As far as the money, that was no big deal. Being a member and practicing when I wanted would be handy. Based on that, I asked what I had to do.

It turned out truly little. It was all a setup. I had to sign some prepared paperwork and write a check. I had to be voted on by the membership committee but was given the impression that it was a mere formality.

I found out later how much of a formality it was when the membership committee hanging out at the bar voted me in. The check had better clear.

The next morning, we met at the clubhouse for our round. Ike was in good spirits as this was his favorite course. After spending some time on the driving range to loosen up and then the practice greens to get a feel for their greens, I was ready to play.

I thought I would tear the course up. Instead, the course tore me up. Ike was incredibly happy with his 81. I was unhappy with a 76. I could see that John and I had a lot of work to do.

I played another round in the afternoon. Since it was all walking, Ike begged off. He certainly was getting on in years.

I did better the second time through, a 72. I didn't think I would ever duplicate Gene Sarazen's shot heard around the world. After playing the par 5 15th hole, I thought getting a birdie would be a fine showing. His double eagle of two shots on the par 5 was incredible.

John was learning the course at the same time I was. He suggested on the second day that we hire a course caddie who knew his way around.

That was genius, as the caddie gave us the ins and outs of every hole. John took notes on every hole and almost every shot.

We stayed a third day. Ike had gone home the next day after our round. He flew back to Atlanta, and my crew took him home. He called me later and told me that was a better plane and setup than the president of the United States had.

He gently hinted that he would like the use of the plane occasionally, especially if he had to go to Europe. Try to tell the ex-president you wouldn't loan out your aircraft.

After playing two rounds on the third day, I had enough of Augusta for a while. I would be back before the Master's, but enough was enough.

I had my trip to China coming up and wanted to be sure I was prepared. The British had sent their ambassador ahead to Hong Kong. I needed to get there to get my internal clock adjusted. It would take a week.

Our flight back to LAX went well. The aircrew, the hostesses, and I had gotten our routine down pat. I was able even to perform the takeoff. I had landed a 707 but never taken off.

Chapter 8

On Thursday, the 25th, we flew to Hong Kong, arriving on the 27th. The coronation was the following Thursday, so I would have plenty of time to get my body clock turned around.

I slept well on the flight when I allowed myself to sleep. I stayed up as late as I could, not that it ended up helping.

A Boeing 707 cruising speed is advertised as 607 miles per hour. I know we did over 600 miles per hour, but our flying time was longer with headwinds.

Then, there was a two-hour layover in Honolulu to refuel. I went for a run around the airfield to stretch my legs. One thing and another, what would have been a twelve-and-a-half-hour flight turned into sixteen.

We left LAX at seven a.m. We lost a day crossing the international dateline, so we arrived early on Friday. I had a long day ahead of me.

I was staying at the Peninsula Hotel once again. I liked their style. I checked in and was taken by one of their limos to the British Embassy. The man who had been named the British ambassador to the Forbidden City met me.

I thought that I would have days to rest up. I was informed that I would immediately start Chinese imperial etiquette lessons.

I realized you had to bow the proper depth for different ranking officials. That and a polite how do you do should do it. Boy, was I wrong.

Some of what I learned made sense; some things I will never understand. Four is an unlucky number, so never give four of anything. Eight is lucky, so that works. Shouldn't it be double unlucky? What about twelve of something, unlucky and lucky? Would that mean twelve is neutral?

Always greet the oldest person first; what if you don't know who is the oldest? If you greet a woman first who looks oldest, is she complimented because she is senior or upset you think she is old?

I was told handshakes were the most ordinary form of greeting with foreigners, but that touching is only acceptable between family and close friends.

Then there is the eye contact thing; don't do it. Look down when being introduced, shoes are preferred. No eye contact is considered reverential. What if I only like them but don't revere them?

You can look at people with your head turned so it is only one-eyed. Is that where the one-eyed Jack came from?

Don't give scissors or knives as gifts, as they can be interpreted as severing a relationship. What do you give your son who just graduated from barber school?

A hairbrush?

No flowers because they go with funerals and no white, blue, or black paper. Don't open the gift at once. Always present gifts with two hands. That one was easy because I knew about business cards.

You can refuse a gift three times before accepting it. What if I want the gift?

Entertainment should be in public places, not the home, particularly with foreigners. We probably would forget to wipe our feet.

Inviting me into a home would be considered a great honor, and it should be accepted if possible. If not, give a complete explanation. Muddy shoes will not work because you must take them off outside.

Bring a small gift to the hostess.

Learn to use chopsticks. Luckily, I could do that because you must eat well to show you enjoy the food. This was the only place where I felt I had an advantage. Teenager here.

Don't place chopsticks upwards in the rice bowl. It is bad luck. I suppose if you fell forward, you could put an eye out.

I was to wear dark-colored conservative business suits. I didn't know they made any other type. Not true, but it sounded good.

Always use a title and last name.

My business card was to be English on one side and Chinese on the other. It also had to say that Jackson Enterprises was the world's largest and oldest provider of cargo containers.

After examining the business cards, you place them on the table until the meeting ends. Never write on the card unless told to.

As far as the subject of the meeting, there could be a problem. They were supposed to be made in writing in advance. There would be an agenda that should be adhered to.

Listen carefully as people speak; they will take an inordinate amount of time, but there will be hints of the concerns that must be addressed.

They would indicate where I was to be seated, presumably across from a senior person, as I would be the senior person representing Jackson Enterprises. In government matters, the ambassador would take precedence.

Only senior members would speak, and as the only one from my team there, it made it easy.

Losing your temper is the loss of face and to be avoided.

The Chinese are very hierarchical, and decisions will not be made if the senior person is absent. These meetings are jumping-off points for other opportunities.

Most of all, they want to learn if they can work with you. They are shrewd negotiators and will skin you alive if allowed.

I was to remember that I was at a severe disadvantage because of the hierarchical nature of the Chinese. The teachings of Confucianism said that there is never equality. Older and senior people command the most respect.

I was taught about these things for three days straight. I was put into practice situations where I had to abide by these rules. It wasn't fun. How I would do when thrust into reality was an open question.

The business portion of my training assumed I would have business meetings. As far as I knew, I was only attending a coronation.

The first two days of the time change were terrible. I felt like I had the flu. On my previous trip, I had made the journey in steps and adjusted each stop along the way a little. This was one giant leap, and boy, was it hard.

By the fourth day, I was doing okay. I had no time for sightseeing as the ambassador was determined to cram three thousand years of Chinese history and culture into one short week.

If I didn't know he was correct in what he was doing, I would have kicked up a fuss.

We debated on how I would dress for the occasion. Since the Chinese respected rank, I would wear the full Coldstream Guard mess dress with all my medals. I certainly would get no respect for my age. I needed every edge I could get. That is even if I was to be in any meetings or negotiations.

I had a not-so-bright idea. I called my parents long distance. It took a while for the operator to get my call through. When I told them what I was thinking, they decided I was mad.

When I explained my reasoning, I wasn't considered mad anymore, just one of the largest gamblers in history. A win would be incalculable; a loss would take time to make up, but it would be made up. It's not like I didn't have time on my side.

They asked if I was telling Ambassador Charles Cathcart my plan. I decided not to if he couldn't take a joke. It was my risk, not England's. If I told him, he would try to take credit for it. That was his job, but this one was on me.

An item on my list was to purchase a present for the new empress. What do you get a woman who has the largest country in the world at her feet? I doubt a day at the spa would cut it.

I already had her large present in mind; now I needed something for the presentation at the public ceremony. I explained my problem to the embassy staff. A young man who worked at the front desk told me he had an uncle who dealt in old Chinese jewelry. At a total loss of what else to do, I accompanied him to a shop that was literally in a back alley.

I kept looking to see if there was an opium den nearby. We entered an old, cluttered shop. His uncle must have been older than the shop. My mission was explained. While I haven't mentioned it, China was in a total uproar about the empress taking the throne.

People were being fed; life was good. When the uncle, who had a name I couldn't pronounce, learned it was a gift for the new empress, he took us into a back room and opened an old safe. He brought out an old box and opened it.

This was a box containing an old necklace with a Fenghuang phoenix. He explained this was the symbol of Chinese empresses. It is considered a symbol of luck and harmony. The fact that it had blue sapphire eyes made it even more powerful.

Wow! It was beautiful. With its beauty and symbolism, it was the perfect gift. It cost a ton of money, but it was nothing compared with my other gift. I didn't have the necklace wrapped because I wanted Lady Ping to see it when I presented it in court.

Chapter 9

On Tuesday, I felt like a human again. My body clock was adjusted to Hong Kong time. Now I had to look forward to the reverse process going home. Not much fun.

I also had been checked off on my Chinese cultural understanding. It was thought that I knew enough not to be a total embarrassment to England. The ambassador told me, "If you have any faux pas, we will blame it on your American heritage."

I started to laugh, then realized he was deadly serious.

I was provided a guide to see the city. One day, we visited the Kowloon Walled City Park, Man Mo Temple, Sharp Island, the Po Lin Monastery, and the Tian Tan Buddha, walking up all 268 steps.

That evening, we went to the Temple Street Night Market. It was fascinating. Noise, smells, crowds, and you could buy anything you could name. Well, almost anything; I didn't see any tanks or battleships for sale. An aircraft dealer was set up with a Cessna 320 in the center of his large stand.

He could speak English, so I asked if I could buy a Phantom F4. He never batted an eye. He asked for my name and number and said he would get back to me with a price.

I backed down quickly. Later I wondered if that was his intent or if he could get me that jet.

We hiked the Dragon's Back hiking trail through Shek O Peak the next day. It took about four hours and had some breathtaking views. Tai Tam Harbor was full of ships waiting to be loaded or unloaded. The wait times should be reduced when my port operations are active.

On Wednesday, I got to play some golf. I always had a set of clubs on board the aircraft. I played at the Royal Hong Kong Golf Club, which had just started hosting a new tournament, the Hong Kong Open.

I needed to put that on my list of tournaments to enter. I didn't set a course record, but I had a respectable 64. I was in a threesome with Bob Ramsey and Gersham Stewart. They were pleasant chaps, though a lot older than me.

They told me the story of the Uganda grass used on the course. It had been brought from Uganda through Cairo and almost got the man carrying it arrested for smuggling. Who would smuggle grass?

There was a reception at the British Embassy that evening. I had to attend in mess dress. I had never given it much thought, but with my size, dressed in all honors worn, I must have been an imposing figure.

That and a half-crown would get me a good cup of tea. The upshot is that even though a younger set was at the reception, they wouldn't come near me. Instead, I was a magnet for all the old fogeys.

They wanted to talk about business or the war, World War I. I managed to dodge them for a few minutes and go out on a balcony where the younger set was gathered. Several cute girls were there; I had nothing in mind except talking to kids my age.

I love business and what goes on, but sometimes I need some nonsense in my life. Teenage jokes are funny to us and no one else. I wasn't going to have that tonight. The kids all started to migrate away, and the oldsters moved in.

I managed to corner one young man and ask him why all the teens kept away from me.

"Our parents have warned us off. You are too important for us to bother."

"What a load! First, I'm not that important, and second, I'm dying to have good company. Those old guys aren't it. Where do you go after this is over?"

"We will sneak out to a coffee shop just around the corner. That way, we can see when our parents are leaving and can catch a ride home."

"Lead the way."

We went out a side door down to the coffee shop. The place was half full of kids who had escaped the reception. A couple of night shift workers were there, but they kept to themselves.

We had an enjoyable hour, talking about everything and nothing. I wasn't made the center of attention, nor was I ignored. It was delightful.

As the last of them were leaving, I rejoined the reception, which was winding down. The ambassador came up to me.

"Did you enjoy the coffee shop?"

"I did; how did you know I was there?"

"Teenagers have been cutting out of these receptions for over fifty years and going there. It is safe and keeps them out of our hair; why should you be any different?"

"How do you know it's safe?"

"Those night workers are all Hong Kong police."

That was the most fun I had in a while.

The next morning, the ambassador, his staff, and I took one of the hotel's Rolls-Royces to the airport. It was a three-and-a-half-hour flight to Beijing, as Lady Ping had told me Beijing was properly called. I had invited them to fly with me to save on logistics.

While on the way, Harold was fussing over my formal dress. I wore a morning coat with long tails, a top hat, white gloves, and miniatures of all my medals. It was some sight. He had a Polaroid camera as Mum had demanded pictures.

Upon landing, we were bundled into a stretched-out Cadillac. We were taken to the Forbidden City. There, we took a confusing route to one of the many buildings to wait to be summoned. There were coffee and other refreshments available. I avoided all liquids, as I knew I would spill them on my white shirt or must pee at the worst possible moment.

After a wait of several hours in which we had a desultory conversation, we were summoned to a great hall. It probably has a formal name, but I had no idea what it would be. To me, it was just a bloody great hall with several thousand people in it. Television cameras representing the entire world were there. China was letting the world know that change was happening.

A grand procession came down the aisle, so we all rose. I could tell by the dress it was Lady Ping. That is, she was dressed in the historical costumes I had studied in preparation for this trip. She had on so much makeup it was impossible to tell if she was Lady Ping.

She arrived at the front of the room, and several men I thought were priests spoke in Chinese. This went on for a while, and then a man came down the aisle. It was Deng Xiaoping. He carried a cushion, and on it was a crown.

He approached Lady Ping and was ready to pick up the crown and place it on her head. He was the General Secretary of the Communist Party and President of China.

Before he could take the crown in his hands, Lady Ping picked it up and placed it on her head. She had pulled a Napoleon!

Deng was going to crown her, showing her power was through the state and that the Communist Party was the state. She had chosen to declare her independence. I wondered how this would play out.

From the gasps and outcries of the crowd, it was a toss-up. The ambassador standing next to me had a cogent comment, "Well, I never!"

Trumpets blared, and Empress Ping led the way out.

We were taken back to our waiting room but didn't have a long stay. The new Empress Ping summoned us to her presence. Going to a much smaller hall, we removed our shoes and made our way to her.

We had debated what honorifics to use. For me, we had settled on an officer talking to a higher-ranking person.

"This official wishes to congratulate you on your accession to the throne."

The newly crowned empress laughed and said, "Nicely done, Ricky. They have taught you well. Now come up here so we can talk."

She was sitting on a sofa and patted the seat beside her. I, being a good dog robber, sat.

"I have been rather naughty, you know; the Communists will want my head, but they don't dare, or they will lose tremendous face."

"I wondered."

"I'm going to open China to the world and bring my people out of poverty. The communist leadership can maintain their decadent lifestyle, but things are going to change for the people."

As she said that, she stared directly at a sour-faced Deng.

I got back on my script and told her I had a gift for her on this auspicious day. I held out the open box with the Fenghuang phoenix necklace displayed. She picked it up and held it for all to see. There were oohs and has all around. Even Deng looked impressed.

Chapter 10

If he were impressed by that, what I shared next would knock his socks off. This was the present I hadn't told the ambassador about and the one that made my parents think I was mad.

"I also have a present for the Chinese people, which I'm asking you as empress to administer."

I handed her a formal envelope that had the fanciest calligraphy money could buy. There were wax seals and ribbons. It was well over the top.

That is, until she read it, she shook herself and read it again. She gave me a look of wonder.

"May I share this?" she asked.

"Yes."

She read the letter to the crowd. It was several simple statements. The one hundred-million-dollar loan was forgiven. It was to be administered by Empress Ping. If she couldn't do so by ill health or her death, the monies would revert to me.

I watched Deng as she read it out; he looked at me with a half-smile and shook his head. I like a good loser.

Then, the impact of what I had done hit him. You should have seen Deng's face change. What a study in contrast. I had just given the empress significant funds independent of the government, reducing their power. I had also forgiven the government's debt.

On one hand, he was happy, and on the other, upset.

I had just upset the Chinese apple cart. My financial moves didn't completely give one part or the other power but made them more equal. Empress Ping wouldn't be a puppet, at least financially. She still couldn't make laws, but she sure could influence them.

It had occurred to me that by forgiving the debt I had taken the possibility of nonpayment off the table and the embarrassments it would have caused.

After that presentation, I made my final bow and backed off, never turning my back to the empress. Once outside the room in the anteroom, I waited for the ambassador.

He had previously given his unsealed credentials to Deng; now, he had presented his sealed copy formally to the empress. England now had an Ambassador to China.

He was furious with me. How could I pull a stunt like that without Her Majesty's government's permission?

I told him, "It's my money, and I can spend it how I want."

"You have influenced the policy between China and England; private citizens can't legally do that."

"Lord Blackhoof, British citizen, did nothing. The money came from American citizen Richard Jackson. That is where I keep my funds."

He sputtered, "But that means the United States, not the United Kingdom, will get credit for the funds."

"Neither will; this was a personal gift."

He sputtered on but had to call for instructions before he could do anything else. He did ask more questions.

"Why did your parents allow you to do this?"

"They think I'm mad, but I'm emancipated and of age in the United States to make financial decisions."

"How can you afford such a sum?"

"It's hard being down to your last one hundred and fifty million, but I'll manage. My accountants tell me my company will earn that back within two years."

"Not only that, there will be enormous favorable tax consequences. Add to that, I'm making a profit on both the wheat being shipped and the shipping itself, and the cost is nearer twenty-five million rather than one hundred million. My Uncle Sam is paying for it."

"What will President Kennedy have to say?"

"He won't like the financial part; I'll make it up to him by having the US ambassador recognized. That means England had better get busy signing trade deals rather than whinging about what I've done.

"The only people I see not getting anything out of this are those in the world that think I should have been feeding their hungry. My comment is there is a difference between hunger and starving to death."

"I have to get instructions from my office, but they won't be happy."

"It's not my job to keep them happy."

He then asked to be escorted back to the embassy. I asked if I could use a phone to make several international calls. I could.

I first called the palace, trying to keep ahead of the ambassador. It was still early in Beijing, 11:00 a.m., so that made it 3:00 p.m. yesterday in London. That is so hard to understand. I know about the dateline, but it still felt like a time machine at work.

I got through to Mr. Norman on my first try, which was just short of a miracle. Heaven knows how this call was routed. I had heard operators talking; I swear I heard French and Russian.

I explained what I had done. The weirdest sounds came over the line, a terrible hollow connection. I realized he was laughing.

"Leave it to you to throw the cat amongst the pigeons. They will be having conniptions over at the FO's office in Whitehall. Douglas-Home will be screaming for the Queen to have your head."

"Will she?"

"Will she what?"

"Have my head."

"What honor have you yet to receive?"

"I have no idea."

"Whatever it is, you will probably receive it. I would settle for no less than an earldom."

"That is for later; I just wanted Her Majesty to know that the empress is on her throne and that she should be favorable to the United Kingdom."

"I will update Her Majesty, Lord Blackhoof. Now, I must ring off if I'm to stay ahead of the FO."

My next call was to the White House. Upon identifying myself, I was put through to the president's chief of staff, Ken O'Donnell. When I told him that I was in Beijing at the crowning of the empress and that I might have an opportunity to ask for an ambassador exchange with the United States, he interrupted a meeting that the president was having.

I brought them up to speed on what had happened. They both commented about my sanity but both wanted to take advantage of the situation. I was told that I had the authority to ask for the exchange. Since nothing was in writing, I would be the one holding the can if things went awry.

My third and last call was home. It was 7:00 a.m. in LA. At least, I thought I had the time conversions right. My parents sounded awake, so I had to be close.

Again, I updated them. Mum wanted to know if I was armed. I wasn't. She recommended that I get back to the British Embassy as soon as possible. Someone had to be mad enough to kill me over this.

That made sense to me.

I didn't get the chance to leave. I was summoned to a meeting. It was with the empress and Deng.

When I entered the room, I didn't know what to think. Since neither was frowning, I thought I might get out alive.

Deng spoke first, "Lord Blackhoof, you have a distinct way of causing problems and also the solutions."

I must have looked puzzled because I was.

"We have long realized that communism is not a solution for our country. However, those in power have stayed in power by espousing that. They will not give up that power. Up to now, there has been no justification for changing the system. You have given China that justification."

The empress spoke up, "We will keep the government structure and party name, but we will be allowing private ownership and encouraging foreign trade. China may never be a democracy, but we have been and will always be capitalist."

What have I unleashed on the world?

"In the meantime, you have been called here because we wish to give you honor. I wanted to give you the traditional nine bestowments, but Deng has correctly pointed out that would mean you are ready to usurp the throne. Currently, there are no other imperial honors.

"Instead, I'm declaring you a Chinese citizen."

Talk about flummoxed; I had no idea what to say. I remembered that when I had time to think things through, I should do that rather than make a mistake by being impulsive.

Deng very solemnly said, "We are also going to make you a high official in the Communist Party."

He couldn't keep a straight face as they both burst into laughter.

"On a serious note, do you have any requests for us?"

"I do. President Kennedy would like to recognize China and exchange ambassadors."

"Yes, we heard him tell you. We are willing."

And just why would I have thought my calls weren't being listened to?

"We will be entering many trade deals; we will ask your advice on who to deal with as you are a known friend with connections in the West's business world."

Was that a license to print money?

Chapter 11

"More of all this later, Lord Blackhoof. We have other people we need to talk to. Return to your embassy where there will be a thousand questions, I have no doubt.

I did, and they did. At least I was dealing with professionals. They didn't cry over spilled milk. They made sure they understood all that had transpired.

From one point of view, not much had happened. I had written off debt, been made a Chinese citizen, and been asked to advise on business deals.

Of course, there was the little matter that my writing off the debt and putting the administration of the funds in the empress's hands was significant. Also, Deng's statement that they would continue to give lip service to communism but were shifting to a capitalist society had some import.

Sir Charles the ambassador was most interested in this aspect. He put it as "A sleeping giant has been awakened."

I thought a sleeping dragon was more appropriate but wasn't going to quibble; either term described the situation.

Harold had stayed on the plane but had a suitcase with a change of clothes sent over. I needed a shower and a change. Until I was sitting and talking with Sir Charles, I hadn't realized how much I had sweated. I stunk!

I asked if I could be excused to shower and change. He told me, "Please do."

When I got out of the shower, I lay down for a moment. Three hours later, a man woke me for dinner.

Dressed in a fresh suit and tie, I joined the ambassador in his private dining room. The man looked tired. I could understand it. This was a stressful day for all.

"Lord Blackhoof, we have seen the reaction of the Chinese people to events. There have been huge gatherings with bonfires and fireworks. The people are overjoyed."

"That's good to know; it is a good sign going forward."

"Yes, it is. Of particular note is the television broadcast of the empress being crowned and her receiving gifts."

"My gifts were in the private reception room."

"There was a still camera recording the event. Your gift of the Fenghuang phoenix necklace was considered both auspicious and sensitive for a Westerner to give.

"Then, your other gift to the Chinese people has made you a hero."

"I'm not a hero for using money, which I have plenty of, to prevent people from starving."

"They don't see it that way."

"The journalists who have been under the communist thumb are emboldened by events. Not by denouncing the old regime, they aren't that foolish, but they are reporting news of world interest."

"One of the stories is about a young girl and her 'Save the Puppies' campaign. It is now being said that her big brother is running a 'Save the People' campaign. They are even selling T-shirts now.

I groaned at that, "Mary will sue me for trademark infringement."

"Surely not her brother."

"Especially her brother."

"You have some family, what with your mum and dad's records."

I didn't even bother to ask what he knew; I was too worn out to care.

We were interrupted by a phone call. It was for me. It was from the US Secretary of State Dean Rusk. He had picked an ambassador he wished to present to the Chinese—Caleb Cushing. Mr. Cushing was considered an old Asian hand and understood the culture as well as any Westerner could.

He was now on an airplane that was expected to arrive in Hong Kong in fourteen hours. He asked for my assistance in providing transportation to Beijing for the new ambassador and an introduction to both Chairman Deng and the empress.

I could tell this was profoundly serious to them as it was only 6:00 a.m. in Washington. Secretary Rusk must have been up all night.

I asked the British ambassador if I could place a call to Chairman Deng. You could tell he would rather not have the US ambassador on the scene so quickly, but he had the call placed for me. The chairman was in meetings which was no surprise, but an aide told me they had anticipated this request and I had permission to fly to Hong Kong and escort the American ambassador to Beijing.

This whole situation made me think of the Oklahoma land rush.

I wasn't thrilled about providing a taxi service but seemed to have no choice.

There was another call for me immediately after I hung up from Rusk. It was the Chinese Minister of Health. Through an interpreter, he wanted to know who I recommended China buy desperately needed medical supplies from. I told him that the British ambassador would put him in contact with Burroughs-Welcome; please hold for the ambassador.

I handed the phone to the ambassador with a quick explanation. He grabbed it from me as though it were a lifeline. In a way, it was; he was beating the Americans to a trade deal.

After that, he hadn't time to talk to me as he had aides chasing down contact information for B-W.

It was a civil time of day in London, so he was able to speak to the B-W chairman, who would be expecting a call from the Chinese Health Ministry. He assured the ambassador that B-W would be delighted to have the business and would cooperate in every way. That is, if the Chinese had a way to pay. The ambassador assured him the Chinese had a large line of credit backed by Lord Blackhoof.

This seemed to reassure the B-W chairman. I didn't realize that people other than the tabloids paid that much attention to my finances.

This should get me some points with the British FO.

I told the ambassador I had to fly to Hong Kong to pick up the new American ambassador. He asked why I was going. I must have looked blank. He pointed out that I was to get him from Hong Kong to Beijing, but that didn't mean I had to be on the aircraft.

That hadn't occurred to me. I immediately had a message sent to my flight crew captain that he was to fly to Hong Kong, pick up the new American ambassador, and return to Beijing. Mr. Cushing was to be given the full use of the plane, including my bedroom.

When they landed in Beijing, I was to be notified so I could meet him at the airport and bring him to the British Embassy, which had offered its hospitality.

The building we called the British Embassy was temporary housing provided by the Chinese government. It was like an old hotel leftover from the Boxer Rebellion. A permanent building would be acquired later.

The Americans would have to do the same. I wondered if there were many of the buildings left over from the 1900s. These would be desirable because they would have western toilets. I hated the hole-in-the-floor concept.

That reminded me to send another message to my plane. While in Hong Kong, they were to pick up some toilet paper, lots of toilet paper!

After that I went to bed early. I suspected that tomorrow would be a busy day.

I had an early breakfast and read the international newspaper. The Chinese kept up with what was going on in the rest of the world without talking to them.

I inquired about going for a run. I was taken to the front entrance, where there was a small contingent of Chinese soldiers providing temporary security. British troops were in transit.

Through an interpreter, my wish to run was made known. I was given a two-soldier escort, and we set out. It felt good to be running after being cooped up in my plane for days on end. I ran about ten miles. I made a point of circling back to the embassy every couple of miles so my guards could be replaced. Long-distance running must not be on the list for the Chinese army.

By the time I got my run in and cleaned up with a fresh suit, it was time to pick up Mr. Cushing.

The flight was on time, and I was told it was uneventful. And yes, they had picked up lots of toilet paper. I snagged a couple of rolls to take with me. The Chinese didn't use any, using the same methods as India.

Mr. Cushing wasn't on board; he had sent several staff members as an advance party. While I wasn't thrilled, it did make sense. We went to the British Embassy, where calls were made to start the process of his submitting his credentials, which were sent ahead.

No one was wasting time. After lunch, we were driven to the Forbidden City and taken to Mr. Deng, who had set up an office there. I don't know where the chairman normally worked, but I think many symbolic shifts were occurring.

I introduced the senior staff person and then was escorted from the room.

I met another official. Through an interpreter, I learned that I was being offered my choice of buildings in the old foreign trade zone. Not for free, but first chance to buy one. I could use it as my Chinese headquarters. This was the first I knew I would have a Chinese headquarters, but it made sense.

He had a list of buildings for sale. It gave the size of the building, number of rooms and types, along with the outside area.

Having a sudden thought, I asked if I was limited to one building. After a surprised look, I was told I could buy as many as I wanted.

"I would like to purchase all of these buildings."

I was going to be the landlord for all the embassies as China opened.

Chapter 12

The Chinese official got a startled look on his face and then did something I had never seen in China: he giggled.

"That is good; the French and Italians will scream the loudest. The British and Americans will end up building their own. It will have to be on these large empty lots here."

As he said that, he was pointing on a map to two twenty-acre lots. By the way, these lots are for sale."

"I would like to buy them."

"Of course, there is a small recording fee."

"Will this cover it?"

I handed him two American twenty-dollar gold pieces. He made them disappear.

"They will do nicely. The only major embassy which will not own the land or the building is the Soviets."

"If it ever comes up for sale, let me know."

"For an honored person such as yourself, I will be glad to."

Right, I thought. You honor my gold.

I immediately saw the need for a Chinese Headquarters. I asked my new Chinese friend which of the buildings I was buying was in the best condition for immediate occupancy.

Without hesitation, he pointed at one. This was the office of a Soviet business group. The Soviets thought that relations between us would permit much trade. The Soviet government never allowed them to make trades, so we repossessed the building.

"Is it ready to move in?"

"Almost. Some carpets need to be replaced and walls painted—the blood, you know."

Some repossession.

"I will need to arrange to transfer funds with the Peoples Bank of China."

"I believe they have arrangements with banks in Canada and Switzerland."

"That will work. Are there any problems holding these until the funds are transferred?"

"There will be a fee for that service."

Fortunately, I had several more gold coins on me. From his office, I returned to the Forbidden City by the car provided by the British Embassy. Once there, I went to Chairman Deng's office, where the helpful official who had sent me to the real estate office waited.

I asked for his help in obtaining my Chinese passport and any other papers I may need. He had them in his desk drawer. There was a passport made up with my picture in it; all I had to do was sign it. He gave it a final stamp, and it was good to go.

There was also a set of travel documents that let me travel anywhere in China as though I were a high official in the Communist Party. I asked him if there were any fees.

"Do you mean bribes? If so, that would be a labor battalion for the bribe-taker or even the death penalty for multiple bribes."

"What about the person offering a bribe?"

"Twenty years at hard labor at best, maybe death."

I hoped the real estate guy was careful where he flashed that gold. How many people were handing out American twenty-dollar gold pieces?

He made a phone call to the Peoples Bank and made me an appointment. My driver took me there; it was literally across the street. All he did was make a U-turn in front of about a million bicycles, and we were there.

At the bank, I met with a senior vice president. It turned out they had handled my letter of credit for the money I had initially loaned China, so they knew the avenues to get money from my bank into theirs.

I opened an account with them and, with his help, sent transfer instructions to my bank in LA. The money would go from the US to Canada to China.

From this route, I thought it would take days. Instead, it would be hours. Of course, each bank would take one percent of the funds as their fee.

I think bribery was cheaper. That is, if you didn't get caught.

While I was doing this, I kept track of the time. From the bank, I was taken to the airport where Mr. Cushing should finally be arriving on my plane.

It was on time. I boarded the aircraft to an almost full front section. The ambassador hadn't come alone. I was met by an aide and taken to my office where the ambassador had made himself at home.

I didn't mind him using the office, but he should keep his damn feet off my desk.

He did stand to shake hands. I decided to let the feet on my desk issue go in the spirit of harmony.

He graciously offered me a seat in my office. This was getting old fast.

"Mr. Jackson, I'm glad to meet you. Thank you for providing transportation. This is a nice office setup you have here. With the copy machine, telex, and typewriters, I think I will use this until we get settled into a new building. It shouldn't take long to find temporary quarters."

What is it with these American officials? First, that idiot general, now this.

"That won't be possible. This is a British-flagged aircraft. It is Queen's Messenger One."

"Nonsense, you are an American citizen, and I need this aircraft."

"What does my citizenship have to do with it?"

"I can have your American passport canceled if you don't cooperate. You will be stranded here with no way home, and the Chinese will make short work of you."

Where do these people come from? From my suit coat, I pulled four passports: an American, two British, diplomatic and civil, plus my brand-new Chinese one.

"Take your pick."

He picked them up and rifled through them.

He handed them back to me, "Obviously, I wasn't given a full brief on you."

"Take your people and get off my airplane."

He left without further comment, his entourage following. I had no idea how they would get to the British Embassy and didn't care.

Using the onboard telephone, I called Deng's aide and told him I would like to find lodging at a hotel, Western-style, if possible. He told me it wasn't, but they had Western-style rooms on the Forbidden City grounds that I was welcome to use. They had been put in for the Soviets when they had good relations.

I figured it was time to move; the British Embassy wasn't big enough for me and the American ambassador.

In the meantime, my Bentley was unloaded. The flight crew hired a local driver. Harold had a new collection of clothes for me to wear, so he joined me on the trip into the city.

My room was an enormous suite. It looked brand new with all the latest in 1940s furniture. Heavy ornate furniture. It was as ugly a room as I have ever stayed in. That said, it had all the amenities.

Harold thought the place was great. Of course, he grew up in a palace that was last updated when Victoria was queen.

I placed a call to the White House; it only took an hour to make the connection. Once connected, I explained to Ken O'Donnell what an ass they had chosen for an ambassador. He was surprised to hear my story as he had been assured that Cushing was the man for the job.

I told them I wasn't worried about me as I could ignore him. He should be concerned about his relating to the Chinese. He was acting as though he could send a gunboat up the river to make his points.

I was told they would talk to Dean Rusk and see what was going on.

The bed was comfortable, and I had a good night's sleep.

The first thing in the morning, I had a call placed to the Bank of China to check on the status of the funds I had asked for. There now was twenty-five million dollars in my Chinese bank account. I would have to do something with it soon as it was illegal for Chinese citizens to hold foreign currency.

I intended to spend a good bit this morning but would still have eighteen million left. I was reluctant to have it converted to Chinese renminbi yuan as they had no official conversion rate with the rest of the world.

I was told that I should put my dollars into gold. It was illegal for Chinese citizens to own gold, but the British Lord Blackhoof could store his gold in their vaults.

I asked what that would take. It turned out to be extremely easy as there were huge amounts of gold in their vaults which changed hands all the time. I could purchase gold for a small fee. This fee wasn't to be confused with a bribe as the bank managers authorized it. It was shared by all employees involved.

I arranged the gold purchase and had a bank draft drawn for the buildings and land I was buying. I did have the smarts to have Deng's aide clear the purchase with both Chairman Deng and Lady Ping. They both wrote back that it was a wise move for many reasons.

I went back to the official real estate office and made my purchase after paying small fees, not to be confused with bribes.

Chapter 13

My biggest issue now was to find someone to run my Chinese headquarters. I would prefer to find a Chinaman here in Beijing who had gone to school in America, an English speaker who had experienced the culture.

Again, I went back to Chairman Deng's office for advice. A different person was manning the front desk. They knew who I was, no surprise there; how many round eyes, as they called us, were in town.

I explained my need. He led me to another room, which was filled with filing cabinets. We stopped at a desk barring the way into the room. Fast words in one of the Chinese dialects had the man at the front desk summon another. After short instructions, that person went out of sight, presumably to find the information.

They returned in five minutes with six folders. They were presented to my guide. Since they were in Chinese, I didn't have a clue what was said.

My guide went through them and handed three back.

He turned to me, "These two are problems; one gambles more than he can afford, and the other drinks too much. The last one has a good job that is valuable to the state, so we won't interview him."

So much for freedom in China. However, it did save me time.

"We will have these three come in for interviews tomorrow."

We went back to his office.

"I understand that the new American ambassador was recalled before he could present his credentials. Do you know anything about that?"

"He flew in on my aircraft. I met him before he deplaned and determined he would not serve the American needs, so I suggested they review his record. It looks like they did, and he was found wanting."

"That is what we were told; the American government seems to respect your opinion."

"I don't know about that, but they are smart enough to listen and double-check."

"It says much that they listen to you and don't dismiss your thoughts out of hand."

"I suppose so."

I spent the rest of the day going through the eight buildings I had bought. As I had been told, some carpet replacement and paint would remove the long-dried bloodstains in the building that would be my headquarters.

All the other buildings needed considerably more work but could be refurbished. Two of them were in better shape, so they could serve as the American and British Embassies until they built their own.

I left a message for the British ambassador about the buildings and that he should detail someone to look at them. I had been given to understand by my Chinese real estate person that the embassy would only be allowed in this area and these buildings.

The real estate office was not like a traditional American company. They were more like the American General Services Administration; they were an arm of the government providing over-the-counter equipment to the various government bureaus.

Among other things, they acquired office space or, as in this case, disposed of unneeded buildings. What they said goes.

The next day, I interviewed my three candidates and ended up hiring all three. They were all American-educated, well-spoken men. One Mr. Wang stood out as he had a doctorate from Stanford in business administration.

Normally I would give preference to someone who had real-world experience. In this case, he had both. He had returned to China to try to save his family's failing shipbuilding firm.

He worked hard for six years before he had to let it go under. A note in his file said that his father had offended the local communist cadre leader and that the business was forced under by the state.

Meeting Mr. Wang was against all expectations. I thought that having a Ph.D., he would be a soft-looking man. He looked as hard as nails with a handshake that would do Popeye proud.

The other two only had master's and hadn't run large businesses, but I thought they would make good assistants to Mr. Wang. I wanted to overstaff a little to help ensure Mr. Wang's success and, at the same time, have a reserve in place if he failed on a personal level.

I called Jim Williamson in LA. That was a hard phone call, not the conversation, the connection. It took over an hour to set the call-up, then it was immediately dropped.

We had to shout to hear each other. I asked him to come to China and help Mr. Wang set up the office here so that he was in close contact with the California offices. The building was in Beverly Hills, but I couldn't break myself from thinking of it as the LA headquarters.

Jim asked if he could bring his wife as they had no children, and she didn't work. I told him to bring her and have a good time. I arranged a suite for them at my hotel, a car and driver, along with a translator.

The hotel concierge assured me that they would arrange a "shopper" to help Mrs. Williamson spend all of Jim's money. I made a mental note to give Jim a bonus for this trip.

With banking arrangements set up, first office staff in place, and support arranged for them, I thought I was ready to return to the US.

To be safe, I checked with Chairman Deng's office to see if there was anything they needed me for. There wasn't, but there was a request from Empress Ping to call upon her.

I had made my calls from the hotel next to the Forbidden City, so I immediately started to cross the street to the complex. That is when I realized that all wasn't well in China. I no sooner than stepped outside the door and gunfire started.

It wasn't directed at me. Rebels were attacking the guards at the entrance to the Forbidden City. I ducked back into the hotel. I had been shot enough.

I wondered how long this firefight would last. It wasn't long before a motorized brigade of the Chinese Army came roaring in from a side street and took down the rebels in short order.

While this was going on, I had been talking to the concierge about the fighting. He informed me state radio was quiet about the events but that from what word of mouth spread, the rebels were fighting across the country and failing at all stops.

From my point of view, that was good news. The rebels weren't a concerted effort but various military leaders around the country who thought they could split off their kingdom.

After waiting an hour sipping tea in the dining room, I was able to cross the street safely. Two soldiers momentarily detained me, but an officer came running up shouting at them. The only word I understood was a mangled Blackhoof. Being six foot five inches in China made one stand out.

My wait to see the empress was short. She greeted me warmly and told me that China would forever be in my debt. The money I had provided would save many people, and they would support the new China.

In the meantime, it would be best if I stayed out of China for a year or more and let things settle down. It was fine that I had an official opening, and she thought it was hilarious that I would be the landlord to all the embassies but the Russians.

She would ensure that all the embassies rented or being built on my properties were given first-class support. The Russians who had failed China would receive nothing.

I know it is petty of me, but the idea of the Russian ambassador not having hot water tickled my fancy.

I promised to stay away until I was told things were settled enough and that I would await her word. There were many sights I wanted to see in China; the Great Wall is at the top of the list, but they would wait. She did ask that now China was open to foreign trade, I start modernizing the Port of Shanghai.

I promised that I would have our engineers survey the port as soon as possible to start the process. An aide standing behind her gave me a card with the office to contact in Shanghai to coordinate with.

That ended my China trip. I boarded my aircraft and flew to Hong Kong. As soon as we landed, we were told that we had to board the new American ambassador and fly back to Beijing.

I called Ken O'Donnell at the White House and explained I wasn't a taxi service. He practically begged me to make the trip. I was in high favor in China, and it would help immensely if I were seen bringing the ambassador to China.

Yes, it would help the ambassador to be seen in my airplane, but at the same time, it would make it look like I was at the beck and call of the Americans. If the government had called and asked, I would have done it, no questions asked.

I was beginning to dislike the "Ugly Americans." As an American myself, I knew that no one from Bellefontaine would act that way; it was those idiots who came to power in the government or Hollywood. Well, maybe Tom Humphreys would, but that was it.

The upshot was I told him no. I had an important event that I had to get back to in California. I wasn't lying; Valentine's Day is an important event.

Chapter 14

Losing a day on the trip back got me into LAX at noon on Tuesday, the 13th of February.

I had slept on the plane but still had to go through the reverse time change. I wasn't looking forward to it.

There was a limo waiting for me with a very pretty girl in the back seat. What a nice welcome home. When we came up for air, I asked her how things were going. She was in a particularly good mood; there was every sign her parents were getting back together.

I asked what the signs were. It seems her parents were using only one bed. Most importantly, they were talking, talking about what had upset them with each other and how silly it seemed now.

Mr. Monroe had told me that he and Karen were getting remarried, but I never heard another word. Something had changed their plans, but now it seemed like they were working it out.

I hope the best for them. I like Mr. Monroe, and Nina's mom seems nice. I agreed with Nina that it was a good sign that they were talking. I hope she isn't too disappointed if it doesn't work out for them.

Nina had a couple of days off school and had flown commercially to spend time with her parents. My being home was a bonus for us.

She had planned to return to Switzerland tomorrow, so I told her to take my plane. The flight crews could end up at their homes in England. I was going to be here for a while.

We had been hitting the air travel heavily, so we were all due for some non-flying time. You can only stay inside an aluminum tube for so long. I don't know how submariners do it.

Upon arrival at Jackson House, there was a welcome committee. Not my family but Secret Service Agents next to our regular guards. This didn't bode well.

Inside, Bobby Kennedy stood with my parents. It looked as though they had been having a tense conversation. When I came into the room, all eyes shifted to me.

Kennedy started, "Jackson, we need to talk. You haven't supported your country, and you are going to change your ways."

He didn't add or else, but it was implied.

"In what way are you asking me to change my ways?"

"When our ambassador needs transportation, we expect you to turn your aircraft over to him. When we tell you to support our policy of nonintervention in Chinese affairs, we expect you, as a private citizen, to follow the lead of your government. Shall I go on?"

"Let's take it one item at a time. You want me to turn over Queen's Messenger One, a British diplomatic aircraft to you? I would think you would need the agreement and cooperation of Her Majesty's government.

"As far as nonintervention, when and where was this policy promulgated, and when was it communicated to me or any other member of the public?"

"We know you are the registered owner of the aircraft, and the call sign travels with you, not the aircraft."

"You are correct; however, you mustn't be familiar with the lease agreement I have with the British government that the aircraft is available to them at their call. When they exercise their rights, the plane is automatically Queen's Messenger One.

"So, I'm afraid we are back to the issue that you need the permission of the British government. Now again, I ask when the nonintervention policy was put into effect?"

"The President signed an Executive Order last night."

"Since I was in the air over the Pacific last night, there was no way that I could have gone against American policy; now that we have that out of the way, what is this really about?"

"You can influence the Chinese, and we need to do so."

"What do you need done?"

"Vietnam is about to explode; the Soviets are backing a popular communist leader, Ho Chi Minh. We need the Chinese to tell the Soviets to back off and, if need be, let us blockade the port of Haiphong.

The civil government in the southern part of the country is so corrupt that it will soon fall, but if the Soviets back the northern part of the country in a civil war, we will have to back the south. We don't want to do that but will if needed to prevent Soviet influence from expanding.

"If we don't have a Chinese commitment soon, we will start training pilots in the south and providing support to their air force."

"Why couldn't you just ask me that in the first place?"

The Attorney General looked embarrassed.

"If I had been able to browbeat you into doing this, we would owe you nothing. Now, you will be doing us a favor, and we will owe you."

"My god, man, some people ask what they can do for their country, not what their country can do for them. I will do this, and there will be nothing owed by anyone.

"If the Chinese are willing to tell the Soviets to back off, what are you willing to offer?"

"Most favored nation trade status and a loan package of twenty-five million dollars."

"A little cheap. I just gave them a hundred million."

I swear he turned green.

"I was told that but didn't believe it."

"It's true but offer what you think is correct. I only suggest you make the offer to the empress. She will have to turn it over to the Communist leadership, but it will improve her value to the Communists and the country."

He looked pensive for a moment.

"You are right, Lord Blackhoof. I see that we have underestimated you. May I call you in the future if we need help or have questions?"

"Yes, you may."

He turned to my parents and thanked them for their hospitality as he left. I lifted one eyebrow at my parents to let them start the conversation.

It wasn't nice. I don't think the Kennedys will receive much in the way of campaign donations from the Jackson family in the future.

Nina had been standing there during the entire exchange. She had a look of almost fear on her face. I asked her what was wrong.

"I'm only a senior in high school. I don't think I'm ready for your world. I thought I knew it, but I don't."

My mum rescued me, "Nina, dear, no one is ever ready for this level. One does what one can."

"But Rick, without saying it directly, told the Attorney General of the United States to go to hell. Won't there be a price for that?"

"There is always a price," Dad told her, "But that goes two ways. They will be angry, but so are we; both sides will weigh the damages we can do each other and most likely do nothing. That is unless a clear-cut opportunity arises.

"If an opportunity comes about, one of us will go for the others' throats. In the meantime, we will smile and work with each other. It is called politics.

"In the world of politics, friends become enemies and enemies the best of friends in a heartbeat, sometimes both at the same time. Just look at Mary and Patty; they are living examples."

We talked for a little longer, but there wasn't anything more to add. I placed a call to Chairman Deng's office. I asked that I be allowed to talk to him about an American government request.

When he came on, I explained how the United States didn't want to support South Vietnam but felt like they would have to if the North accepted aid from the Soviets.

He told me that he thought that was how it would play out. I told him what the American government was requesting and that they were willing to offer a foreign aid package.

Since I was peeved at the Kennedys in particular, I suggested that they not accept the original offer.

He said, "*yào bú bān mén nòng fǔ*," which the translator expressed as don't teach your grandmother to suck eggs. That put me in my place.

I didn't bother to tell him the offer would probably be extended through the empress. First, I didn't know they would do that, and second, let them be the bad guys.

My parents and Nina had heard my end of the conversation, and I shared what the chairman said.

I called the number that Bobby had left me and told whoever answered that Chairman Deng's office was expecting their call on Vietnam.

After that, Nina and I looked up my siblings. They were all watching TV. It was a new show about weird situations. The announcer, Rod someone, looked familiar to me, but I couldn't place him.

We watched it with them; then we all went up to change for dinner. This had become normal at our house. At times, it was a bit of a pain, but it seemed classy most of the time.

After dinner, we played a rousing game of Monopoly. Nina and Mary teamed up and broke the bank. You could tell Mary wanted Nina's approval as she was a big girl. In turn, Nina was understanding with Mary. This was a deadly combination if let loose on the world.

The next day, Wednesday the 14th, was Valentine's Day. Dad had gone the traditional route with flowers and candy accompanying the card. Mary got cards from all the guys.

I gave Nina a small box. It was great to see Mum's eyes get wide when she saw it. This was accompanied by a look of relief when Nina opened it to a set of Ferrari keys. I told her the car had been shipped to Switzerland, and I had bought a garage next to her apartment to house it. I had to buy the garage as it was the only one available in the area, and they would only sell, not rent. The price wasn't that high, so I went for it.

It was treated as a big deal, and I tried to downplay it as the car was gathering dust in England. Mum gave Dad a look like, see, that is how it is done. I suggested to Nina that we go horseback riding, anything to get out of the line of fire.

Chapter 15

The next morning, Nina left for Switzerland, and John Jacobs came to my house along with Sam. We piled into the old Jeep we kept for this type of jaunt and took the back way to the Forestry Station.

For some reason, the guys kept telling me to slow down as we bumped along. It was an original Jeep and wouldn't go over sixty-five, and I kept it below fifty on the dirt road, but it was too much for them. Wimps. This wasn't even a Leaping Lena.

The crew who moved the practice putting green and the driving range had done a wonderful job. You couldn't tell the setup had been many miles away not that long ago.

It was getting a good workout as there were people on the driving range and several on the greens. No one said anything to us as we got out. There was a small shed to one side.

It was locked because John was using it to store my gear. There were also a couple of chairs and a small table, which John and Sam pulled out and used. They weren't going to suffer as I worked.

I went through the same steps as I had before my trip to China. It didn't take more than an hour to get back to 98% at three feet and 20% at fifteen feet.

It took another four hours to get to 99% and 24%.

I alternated every hour with using the driving range, working my way up from a chip shot to my driver.

When I started hitting the driver, I noticed that I was gathering an audience. Anyone who plays golf loves to see a long-hit ball. I didn't mind, but as a taxpayer in the ninety-one percent bracket, I had to wonder if these government workers had anything to do.

I kept my mouth shut as I realized these were the people who would have to go into a raging fire to put it out. Their lives were on the line. They should have some perks with their job.

At noon, I had enough of hitting golf balls for the day. John and Sam sat there and watched me the whole time. John at least had a clipboard and kept track of my putts and calculated my percentages as I completed each practice session.

Sam just sat there beaming. Part of his beloved course was living on. I wasn't going to rain on his parade. When John and I started to leave, Sam got some equipment out of the shed.

He was going to tend our little golf course. He had met John here this morning, leaving his car here, and rode with John to my house. I told them I would meet them here tomorrow morning. They seemed relieved to hear that.

After cleaning up and changing clothes, I joined Mum and Dad at a restaurant on Sunset Drive. It had become a favorite of theirs. It hadn't been "discovered" yet. They had mixed feelings about that. They loved the good food and service without the crowds but wanted to see the owners succeed.

Mum had something green that looked like it was grown in a cow pasture. Dad and I kept with good old American cheeseburgers; you couldn't go wrong with those.

We talked about the Kennedys and if we would have any problems with them. I had been harsh with Bobby the day before.

As Mum said, "They started it; you finished it. That is the way it is supposed to be."

She is gentle in her approach to the world. Not!

Dad didn't think it would be an issue as the Kennedys were well known for being pragmatic. Also, they had enough skeletons in their closets that they didn't want to tangle with the owner of as many newspapers, radio, and TV stations as he had.

Dad was also gentle in his approach, just like Chuck Bednarik.

If they weren't concerned, I wasn't either. At the same time, if I could do anything reasonable to get back in their good graces, I would.

After lunch, I stopped at my office and spent most of the afternoon signing cards to be sent to my many workers. There were a few that were noteworthy enough that I penned a short letter of congratulations.

One of our worker's children had won a statewide spelling bee and was on her way to the nationals. We knew this because the father was noted as working for Jackson Transportation, so the clipping service picked it up.

Besides the note to the young lady, I also dropped a line to Todd Goodson to let me know when the nationals were occurring. If she made it to the finals, I would like to be there. Also, we needed to ensure she was included in our scholarship fund.

It would look good in the company newsletter. Besides, I admired anyone who could spell that well. I knew how hard it was from all my typing. Typos were bad; not knowing how to spell a word was a time killer. The fact that I was taking an interest in these sorts of things should send a signal to my management that they should, also. This is how you prevented unions.

After generating a decent case of writer's cramp, I went back to Jackson House after promising to come back this week and finish the job.

Clark Miller had called for me and left a message. I returned his call. He was excited he had just received the movie offer from John Wayne's production company.

There was a real kicker: the script I had read in Hong Kong was a spy-type movie. Now they wanted me in an oater, a Western. I just about hung up the phone but remembered in time that this wasn't Clark's fault. I decided to hear him out. I did need something to do.

They were offering an incredibly low salary but five points in the movie. I had told Clark he was a winner if he could get five points, not telling him that I would be impressed with three.

I asked him what sort of production schedule they were looking at. He told me they wanted to start as soon as possible with a five-month shooting timeline and another five months in post-production.

This sounded very doable as it was set in the Old West and wouldn't have a lot of high-tech stunts like jumping out of airplanes or car chases. Filming a runaway stagecoach could get interesting.

Then there were cattle stampedes. Strike the thought that it would be easy. Things could go very wrong.

I read the script several times, and I thought I understood the movie they were trying to make.

There was a cattle drive involved. It was based on one of the last great cattle drives from the Texas Panhandle to Montana. The movie was called *The Chisholm Trail,* which was completely inaccurate but recognizable by theatergoers.

The Panhandle to Montana drive was enormous. They had ten herds of 2500 cattle to move. There were over 100 hundred cowboys involved. John Wayne was to play trail boss Tom Coffee; I was to be a young Charles Goodnight. As I said, accurate history isn't Hollywood's strong suit. At least I wasn't Bill Pickett.

As Charles Goodnight, I would be a messenger for Tom Coffee. I would spend my days riding back and forth between the ten herds, reporting on and trying to solve problems.

There would be a young lady named Molly hired as a cook on one of the herds, and she would be my love interest. That was about the only thing in the movie true to life: the real Charles Goodnight married a Molly.

We would have to turn stampedes, ford rivers and quicksand streams, and fight Indians and cattle thieves. We would endure hunger, thirst, and other physical hardships.

There would be a stopover in Abilene. Hey, I know that's not accurate at all, but we had to have some saloon scenes and a showdown on Main Street. We might even have a jailbreak, but that was under discussion.

It was a movie to make money, not win an Oscar. I was typecast as the young cowpoke but didn't care. I wanted something to do, and the movie set was always fun.

There was mention of a town named Shawnee. I wondered if I could get some work for my real Shawnee friends. Maybe even work in a cute-looking Shawnee Indian girl to make Molly jealous.

There was a note on the edge of my script that they should check on the Easterly ranch and see if that would be a good setting.

If nothing else, they had an ornery herd of cattle. It would be good to see Mr. and Mrs. Easterly again, though I would skip the bank robbery reenactment this time.

I decided to get ahead of the curve and ask if my siblings could audition for bit parts, and maybe Nina could play Molly.

Nina being in the movie meant that I would have to be careful about a good-looking Shawnee girl. Someone might get scalped, and it could be me.

Chapter 16

I had second thoughts about trying to get family members and Nina in the movie. I had seen others try, some succeeding, others failing. It never sat right with me when I saw it happening, so I shouldn't do it.

Now, if someone else brought it up, that was fine.

Monday morning started with my usual run and exercises. I had fallen behind on weights while in China. Considering my schedule, I felt lucky about even getting to run.

After cleaning up, I went over to the Forestry Service for my golf practice. I had a surprise waiting for me. The sod people were back and unloading what looked like a massive practice green.

Sam and John were there. Sam was rubbing his hands together in glee.

"What's this about, guys?"

"Your dad heard about two more golf courses being torn down for housing projects in the Valley, so he bought the practice greens and the actual greens."

"Why did he do that?"

"He was here earlier to get it started. Sam has been given the project of recreating the major greens or at least the obstacles like shelves, tilts, and curves of all the greens on the four tournaments in the Grand Slam this year."

"Because of grass differences, he won't be able to get the speeds to match, but they will still give you a good insight on how to play the shots. Once you are at the actual course, you can factor in the true speeds."

"Wow, I would have never thought of this. I must thank Dad. How are you going to find out how all those greens are shaped? That is four times eighteen greens with at least four possible pin placements on each one. That is at least 288 possibilities."

John spoke up, "Your dad and I talked about that. I will be making contacts with several caddies at each course, and we will build a model of each green."

I could see a lot of travel in John's near future.

"Take good notes on your trip; you will be able to write a book on this project."

He got a look of wonder, "Who could imagine that? Me, an author."

Then a look of frustration appeared as he stated, "But grammar, spelling, and punctuation have never been my strong suit—just the opposite."

"That's why God invented editors and proofreaders."

Sam frowned at my blasphemy but let it pass. He seemed to appreciate that he had a good thing going here and wasn't going to mess it up.

While those two went over to supervise the sod people, I got to work. I was still improving my percentages, but it was slow. My progress now was measured in tenths of a percent of shots made.

The driving range was being kind to me. My drives, pitches, stock shot, pitch and run, knockdowns, and blind shots were coming together. I could even hook and slice the ball pretty much where I wanted it.

I also knew that any of these shots could go away from me on any given day. My practice area was set up for everything but bunker shots. I suspect John and Sam had a plan for that as well.

No sooner than I had the thought, dump trucks started pulling into the area and dumping piles of sand. I didn't even bother looking for the front loader machine that would be digging the bunkers out and hauling sand. It would be here.

Several of the Forest Service people wandered over and asked what was going on. My operation was taking a lot of space. Not that it was a problem. We were next to a mile-and-a-half runway with the fencing at least a quarter mile from the runway. That is a lot of room.

I updated them on the plan. I asked them not to spread it to the press. If the press got wind of this, then the Forest Service would take a lot of heat for a problem they didn't create. Besides, I had paid for all of this, including the airport itself.

They saw the wisdom in not talking about it outside of their group. It also would be cool to practice the putts the pros faced on the tournament trail.

I spent half a day, putting hundreds of times. I didn't have anyone keeping track of my shots as both John and Sam were engrossed in the new greens being installed around the area.

As I was getting ready to leave, they came over and we talked about what was going in. There would have to be water lines put in so all the greens could be watered. Here in California, you could lose a green almost overnight in the dry season. It looked like Sam had a lifetime job.

I went back to the house, driving the Jeep at my speed. I managed to bounce it into the air twice on the way back.

After cleaning up and lunch, I headed over to the Warner Brothers lot for the first meeting on the movie.

In this meeting, we would talk about the schedule and locations and start the costuming process. From what I read in the script, I suspected there would be more dialog changes than normal. The action scenes in a Western were standard.

What could you do besides gunfights, bank robberies, stagecoach robberies, stagecoach runaways, jailbreaks, stampedes, and, oh yes, throwing Rick into a water trough? That last had been a staple of every movie I had been in, and I doubted it would change now.

They managed it even in OTO. Not when in Death Wind mode, but as Lew, the cheerful fiddle player.

Mr. Wayne laid down the law about budget and schedule; we were to meet both. At one point, the discussion turned to the movie cast. With a need for a hundred cowboys, it would take a lot of people. The casting people pointed out that it wouldn't really. There were only a couple of times in the movie when they would show all of them as a group.

For that, they would hire extras. For all the other shots, twenty full-time actors could change costumes and horses, and no one would know the difference.

Speaking of real cowboys, some of those would have to be hired to manage the livestock, both cattle and horses.

John Wayne asked me if Mary and a friend would be available for bit parts. It seemed that cute seven-year-olds helped the human dimension of the movie. The audience could relate to them.

Their parts would be skipping rope as the cowboys rode past or some such scene. It showed that the cowboys were part of what we considered the real world.

I told him that Lady Mary would be all for it, but I thought she was only six. He gave me a funny look.

"How old are you?"

"Seventeen."

"How much older than Mary are you?"

"Ten years."

"Math wasn't your strong suit, was it?"

"I guess I just got used to thinking of Mary being six and have never changed. Anyway, it is Countess Jackson who has to be asked if seven-year-old Mary can be in the movie. I'm sure that you will ask politely."

He muttered, "Coward."

I thought discretion was the better part of valor.

The girl who was to play Molly was there so that left Nina out, which was probably for the best.

One interesting thing happened. One of the writers who had worked on OTO with me asked if the Indian chief would be available to help. There was a town named Shawnee on the way. It was a good bet that the chief could help there.

John Wayne wanted to know who the chief was. I told him and the others present about Chief Redfoot, who was director of the Shawnee Heritage Museum, and how he had given technical advice on *Over the Ohio*.

Wayne was interested and asked me to make a phone call. I agreed; it wasn't like having to ask my mum to do something that I knew she wouldn't be wild about. Heck, the chief probably wouldn't even scalp me.

That meeting took up the rest of the afternoon. We all got to know each other a little in the breaks. The actress playing Molly was new to the business but seemed to have her act together. I liked her and thought we could work with each other.

I found out she was two years older than me, single but dating a guy steadily. He was a senior at UCLA by the name of George Takei. He also hoped to be an actor.

Not being a complete rat fink, I told Mum before dinner that she would be getting a call from John Wayne. He would be asking if Mary and a friend would be interested in a bit part in the movie we were about to make.

To my surprise, she thought it would be okay. Before, she had restrained what Mary could do as she wanted her to be a little girl.

I asked her about that, and she told me that the ship had sailed. Now, she was trying to help Mary adjust to a life of fame and fortune and not have it turn into a life of sex, drugs, and alcohol—her words, not mine.

Wow, that is a burden for a seven-year-old. Now, I'm not sure that I want Mary in the movie.

I asked Mum if she would ask her friend Patty to be in the movie with her or if it would depend on what day of the week it was.

Mum told me that Mary was realizing she couldn't count on a stable relationship with her best friend in the world. She approached Mum and told her she wouldn't be inviting Patty to be a model because she never knew when they would be fighting. My little sister is growing up.

Instead of Patty, she probably would invite her new friend with whom she was on the phone almost every day.

"Who is that?"

"Princess Carolyn."

Chapter 17

The young princess keeps calling Mary. Mary is very patient with the younger child. I spoke with her mother. She is more enthused to talk about fashions with Mary than anything else going. They have used it as a method to teach her to read and her numbers; you must use both to be a fashion designer, you know.

At first, she was forbidden to make calls. She would sneak off and do it anyway. The Grimaldi Palace staff humored her until Princess Grace said no and stopped placing the calls.

Then Princess Grace saw how Carolyn was improving in her studies, so she told the staff to put the call through, but it was to be as though Carolyn was getting away with sneaking. Let her have the fun.

Mary was part of the plot as she would ask questions she had been fed, which the young princess would have to do her homework to answer.

I wondered what the Monacan orders of merit were. I asked Mum more as a joke and found out that Mary was being considered for the Order of Grimaldi for her contribution in getting a stubborn little girl to learn.

This took me aback; I was happy for Mary, but a seven-year-old being given an award people would spend a lifetime earning didn't seem right.

I voiced that to Mum. She laughed at me.

"Rick, at times, you are so easy. She is being considered for a lesser award but not for her actions with the princess.

"Her foundation has opened a shelter in Monaco. This is of note as the people of Monaco voted not to put down any healthy animals. Both the French and Italians have been using them as a dumping ground for unwanted pets."

"Won't her shelter fill up?"

"A network has been created between all of Mary's shelters; they share Polaroid pictures between them. If you adopt a Mary save, it will have had its shots, and if old enough, house training started."

"I didn't know that she had such a sophisticated operation going."

"You do know that she is only the front person. Her money supports it, and she does the ads, but professionals are running the shelter program."

"I hadn't thought about it, but it makes sense."

"As to Princess Caroline appearing in a movie, her mother won't allow it. I have heard and respect her reasons for not wanting her daughter to go into show business. The only reason Mary is allowed is that we can protect her in ways the Rainiers can't."

The way she said it, I thought of Popeye and sterling silver. I will never forget my thinking a Sterling machine gun was silverware.

The next morning after my usual exercises, I went over to the Forestry Service practice golf course. For short, John, Sam, and I had taken to calling it The Greens.

They had beaten me there. Sam was supervising crews unrolling the sod for the greens. This was so he could duplicate the different greens. John wasn't there as he was visiting the various courses. I think he was in Augusta right now.

Someone had been thinking because Denny was there taking photographs of the work in progress.

Earlier crews had been in and dug down for the underlayers of sand and gravel. Drainage tile and irrigation had been put in. The light fixtures were still set up on stands where they had worked through the night.

This had all been done on an urgent basis, so it was costing Dad (really me) almost double. When he told me at breakfast that it would be close to two million dollars, I almost choked on my toast.

I could see the potential of all sorts of screams of rage if I did well in the upcoming tournaments. I was cheating! No other golfer would have my advantage.

Nothing would be said about all the other golfers who had the time and privileges to practice on the real courses.

Oh well, they would get over it. It might even start a new industry. Maybe John and Sam could run a camp every year for the upcoming Grand Slam tour. There might be issues about it being on Forestry Service land. I think I will leave the whole issue alone. This is one battle I don't need.

I went ahead and started my daily routine of practice greens, then the driving range. The improvements were incremental, but they were there as my muscle memory improved.

Finishing up, I chatted with Sam a bit. He was concerned about fitting the sod from the greens so that a seam wouldn't interfere with the putting line being practiced.

I next returned home, showered, and then had lunch. I cleaned up, refueled, and headed over to Warner Brothers. Today, I would spend hours putting on and taking off costumes for lighting checks and comparisons with others in the same scene.

Boring was the best I could say about it. Why couldn't they use stand-ins? Too cheap, was my guess.

It was a wonder of wonders; I finished up an hour early. I stopped by the stunt lot on my way out. I talked to a few of the guys but didn't get involved in anything.

It did make me realize that I hadn't done any boxing, martial arts, sword fighting, or using a staff for months. I had done some archery, for real, not practice.

I needed to get back at it soon. It made me think about the upcoming movie and the hours on horseback. Just thinking about it made my thighs sore.

Later at home, I went for a ride on George. It only confirmed that I was in for some pain. I pledged to myself to ride him every chance I got from now on.

I made good on my promise the next morning after completing my daily routine. I rode George over to the Forestry Service. I had a stake and long lead line for him, so he was happy to spend the morning munching on a new set of grass.

I set up for my putting. I was focused on putts at about thirteen feet when an object thudded down between me and the hole. It took a moment to put it into context.

I realized it was a smokejumper who had drifted off course. They were doing practice jumps on the other side of the field, but a wind gust caught this one and dumped him on my green.

After I got over my shock, it was interesting to see what all they carried. The guy could barely walk with all the gear he had on him.

I helped him bundle his chute up. A Jeep came driving up to collect him. He thanked me and apologized for interrupting the putt. It seems he also played golf and had his priorities in order.

I told him "No worries." I learned that saying in Australia.

He invited me over to their little field canteen set up for a beer after work. I told him I would be leaving at noon, so I couldn't take him up on it, but I would like to talk to him about his job.

It was decided I would join Rob and his friends at lunch. I went back to my grind as he roared off for his. Jumping out of an airplane had to be more exciting than stroking the little white ball.

That thought made me introspective. Then I realized that I did get a thrill out of a well-placed shot or a long putt that looked like it had eyes.

Sam didn't even acknowledge my presence as he worked on the greens. The man was in greens keeper heaven.

I did join Rob with his friends Steve and Dave for lunch. They had some good tales about some jumps that turned hairy. If they misjudged the speed of a fire, they could get in an updraft with terrible results. You don't want to land in the middle of a raging fire.

I asked about their training program. They would spend a week a year here to keep their certifications. It wasn't something to look forward to. They loved the jumping part. Someone else paid for everything.

It was the quarters or lack thereof. They had to sleep in whatever tent they brought. A lucky few had the little popup campers, but even they grew old after a week.

There was a communal shower. Food was served in this, what they called a canteen, but I had seen better field kitchens with the Ohio National Guard.

That gave me some food for thought. I had put a lot of money into this facility so I could use the hangar and runway. Now I was having a personal golf practice range put in.

Yes, I let them use it, but I was imposing it on the facility. I didn't have time today, but I had to talk to the chief ranger of this base. I had a golf course where these guys could cut, plow, and dig a firebreak out of it in short order. I better keep on their good side.

Chapter 18

At Warner Brothers, I spent the afternoon dodging seamstresses' pins and needles as they took my costumes in and out for the proper fit. One comment made about one of the outfits caught my attention.

This is the one that will get wet, so give it some extra room. What did they mean to get wet? There were no scenes in my script that called for me to be in the water.

Oh no, not only no, hell no! If it was what I thought it was, there was no way. I had enough water troughs to last my career.

I realized all I could do was be on guard the day that I was handed that costume. The evil people behind this would never come clean about their plan.

I did manage to get over to the stunt barn and wave my sword about like I knew what I was doing. It surprised me that I hadn't lost that much skill in my long layoff.

I would try to work on the others when I could.

That evening at dinner, I brought Mum and Dad in on my plan for the Forestry Service base. They both thought it was reasonable. It wouldn't hurt to have the facilities I was going to propose in the area.

The next morning, I rode George directly to the headquarters to make an appointment with the chief ranger.

It turned out that he came out of his office to get a second cup of coffee when I was talking to the guy at the front desk.

He told me to grab a cup and join him in his office.

Once we sat down, he asked what I had in mind.

I explained that I had talked to some of the smokejumpers here on their annual certification course. They weren't complaining but told me about the lack of quarters.

They were in a catch twenty-two. If there were housing like a hotel, they would be given a housing allowance. Since there wasn't any such facility, they were expected to camp out. This was a hangover from the old days when that was the only practical thing to do.

If there were a hotel nearby, they would get enough to pay for it.

I did a quick revision of my plan. I had intended to provide housing for free.

"So, if I built a hotel outside of the front gate, they would be given the money to pay for it?"

"That's correct."

"Then I propose that I build the hotel or at least hire someone to do it."

"It would be nice if it had a swimming pool."

"It will, and that brings up another subject. I feel like I'm pushing it with my golf range. How do you feel about that?"

"I have no problems with it, but if some politicians got involved, they could make a deal out of it."

"I already allow your people to use the range. What if we expanded to other sports?"

"Such as?"

"A shooting range, baseball diamonds, and tennis courts for one. I'm open to ideas."

"Instead of being considered a hardship posting, this would become a sought-after training center."

"That's another thought. There isn't much in the way of classroom space here; I could have a conference center added to the hotel."

"You just changed this from a hardship posting to one directors would fight over. I love it. I was moved here for five years as an unspoken punishment. This would stick it in their eyes."

I held my tongue, but I would have to find out why he was being punished.

We ended our chat, and I told him I would get back to him with firm plans.

I went back to my golf. My drives were noticeably longer. I had added fifteen yards on average since I had started.

I made a point of joining Rob and his friends at lunch. I had some questions for them.

"Hey, what do you guys think of your head ranger?"

"He saved our lives."

"How so?"

"It was a windy day at the El Centro fire. Some politicians had shown up to get a sound bite as we were supposed to take off. It wasn't safe, and our boss said no jump today.

"The politicians got bent out of shape and insisted the jump go forward. He told them where to go. That's how he ended up at this hardship post. I would do anything for him."

That answered my concern about the head ranger. I would be delighted to work with him.

Dad was home at lunch, so I told him that if I had a hotel built, they would pay to use it. I had thought I was going to build it and let the jumpers use it for free.

Dad thought that was wonderful. He asked what I knew about the hotel business. I knew they rented rooms, and that was it. He pulled out his black book. Unlike mine, his was tattered from use.

He called a man he knew from Bellefontaine, a Don Hilliker. He and Don had served on the board of the Bellefontaine National Bank together. That is how Dad knew him.

I didn't know it, but since then, Mr. Hilliker had gone into the hotel business. Not only building them but running a chain.

Once Dad explained what I had in mind, Mr. Hilliker expressed interest. He liked the idea of a captive audience.

Dad handed the phone to me after telling Mr. Hilliker who he would be talking with. I asked him who my business manager, Jim Williamson, should call. He gave me a name and number, and we were in business. He told me that the way they build them these days, we would be renting rooms by September of this year.

We exchanged some pleasantries. He told me he had watched me win the Ohio State Youth Championship in Columbus. He wanted to know if I intended to repeat the US Open. I told him that I intended a Grand Slam Bobby Jones style.

I probably shouldn't have bragged like that, but it was my intention.

At the studio, I ran into Mr. Monroe. He asked if I had a minute. I did.

"Rick, I want to tell you that Karen and I are getting back together. We will be having a small wedding, but we will be inviting you and your family."

That didn't sound small to me.

"What do you call small?"

"No more than two hundred people."

"Intimate then."

"Yes."

He must have it bad to not even recognize my sarcasm.

He continued, "Another thing, are you and Nina getting serious?"

"No wedding or even engagement plans, but there is no one else on my horizon or hers; at least, that's how I see it."

"It is Rick this and Rick that, so I think you are safe there. I want you to know I wouldn't stand in your way, but I do hope you guys will wait a few years."

"Why, if I may ask."

"You two are still in the first love stage. It would be better if you waited until you are best friends in the world forever."

"I thought we were friends a long time ago."

"Puppy love, young man, puppy love."

Puppy love reminded me of another romance that was doomed by their elders, who thought they were too young. Maybe they were, but they should have been the judge of that.

With that downer of a conversation, I went to makeup, where they got me ready for some lighting tests. I just thought trying on clothes was boring.

At least the makeup artist would talk and make jokes. That helped for the first hour, but even that soon grew old.

By some twist of fate, a light got knocked over on the set, and we had to end the day early. It wasn't me, honest.

I managed to round up a couple of guys to box with. The first guy made me think I still had it. The second guy just about knocked my block off. I thought Don Palmer was going to laugh himself silly.

When I got home, there was a call from Jim Williamson. The Hilliker group wanted to do the whole hotel project by themselves. They had made a couple of phone calls and found that the Forest Service would front the loans to build the place.

That was fine with me. They were welcome to the whole show, that is after they bought the land at the front gate, which I owned.

Dad thought it a hoot; Mum had little interest. Mary asked what the ROI would be on the hotel.

Chapter 19

The next morning, it was back to the golf range. I was working at reading the grass on the greens. Not the slope but the way the actual grass blades faced at different times of the day. They tended to follow the sun.

When the blades faced me, they would slow the ball down. When they faced away, it sped the ball up; we called this a slick green. It influenced how hard you stroked the ball.

It is peaceful in California in March; the weather is mild; it must be just 72 today. This early, there is dew on the grass. This gives a nice feeling to the day but is hell on putting.

My putts were slowed down even as I stroked the ball hard enough to leave a rooster tail as the ball traveled. I just hoped I never had a tee time so early that I faced this in a tournament.

It was so frustrating that I went over to speak to Sam to see how he was doing with building the new greens.

He was down on his knees on the wet green. He looked up when I approached. His trousers were damp and muddy, but he had a grin on his old, weathered face.

"This mud makes it easier to pull the seams together."

I saw what he was working on. He was right; where he had hand-smoothed the seam, you could hardly tell the grass had been separated.

"Looks good. How many miles do you have to do?"

"Not miles, but quite a bit. I will keep the greens damp all the time so I can do this all day long."

True love is a wonderful thing. I wished him the best of it and got back to one of my true loves, placing a little white ball where I wanted it.

I think he had the easier job.

I could hear dozers in the distance. The Forest Service had decided to expand the base. Since they owned the forest land, all they had to do was take down the cyclone fence, remove the trees, and put up new fencing, and they were good to go.

I may have created a monster here. Originally, it was to be an airstrip close to our house that would be convenient and provide a quick getaway if the family needed to leave Jackson House while under attack.

Today, that seemed like paranoia, but we had just moved to Jackson House for safety after the KGB had kidnapped Mary. They paid dearly, but we didn't want to give them another opportunity. All was quiet on that front now, but it may not be in the future.

I had set in motion another obstacle to Soviet plans by providing aid to China, which, in turn, was letting the Soviets know they weren't welcome in Vietnam.

They would find out about my involvement, and then who knows what would happen?

I shrugged. There wasn't anything I could do about it. What I could do, though, was practice hitting fried eggs out of the new sand traps Sam had put in for me.

Using the same technique I used while practicing putting. I shoved five balls into the sand in a row, with just a quarter of the top of the ball showing. I then proceeded to hit them out.

Hit them out, I did, and ended up with a mouth full of sand after each shot. By the time I had hit twenty-five balls, I was a mess. This would never do! One had to look good on the tournament trail.

I tried opening and closing my feet and varying my speed, all to no avail. You had to have the proper stance, open the clubface, and hit about five inches behind the ball.

When I did this, the ball came out of the trap. I worked on the proper force, knowing that it would vary under wet or dry conditions.

I finally figured out how not to get sand all over me. Stay out of the trap!

When I went home for lunch, I found that I had sand in my hair and, worse yet, in unmentionable places. Yes, stay out of the trap.

The movie studio was a pleasant day for me. They had little to do for me on the set. My costumes were ready, and after trying them on, I was given the rest of the day off.

I didn't just run off. I spent time talking to some of the cast members to get to know them. Nothing deep, just how is it going? It was early days. From previous movies, I knew we would be like a family before it was over.

John Wayne wasn't around. I asked and found out he was back in Hong Kong working on the action movie he was producing. I wish I were in that one. Westerns were getting a little old for me.

Besides, there were early signs that the Western boom on TV was dying. There are only so many ways to show a theme. The industry was ready to move on.

It would be neat if it went in the direction of spy movies so I could be a James Bond type. That was my wish; what I had was another oater, and I had to give it my best.

In a way, it was a letdown after *Over the Ohio*. Even though my involvement in the movie was minimal, it set a standard in dramatic possibilities and money earned. The fact that the Oscar committee snubbed it was a plus in my mind.

With the rest of the afternoon off, I went back to the stunt area. I was able to get a sword fight in. I felt that I had lost a step but still won handily. It wasn't that I was so good; the other guy was bad. I think it was the only time I ever saw Jim Garner with a sword in his hand.

After that, a director's assistant came up to me and asked me to take part in a fight scene in some sort of Western. I'm not even certain what the movie was about.

I found out that this was a rehearsal for the real scene and that I was standing in for John Wayne. We walked through it a couple of times, then went at it for real.

The fight was on a big dirt pile, which was half mud. Maureen O'Hara came in and helped me, Wayne's character, by stabbing an opponent with a hatpin. She was to do the same to me, but I accidentally (by plan) elbowed her down a mudslide face first.

I loved it; she didn't but was too much of a professional to refuse to do it. We were told we had to do the scene over, so we all had to shower and change using the portable showers that were in place for this scene. The third time through, I missed her with my elbow, and she got me with her hatpin, and I was the one to slide face-first in the mud.

From her look, I think her revenge was served hot. Her role had her acting as a termagant, so I wondered if we were doing a remake of *Taming of the Shrew*.

I didn't care enough to ask. I signed the papers to get paid scale, took a shower, dressed, and left. At home, I showered again and found I still had mud in unmentionable places and even some sand.

I related my tale at dinner. Of course, Mary had to ask what unmentionable places were. Mum whispered in her ear. Mary's eyes got big, and she asked, "Won't your bum get sore?"

For some reason, this cracked the table up. I didn't think it was funny at all. The hand lotion I had used wasn't doing the trick.

What a messy day.

I spent the evening reading quietly in my room. I was going to suffer in silence. Even that wasn't to be. Denny knocked on my door and let himself in.

He had a business proposition for me. His work was a little slow right now, and my publicity pictures were getting stale—his words, not mine.

He was right, and more importantly, I had a chance to help my brother. Yes, I would devil him to no end, but when asked for help, I was there.

Since today was Friday, it was easy to agree to do it tomorrow. The only thing I had thought about doing was going to the beach.

Saturday morning, we went down to the first basement, where he had taken over a corner for his studio and darkroom.

Since I had a complete wardrobe here at Jackson House, he and Harold had picked a selection of clothes or, in this case, costumes for me to pose in.

In my opinion, three of them came out exceptionally well. One was a dark and brooding Death Wind. The next was a debonair spy in the making. Lastly, I was in my full Coldstream uniform with all my awards and medals. I even had a dress sword at my hip.

My luck was that Mum came in right as we were finishing up. Denny had quickly developed the pictures, so we all had a good look. When Mum saw me in the Coldstream uniform, she decided then and there that she needed a full-size oil painting of me dressed just like that. It would look great in the library.

Chapter 20

There was no way that I was going to spend hours posing for a painting. To my relief, Mum explained that an artist could use the photograph as the model and paint from that.

Later in the day, I did get to head out to the beach. I was able to drive my T-Bird with the top down. It was on the cool side at 68 degrees, but the heater took care of that.

With the radio blaring out the latest songs like "Runaway," "Pony Time," and "Hit the Road Jack," it was a great drive down 101.

Even with a wet suit, I wasn't going out into the Pacific. It would be cold! I did stop by Katin's to see if anything was going on. I got an update on Corky; he was doing great, and he had a good chance of being the World Champion of Surfing this year.

He sported the Jackson Transportation logo. I wondered if I should sponsor any other teams. I asked some guys who were sitting around the surf shop. They thought I should sponsor a girls' volleyball team. They didn't get much advertising exposure, but the girls' exposure would make up for it.

On the surface, that sounded good, but I figured it could get me into a lot of trouble.

On the way back to Jackson House, I listened to "I Fall to Pieces" and "Where the Boys Are." They were good, but "Mother-in-law" made me think. What would Nina's mother be like as a mother-in-law?

I didn't know Karen that well, so I couldn't guess. It was too soon to be considering a mother-in-law, but for some reason, I couldn't let it go.

Back at the house, I washed the T-Bird down as it had salt spray from my trip. Once I had washed it, it made sense to wax it, too. Then, I had to clean the sand out of the interior. That took care of three hours in the late afternoon.

It was nice doing ordinary things for a change. This being a world traveler, mover, shaker, and world-class golfer was all well and good, but I still had some kid in me.

Thinking of that, I wondered what I could do tonight. Sometimes, fate does take a hand. There was an advertisement on the radio. It seemed there was an outside sock hop at the public tennis courts in Beverly Hills.

I decided that was where I had to be. I told Mum and Dad I was going out for the evening. I would grab a bite to eat from an In-and-Out. They thought it a good idea that I go out to a group my age that knew nothing about me.

In-and-Out was excellent, as always. I loved the stuff on the secret menu. I managed to avoid getting sauce on my sports coat. It was a new one picked out by Harold.

It made me look like a professor as it was a brown tweed with elbow patches. I kind of ruined the professor's look by only wearing a yellow polo shirt under the jacket instead of a white shirt and tie.

That and a lighter brown pair of slacks completed my ensemble. I was trying to look more sophisticated than your normal high school-age kid but not so far out as to be an oddity.

It must have worked because while no one stared, I saw a bunch of the girls checking me out. Score! Not that I wanted any girl but Nina. It was nice to be appreciated.

The guys, of course, ignored me. I was shocked at how young everyone looked. I had been hanging out with older adults so much that I forgot what my peers looked like.

It also explained why many of those adults had trouble accepting me as serious.

There was a slightly older group hanging off to one edge. From the way they dressed, I identified them as the college group, come to a slum with the high school kids and maybe impress a girl or two.

They had on sports coats and ties, but most of all, they had either pipes or cigars. I hate to tell them all they managed to do was look silly or at least pretentious.

Despite that, I wandered over to the edge of the group. I wasn't shunned, which I considered a victory.

Two guys standing there nodded to me. I could tell they were from UCLA because they wore sweatshirts from there. I liked their straightforward approach to advertising.

One of them asked, "Where do you go to school?"

"Oxford."

"As in England?"

You would have thought the British accent I was using would have given me away.

"Yes."

There was no need to tell them that I had been kicked out. Though that might have gained me some points.

"What are you doing here?"

"My parents live here, and I'm visiting. I felt like getting out of the house tonight and heard about this on the radio."

"They do this every week, rain or shine."

Not that it rained that much in California.

"What's the drill? You just ask a girl to dance?"

"Yes, but you have to be careful. If you ask a girl to dance and she turns you down, all the others will."

"You mean every girl watches every other girl, see who asks her to dance, and if she turns you down, everyone else will?"

"Well, it is a group thing. They watch out for each other. The way to do it is to start with low expectations, either social or looks, and work your way up."

That seemed like the dumbest thing I ever heard, but at the same time, I could see where it worked.

"Who here has the highest social rating and best looks?"

They pointed to someone I recognized. An old classmate of Nina's, Tuesday Weld.

"Thanks, wish me luck."

"Luck, but you are insane."

I walked up to Tuesday.

"Tuesday, Rick Jackson; Nina Monroe introduced us."

She went from a keep your distance look to a quick hug.

"Rick, I remember you; I read about you and Nina all the time; how is she?"

"Right now, she is probably collecting another speeding ticket in her Valentine's Day present."

"That was in all the scandal sheets. You are making it hard on all the other guys."

I smirked a little as I said, "They will just have to try harder."

She laughed, and I asked her if she wanted to dance. They had just started playing "Puppy Love." We went out on the dance floor, well the tennis court, and slow danced. It was done as friends, nothing else.

She did comment on the hard protrusion, not that one, the one on the left side of my sports coat. As normal, I wore my shoulder holster with the .38. I still had to find a better weapon.

Afterward, I walked her back to her friends, who promptly descended upon her. To think I had come here thinking I could be anonymous.

I went back to my new UCLA friends. They had watched me in action. They were also smart enough to know I knew her.

Since Tuesday was probably spreading my name all over the place, I decided to come clean with them.

"I do know Tuesday. She is a good friend of my girlfriend, Nina Monroe. I used to attend Oxford, but they gave me the boot."

At that, you could see the coin drop, at least to one of them.

"You're Lord Blackhoof, aren't you?"

"Guilty as charged."

Before the conversation could go any further, I was shoved from behind. I turned to face a big guy, a linebacker. At least that is what his Hollywood High letterman's jacket had on it.

"Who do you think you are dancing with my girl?"

"A friend."

He had two other guys with him, so I decided to get this over with as fast as possible. I opened the left side of my sports coat so he could see my shoulder holster.

At that, he turned and walked away. I went back to talking to the guys from UCLA, but within two minutes two uniformed policemen had me bracketed.

Before they could say anything, I told them, "Yes, I am armed, shoulder holster; if I open my jacket slowly, you can see that and my creds.

The lead cop nodded, and I slowly opened my jacket. He could see my shield attached to a leather wallet. I slowly handed the wallet to him.

He examined it and handed it back to me.

"What happened here, Marshal?"

"I danced with a friend of my girlfriend, and a guy who said he was her boyfriend took exception. I gave him a peek at my holster, and as I thought, he went straight to you, which wasn't a bad idea on his part."

The policeman started to say something but was interrupted by a screaming voice and a hard slapping sound. It seems like Tuesday no longer has a boyfriend, as she had just slapped him silly.

The police excused me after cautioning me about using my weapon to intimidate. I thought that rich as they wore theirs on their hip, but I kept my mouth shut.

I told the UCLA guys good evening. So ended my trip to the sock hop. At least I had one dance.

I rushed home to call Nina, no matter the time in Switzerland, to give my side of the story before some reporter made his up.

Chapter 21

Nina was a little peeved when I woke her at six in the morning her time. She had a day she could sleep in a few hours. I told her about the sock hop and its outcome. She didn't think it was that big of a deal but did agree that I did the right thing in calling her.

She was going to call Tuesday and give her hell about trying to steal her boyfriend. All in good fun, of course.

After hanging up with Nina, I went back downstairs, where my parents were still watching the eleven o'clock news. I told them about my evening.

Mum was not happy about my opening my jacket to show the weapon. She was very much of the school that you did nothing with your gun unless you intended to shoot it, and you shot it with the intent to kill.

"Rick, did you intend to kill the stupid jock?"

"No."

"Then you were in the wrong."

I had to agree it went against all the training I had ever had. I promised to be more careful in the future. I will just deck them. Mum agreed that was a better plan.

My mum knows when to choose her battles. She saw a weakness in my position and chose to attack.

"Rick, we are having a charity auction here tomorrow night. I would like you to attend and, if needed, keep the bidding going on items."

How could I say no when I was in the doghouse over my weapon usage? I started to try to wiggle out of it when Dad shook his head. I yielded to his superior knowledge of when to go against Mum's wishes.

"I would be delighted to assist in any way I can."

This got me a dad thumbs up.

The next morning, after my normal routine, I rode George over to the practice range. I needed to get my legs and thighs in shape for extended riding in the movie.

Sam was there waiting for me. He wanted to show me a particular green he had come up with. It was a right-to-left sloping green that fell off sharply on the left, the dreaded number ten at Augusta.

I had to practice chipping on and having the ball stick below the pin. This was an almost impossible shot. The green fell off sharply here, and the ball wanted to roll away.

Sam told me, "I want you to chip in from the left side of the fairway as though your hit had a long drive with a draw. That is the best position to have a good landing on the green. Anything else, and you stand a good chance of rolling off."

Sam was right; even hitting from that area, I had to be careful to keep a good spin on the ball to kill it as it landed. If I did it right, I had a ten-foot putt uphill, which I was now making fifty percent of the time.

That didn't sound great, but if I could do that consistently it might win the Masters on this hole alone.

I hit several buckets of balls, then quit before I made my shoulder sore.

"Sam, you have outdone yourself here."

"Thanks, Rick! It is fun for me to do this. Considering I thought I would be sitting at home drinking beer about now, this is heaven."

"I'm glad it has worked out for you. Are we paying you enough?"

"You're paying me?"

He started laughing at my stunned look.

"Got you. Yes, I'm being paid more than fairly."

From there, I spent until lunchtime working on putting from seven feet and out. Inside seven feet, I was almost at a hundred percent. There was always the odd blade of grass or such that would ruin the shot, but I had the distance dialed in.

My drives were now at a consistent three hundred and ten yards. Some people could outdrive me, but none were as accurate.

After lunch at home, I drove over to the studio. I had the top down and music blaring. The songs told me to: "Put another nickel in, in the nickelodeon;" "Make me loose as a long neck goose;" "And I opened the door, and then splish, splash! I jumped back in the bath."

I was jiving as I drove through the Warner Brothers front gate. This year, I had the proper stickers on my bumper, so the guard waved me through.

It turned out I didn't have a lot to do today. I had to walk through a couple of scenes, but they weren't ready for filming yet. The writers were still arguing about the dialog. The actress playing Molly, a girl a little older than me by the name of Sally Fields, and I got tired of their bickering.

We had just met and were supposed to be arguing. This was to set the scene for our coming romance.

While they dithered about the words, she started with, "You are the typical knuckleheaded cowboy that wouldn't know a good meal if it bit them in the ankle."

"If your meal bit me in the ankle, I would shoot it."

"More likely you would shoot yourself in the foot."

"I'll have you know I'm a good shot."

"And I'll have you know I'm a good cook!"

"Couldn't tell it from this plate of garbage."

"Ninny, that's because it is a plate of garbage. It is the burnt potato I wouldn't serve to anyone and the fat trimmings from the steaks I'm serving."

"Why did you let me eat it?"

"I didn't let you do anything. You came into my kitchen, grabbed the plate, and started eating."

At that, I turned and walked away being heard to say, "What a hard-headed woman, she has to be right no matter what."

She was heard saying, "I have never seen such a stubborn man who won't admit he's wrong even as he eats garbage."

The stagehands applauded our little improvisation. The writers were busy getting it down. They changed the words a little, but not much. I could work with this girl. I think she would be going places in the business.

After that, I went over to the stunt area and practiced my archery. This and swordsmanship were probably my best movie skills. Though archery was proving to be a useful skill in my non-movie life.

At home, I had dinner with the family. The kids didn't have to participate in the auction tonight. This is a shame, as I could see Mary in a bidding war.

Denny and Eddie not so much. Denny was too cheap, and Eddie wouldn't see anything he liked. He was into collecting model airplanes, the latest jets being his favorites.

Donning a suit and tie, I went down to reception to help my parents greet the arriving guests. They had this down to a science now. Everything from valet parking to coat checking was under control. I kept an eye out for anyone carrying a violin case, but we seemed to be free of robbers this time.

I registered like all the other bidders and collected a numbered paddle. To say it was down to science was an understatement. Even the paddles were labeled Jackson Charity Auction 1962. I mentioned that to Mum.

"Rick, they print these as fans for funeral parlors all the time."

Live and learn.

My job was to keep the bidding going as needed, acting as a shill. If a lot was not meeting its reserve, I had to place a bid. The trick would be to keep the bid moving without winning!

I didn't have to raise the bid very often. This was a lively crowd.

There was one item from Boehm, a porcelain brown bear. It wasn't bad looking but it certainly wasn't anything I would be interested in.

The bidding slowed well below the reserve price of one hundred dollars, so when eighty was called the second time I raised my paddle. Another guy in the audience had raised his bid at the same time, so it became eighty-five dollars, still not enough. He and I bid back and forth briskly. The way he bid, I thought he wanted it, so I kept running him up. He returned the favor.

I turned around to get a look at him; he was behind me and across the room. When I did turn to look, I realized it was Ben, our in-house ranch hand.

He saw me at the same time I saw him. He had a look of panic as he realized the bid was to him. I was into the spirit of bidding so much that I raised my paddle one more time before I thought.

Ben was smart enough to stop; that is how I bought a porcelain brown bear. I cornered Mum later and told her she owed me and that she should have told me that Ben was also shilling for her.

"I will do no such thing. You have to learn to pay attention at auctions. You got off cheap at three hundred dollars. If it had been an art auction, it could have been thousands."

She was right about that, but I still felt used by my mum, a hardhearted woman. If Ben had won the auction, she would have repaid him. I tried to enlist Dad's help, but he suddenly found he had other things to do. Coward!

Chapter 22

For the next week, my days were the same: golf practice in the morning and the movie in the afternoon.

My golf improvements had come to a standstill. I decided to back off from an everyday session to alternate days. I didn't want to burn out but wanted to keep the edge I had developed. I was hitting and putting better than ever before.

Now, it would be course management and sheer luck.

Sam was making progress on his greens project. I was able to practice the most difficult shots at the Masters and the US Open. He was working on the next two tournaments.

In the meantime, John Jacobs was learning everything he could about the four courses I would have to play.

On my first day off, I spent the morning surfing. I hadn't surfed in a long time, but it was like riding a bicycle. It is easy to fall off if you aren't paying attention. I fell off a lot that day.

The movie was going well, almost too well. All the actors were on the set on time and knew their lines; this was almost unheard of. The unions were in a sweet spot in their contracts, so they weren't disgruntled. Even the weather cooperated.

Things seemed too good to be true. They were.

Major fighting broke out in China between the old hardline communists and the new soft-liners, as they were being called. It was a tense week as things played out. In the end, Deng's forces won the day.

While nasty at the time, this was good news in the long run. Those forces against a transition to a form of capitalism were now nullified. By nullified, I meant probably stood against a wall and shot.

The Chinese tend towards hard finalizations. Unlike the US, they don't have a tradition of peaceful transitions of power.

One evening at dinner time at Jackson House, a phone call came in. A new kitchen maid grabbed the phone and answered it. She said something rude and hung up.

"What was that, Rosa?"

"It was a prank call, someone claiming to be the empress of China."

The phone rang again. I pushed Rosa aside in my haste to answer it.

"Jackson House."

"Lord Blackhoof, I'm glad to get you. I think my aide dialed the wrong number before."

I threw the aide to the wolves.

"I'm sorry to hear that, Empress Ping; now that you have me, how may I help China?"

"You must be aware of our recent unpleasantness. It was very costly in weapons, munitions, and other infrastructure. Are you in a position to expand our letter of credit?"

"I thought that might be needed, so I have already instructed my staff to shift funds around so we can do another one hundred million dollars. This time, though, I will need to be repaid."

"We can do that. We will ship gold to England. Our loan will only be for a brief time. It's just that we need hard currency immediately."

"We can do that; I will make phone calls and arrange for the letter of credit to The Bank of China tomorrow. Also, we need to look at how we can establish the yuan as a hard currency."

"I will talk to my advisors, Chairman Deng, and others; if you would do the same, it will be appreciated."

"I will. Is there anything else?"

"Not at this time."

I hung up the phone and turned to a stunned-looking Rosa.

"We receive some very important phone calls; treat them all seriously, and I or my parents will decide if they are prank calls."

Dad spoke up, "Rick, did you just loan the Chinese another hundred million?"

"Yes, sir, I knew this would be coming after the fighting broke out."

Mum chimed in, "You need to let the Queen know what you have done, and I suppose those Kennedys."

Bobby had made a not-so-indirect threat to our family. He was treading on thin ice with Mum.

It was seven o'clock in the evening, so I waited until the morning to place my calls. I hoped if I called early enough, my news would beat the morning briefings.

I called the White House first as that was the place that would be the most upset by my action. They would probably be upset by any action I took.

I managed to get through to Ken O'Donnell. He took my news well. I suggested that the White House issue a press release saying that they had approved a major loan to China from a private citizen. That way, they would get some credit and none of the risk.

That seemed like a good idea to him, and he would talk it over with his boss.

Next was Mr. Norman. He wondered how much I could afford to give. I told him that I had that much cash on hand in various accounts. If I had to liquidate Jackson Enterprises, it would be approaching a billion dollars.

Once he wrapped his head around that number he asked if he could borrow a measly ten thousand pounds or so.

"Certainly, Mr. Norman. How shall I make out the check?"

"I was just teasing, Richard."

"Oh, I never know these days."

"That doesn't make things easy, does it, lad?"

"No, sir, it doesn't. I never know who a friend is or just out for money. I tend to keep my distance from people unless I know them. That is not healthy."

"No, it isn't. I wish I had an answer for you."

"I don't think there is an answer. I have found just because someone is rich doesn't guarantee they won't be after my money. I have more luck being friendly with middle-class people. Maybe because I was there not that long ago and know how to talk to them.

"There is something to be said for that, but at the same time, how can they relate to what you face on a routine basis? I could see you at the soda fountain with your friends, "I was talking to the Queen the other day."

They wouldn't begin to understand.

"I have another situation I would like your advice on."

"What is that?"

"I need to get a group working on how to make the Chinese yuan a hard currency."

"You don't take on little projects, do you?"

"It has to be done, if nothing else, to protect my investments."

"The London School of Economics would be your best place to take that problem. I will have some calls made to see how to proceed."

"I would appreciate that; if needed, I will fly over."

"I would plan on it if I were you for no reason other than that you haven't robbed any dogs for the Queen recently."

As a joke, it was getting old, but it did hold some truth. I had to be seen doing something for the queen, or the press would be complaining that my job was a meaningless one given as a favor.

I then called Hastings Aviation to put them on notice that I would have to fly from LA to London and back shortly. They told me the plane should be free for the next week or so because Lady Nina had told them she had no work for the next two weeks.

When had she become Lady Nina, and whose aircraft was it anyway? I did ask about the lady bit and was told that they just assumed we were going to get married and that she would then be a lady, by marriage.

What do you say to that?

After all my calls, I rode George over to the Forestry Service station to practice my golf. Somewhere along the way, the fun had dimmed. I was glad that I wasn't doing this as a career.

In the middle of a scene on set, I realized that this, too, was becoming tiresome. It wasn't what I wanted in life. What did I want to do?

I wasn't about to walk away from either the golf or the movie. That wasn't my style. If I could win the Grand Slam, that would be the end of tournament golf for me. I would play rounds for fun, but that was it.

As far as movies went, we would see. It would have to be a demanding role rather than another B-level money-making effort. Maybe I could direct a movie. That might be fun. No one in their right mind would hire me to do it without any experience; however, I could fund my projects.

When I got home from the set, and before dinner, I received a phone call. Rosa answered the phone. She nonchalantly handed me the phone and said, "It is Buckingham Palace for you."

She learned quickly.

As expected, it was Mr. Norman. He had talked to the chancellor at the London School of Economics, and they would like a meeting on my project. Would the day after tomorrow work?

It would. I would have to let the studio know I wouldn't be available. I needed to let Sam and John know I wouldn't be here to practice. George would just have to figure it out himself.

Chapter 23

I called Hastings Aviation and confirmed my flight to England for the next day. The aircraft would have to be moved here tonight. Next, I let Mr. Norman know when I would be flying over, and could he please set up meetings after that?

He reminded me that today was Thursday and that I would get there on Friday, so Monday would be the earliest that a meeting could occur. I hadn't paid attention to what day of the week it was. When you don't have a real schedule, it is easy to lose track.

Since I would have the weekend free, I called Nina to see if she wanted to come to England or me to Switzerland. For some reason, she was evasive, saying she had things to do and couldn't break away.

I agreed not to come over, but after I hung up, I wondered what was going on.

Riding over to the Forestry Service, I told George I wouldn't be around for the next few days. He didn't act disappointed, so I guessed it was okay with him. Hey, I can talk to my horse if I want to. Now, if he answers me, I'm in trouble. Aside from Mr. Ed, horses don't talk. Mules might, but not horses.

Sam and John were both at the range, so I informed them of my plans without going into why I was going to England. Not that I didn't trust them. There wasn't a reason to tell them.

Sam told me, "Good, that will give the greens a rest. They could use a couple of days without you tramping all over them."

I wasn't certain if he was serious or pulling my leg, so I just nodded.

John asked, "Do you have time to see the Troon course in Scotland, where the British Open will be played this year?"

"I don't think so, John. I have to get back here right after my meeting to work on the movie. They won't be happy that I will be missing a couple of days shooting."

"I bet; it would be okay if you were doing something big like helping that mess in China."

"Yeah, it would."

I was correct in thinking that the studio wouldn't be happy with me being gone for a couple of days.

I finally had to take Mr. Monroe and Mr. Wayne aside and explain why I was going. They understood why I had to do it; it didn't mean they had to like it.

"Rick, you have too many irons in the fire; one of these days, you are going to have to decide what you want to do and stick to it."

"John, I agree. I have been wrestling with that for a while now. One thing I know is that this will be the last B-movie I make. I don't need the money, and it takes a lot of my time. I enjoy the company, don't get me wrong, but this isn't what I need to do in life."

"Are you going to turn professional as a golfer?"

"No, this is my last year of tournament golf. No matter how it turns out, I'm done. I will only play for fun."

"Then what do you see yourself doing?"

"I don't know, but projects like China are giving me more satisfaction now than either golf or movies."

Mr. Monroe spoke up, "I hope you aren't upset with Nina right now."

"Why should I be upset?"

"She told me she can't see you this weekend."

"I don't see that is a problem. We both have lives to live."

From the look on his face, I could tell there was something he wasn't telling me.

I decided I would talk to my inside person, Mary. She knew all the gossip about the models.

I left the studio and returned home. Mary was out of school, so I cornered her.

"Mary, how are you doing?"

"Fine, and what do you want?"

Suspicious little kid.

"Nothing, just paying attention to my favorite sister."

"I'm your only sister. I figured that out when I was three."

"You've got me. Any good gossip about the models?"

"I knew it. You have heard about Nina."

I hadn't heard anything about Nina, but my little sister had just spilled the beans.

"Sure, short stuff. I heard all about it; what do you know?"

"Well, she has only been on two dates with him so far."

"I don't know his name, do you?"

"I don't know his real name; all the girls call him Prince McDreamy."

"Thanks, Mary, you are the best sister I could ask for."

"I'm sorry I didn't tell you before."

"That's okay. I found out anyway."

She got a funny look on her face, and her hands flew up to cover it.

"You didn't know, did you!"

"Not for certain until you told me."

"I'm so embarrassed. Mum told me that this was something you had to work out and handle by yourself."

So much for family support. Though Mum was right, this was my problem to sort out.

The next morning, I flew to London. I directly asked the head stewardess if Nina had anyone accompany her on her flights for modeling.

"Some of the other models and that prince guy. He was a pain, acted as though he was owed all the service in the world."

"Did he try anything with any of the girls?"

"He and Nina seemed close, but I never saw anything untoward."

"Let me be blunt. Was the bed ever used?"

"No, we always change the sheets after a trip, and I can tell you no one used them."

"Thank you. That's what I wanted to know.

We arrived at the Oxford airfield on time. During the whole trip, I kept thinking of things that could be going on. There was no way that she would be seeing another guy. I kept denying the possibility, but black thoughts kept running through my mind.

We arrived early Saturday morning. I went to The Meadows to say hello to Grandmum; she and Elizabeth, the Queen Mum, were having an early cup of tea.

They were going to spend the morning at the Roman digs. I joined them to catch up on what was going on. It turned out not a lot, as the weather had not cooperated, and even though everything was tent-covered, it was a muddy mess.

I excused myself and returned to the house for a nap. Even though I had used the bed on the way over, I hadn't slept well. Nina kept going through my mind. What was going on with her?

At two in the afternoon, I returned to the Oxford airfield and filed a flight plan for Zurich using my Cessna. By the time I had a fuel stop in France along with dinner, I arrived in Zurich at about 11 p.m. local time.

I hired a cab for the ride to Nina's. I wasn't going to mess around. I wanted to know if we were still a couple.

As the cab pulled up in front of her apartment, a Ferrari cut the cab off and came to a sliding stop. It had British tags; it was mine. Nina got out of the passenger side, and a guy got out of the driver's side.

He wasn't much taller than Nina and lightly built. I could break him in half. He left the engine running, got out, and went to her. She grabbed him and got him into a lip lock.

That gave me all the answers I needed. I told the cab driver to wait. Then I went over to the Ferrari while the two were still going at it. I got into the car and buckled up the five-point harness that I had installed.

I then stepped on the gas and, after fifty feet, ran the car into a stone pillar.

Getting out, I heard the guy yell, "Hey, you jerk, what do you think you are doing with my car?"

Nina didn't say anything; she just ran for the door to her apartment. I got back into the cab and asked to be taken to the airport.

The driver never said a word.

Back at the airport, I called the Zurich police.

"This is Lord Blackhoof. I wrecked my Ferrari tonight. There were no injuries, and the only damage was to the car. I will be responsible for any charges."

Of course, they wanted me to come down to the station and file a report. I told them that wasn't possible as I had to leave for London.

I flew back to Oxford, arriving at daybreak. I stopped by Hastings Aviation, which was in the process of opening. I informed them that Nina Monroe no longer had flight privileges on the 707.

I drove the estate Bentley back to The Meadows and went to bed. When I woke in time for lunch, Mr. Hamilton had a stack of phone calls for me. They were all from Nina.

"I won't be accepting any calls from her. Please inform her of that the next time she calls."

I was numb inside; I wasn't mad yet. I had a feeling that there was great anger in me ready to break loose.

Chapter 24

I had no direction for my anger. That guy, Nina, the world, myself? Instead, I went for a long walk around the property. I thought about horseback riding but decided I might end up hurting the poor horse.

I carried a stick in case of a snake, not that I had ever seen one. I did beat up on a lot of innocent plants. I could have cut a path through the thickest jungle.

I kept replaying the scene with that prince whatever and Nina in my mind. It wasn't very adult to wreck my car, but it was satisfying at the time.

That reminded me that I needed to notify my office in London and have them retrieve the car and sell it as is. It had been nothing but trouble since day one.

I must have walked twenty miles or more that day. I was exhausted by the time I got back to the house. There was another stack of notes from phone calls from Nina, which I dumped in the trash.

The news had caught up with Grandmum.

"Rick, you are young. This is normal in early relationships. Take some time to get over this, then remember there are many, many fish in the sea and that fishing can be fun."

Intellectually, I knew she was right. Why did I feel like my heart had been ripped out?

"Grandmum, what do you do to get over being betrayed by the one you love?"

"You don't, ever. Time will soften the memory and the hurt, but it will always be there. It will be a reminder to never do that to one that loves you."

Again, sage advice that had no meaning right now. It did nothing to ease my pain.

I retired early and had a fitful night's sleep. I kept dreaming of smashing that guy's face. After that, Nina would fall into my arms and tell me she knew how wrong she had been.

When I woke up, I realized that all those phone calls from Nina were her trying to tell me that she was wrong and sorry.

That realization focused my anger; she was the one who had betrayed me, and I wouldn't accept a mere apology. We were done.

Monday morning, I flew back down to London and met Mr. Norman at the London School of Economics. He was accompanied by an expert in economics from the foreign office.

I had never been to the school before and was surprised it was just off the Strand in Clare Market. I had been there several times and never noticed the full-blown university plonked down beside it.

We met with Sir Sydney Craine, the school chancellor. After introductions, we explained that we were part of a group trying to figure out what had to be done to have the Chinese yuan accepted as a hard currency.

"I can see mighty things are afoot in the world."

He did speak that way.

"Yes, they are," I replied. "Do you have anyone who can guide us through this?"

"There is one man, one of our dons who wrote a paper on that very issue. I would like him to meet with you, and I would like to add one other person."

"Who would that be, and for what reason?"

"A senior student by the name of Lee Kuan Yew. I reason that it would be helpful to have someone who understands the culture."

"Agreed. When can we talk to these men?"

"I will have my secretary see if they are available for a lunch meeting."

We had an hour before lunch. The chancellor spent it trying to recruit me as a student. He knew my history and wasn't a fan of Oxford since his school had a historic association with Cambridge.

He also let me know that he thought Oxford was frivolous in its actions and that I should be going to a serious school like LSE.

I made noises as if I would consider it. There was no reason to alienate this man, but I had no intention of returning to school at this time.

At lunch, the answer proved to be simple, as the professor explained.

"A hard currency is one in which other nations have faith. The simplest method for the Chinese to create a hard currency is to withdraw all notes in circulation and replace them with ones that are payable to other countries in gold."

"What would that mean for their economy?"

"It would immediately give them a currency that would trade anywhere in the world at a fixed value with other hard currencies, such as the American dollar."

"Do we have any idea of how much gold the Chinese may have on hand?"

"The best estimates say about 9,000 metric tons."

"At that rate, how many dollars of the currency could they issue?"

The professor took his pen and made some calculations on a notepad.

"At thirty-five dollars an ounce, I would say about ten billion dollars. If that were infused into the Chinese economy, it would cause rampant inflation."

"For example, right now, the US has about 17,000 metric tons of gold backing thirty-two billion dollars in the economy.

"However, they would only pay out in gold to other nations who want to redeem their dollars.

"There are many details that would have to be addressed, like the Breton Woods Accords and joining the World Bank and the International Monetary Fund. Plus, shipping thousands of tons of gold to a neutral central bank to keep in their vaults. But those are just that, details. They can be worked out."

The don continued, "From that example, I would think that if careful, the Chinese could have a hard currency. The problem is that politicians and central banks do not like hard currencies because they are difficult, at the least, to manipulate."

At that, the student Lee Kuan Yew spoke up,

"A strong leader would have to enforce the policy. The Asian people are generally in favor of a strong leader who keeps peace and order in their lives. They need to be guided like the children they are."

I wondered what sort of leader he would make when he returned to Singapore.

We talked on for a while, but there were no other ideas presented that would quickly give China a hard currency.

I was flying out of Heathrow in the morning, so I stayed the night at the Plaza. It was only 2 p.m. in London, which would make it 10 p.m. in Beijing. I decided to try a call.

I was lucky in that a night aide recognized my name and put me through to Chairman Deng, who had left orders that my calls were to be forwarded to him.

"Mr. Chairman, I apologize for calling so late your time. I had an interesting meeting at the London School of Economics today. They feel China can have a hard currency if you are willing to go to a gold standard."

"We have reached the same conclusion."

"The professor we talked to used a baseline of 10,000 metric tons at thirty-five dollars an ounce. He thought you would have to regulate how much was to go into the economy; if dumped overnight, China would end up with rampant inflation."

"Again, we agree. Who was the professor you talked with?"

"A Mr. John Hicks."

"I think we will contact him directly. As usual, Rick, you have helped China. We thank you."

"My pleasure. If you think about it, I'm protecting my investment."

"A wise move, young man. I hope you make a wise move in your personal life; don't let disappointment cause you to give up."

Is the whole world spying on me?

The first thing in the morning, I was on the 707 back to LA. I had a movie commitment there, and I wanted out of Europe.

The flight seemed quick. The three flight hostesses only had me to look out for on this flight, so it was an easy duty for them. We ended up debating such important questions as who would name their daughter Rama Lama Ding Dong, and why they would do that.

Some of the conjecture was out of this world, and some downright lurid. After that, we tried to figure out what was behind the green door. One of the girls had been behind the green door in Dallas, Texas. You needed a card to get in, and there was almost always a piano playing while people had a good time. It sounded like a speakeasy to me.

The one that tied us up was "Who put the Bomp in the Bomp, Bomp, Bomp?" We couldn't come up with a reasonable explanation. Not that any of ours on the flight was reasonable.

It did make the flight time go fast, and most importantly, it took my mind off Nina, if only for a few hours.

Once in LA, I was taken to Jackson House, where my family waited. I had been dreading this ever since we landed. I didn't want pity. I just wanted them to ignore me and let me suffer in silence.

It wasn't to be. Mum and Dad were waiting for me to tell them what had transpired. I also figured they knew exactly what happened. If they knew in China, they would know in the US. It probably was in all the tabloids.

I was wrong about the tabloids; the story didn't make the headlines until the next day.

Mary opened the subject with, "I fired her and her friends."

I replied with an intelligent, "What?"

"I had a telegram sent to Nina telling her that the clothing company no longer required her or her friends' services. She can tell them they are all out of a job."

I didn't know what to say to that. On the one hand, I was glad to see Nina getting punished. On the other hand, well, there wasn't another. I was glad to see Nina getting punished.

"Thank you, Mary."

"You're welcome, Rick; we have to stick together."

I looked at Mum as I knew she was the source of Mary's actions. She just said a mysterious, "Hot chocolate."

I think I knew what she was referring to.

Denny spoke up, "What's the big deal? I have a new girlfriend almost every week."

I ignored him. There wasn't an answer that wouldn't get me in trouble.

Eddie gave the best response of all, "Nina probably has girl cooties, and that is why she is acting crazy."

That made sense to me.

Chapter 25

I practiced golf with a vengeance on Wednesday morning. I was rushing my putts. The harder I tried, the worse I got. John finally told me, "Rick, give it a rest. Something is bothering you, and it is ruining your game. Stop before you ingrain bad habits."

That brought me up short, and I did stop. Frustrated, angry about Nina, whatever you want to call it, I'm not totally stupid.

I thanked John and went for a long ride on George. He is a very patient listener, and I certainly gave him an earful on the trails in the park.

I had to go to the studio, which I had been dreading. I hoped against hope that Nina's dad wouldn't be there. I didn't get my hope. The guard flagged me down at the entrance and told me Mr. Monroe wanted to see me in his office.

His new receptionist escorted me in immediately. The guard had called, so they knew I was on my way.

I entered to a stern-faced Mr. Monroe. I had never seen this side of him before. I wondered if I was going to get thrown out of the movie and escorted from the studio.

"Rick, this is difficult for both of us. I have had a long talk with my daughter. She has messed up big time. What I need to know is whether this is going to affect our movie going forward."

"I hope not. I would like to continue."

"Good, I say good as a businessman and as a father. My daughter has made a mess of it, and I would hate to see it affect you to the point you couldn't work with the studio."

I had to ask the question that had been running through my mind like a runaway racehorse, "Why did she do it, two-timing me, letting him use my car, taking him on my airplane? It was as though she wanted to burn me down, salt the earth, and plow me under."

His eyes got a little wide at that.

"I have forgotten how serious these things are at your age. Funny how we forget as we grow older. I have no idea what she was thinking. I'm not certain she does either."

"I feel betrayed by someone I loved."

"And now she is paying for that betrayal. She got a telegram from your sister's company telling her that she and her friends' services are no longer needed. She was riding high with the Ferrari, using a 707, getting to choose who would model and who wouldn't. On top of that, she had a titled boyfriend who was extremely rich.

"Now she has lost it all. She is having to tell her friends they are no longer models. Unfortunately, that was what upset her the most."

"I see; I think she is not upset about losing me, but the things I provided. I think I have gotten off lucky."

Why didn't I feel lucky?

"Rick, try not to get too cynical."

"I can't help it. I have been learning that people want to use me for what I have. I considered Nina my haven. She knew me before I had all of this. I thought she liked me for me, but now I know better."

At that, Mr. Monroe told me that I had better get to the set as they were waiting for me.

The set proved to be a blessing, at least for me. I was able to submerge myself into my role. For a while, I was a single foot-loose, fancy-free cowboy roaming the range.

Today's scene had been storyboarded out well, so it was easy to see what our director wanted. Miss Molly and I had gotten off on the wrong foot, and now we had to make up a little. A bad hombre thought he could have his way with her or at least steal a kiss; it was never made clear.

No matter what, I saved the young lady from a fate worse than death or a stolen kiss. She thanked me half-heartedly. I think it is called mixed emotions; Miss Molly wanted no part of the bad hombre, and Miss Fields, the actress, made eyes at him.

The result was a grudging thank you after I threw the lout to the ground and then kicked him in the rear as he slunk away. We didn't see him anymore in the movie. Maybe the cows ate him.

Miss Molly and I had started a relationship that would grow stronger as we faced the adversities of the cattle drive.

There was one pleasant surprise. Chief Redfoot had arrived. He applauded me for giving the lout the boot. We only had to do that scene six times before I got it right. The first time I went to kick him in the rear, I missed him completely and ended up in the dust on my back.

When I did it, I glared at everyone to dare them to laugh. They didn't. On the next take, when the lout turned to run off, someone had attached a kick me sign to his rear. That is when they all laughed.

I'm ashamed to admit I laughed harder than anyone.

Chief Redfoot had been hired to inject some realistic Indian scenes into the movie. After he and I greeted each other and agreed to meet for dinner, he was talking to the writers while waving a copy of the script. I don't think he was complimenting them.

The day's shooting continued in the usual fashion. We would do a scene over and over until we got it right. The most frustrating part was that a good deal of it would end up on the cutting room floor. We just didn't know which part.

Chief Redfoot came to our house for dinner. He hadn't seen any of the family for a while. Everyone updated him on their busy lives. When asked about his, he answered that the sun rose and then set every day, so it was all good.

That is a different take on life, especially with what I was facing. The good part of my day was that when I was involved on the set, I never once thought of Nina. Do you know how little time an actor is involved in the set?

It seemed I was truly an actor; I could become someone else while performing and forget Richard Jackson.

Chief Redfoot told us that the little boys on the reservation had a new game. They all wanted to be Lord Blackhoof.

He also updated us on the programs that my parents and I were funding. We had donated money to improve the schools and endowed a health care clinic for the young and the elderly. My dad was interested in endowing a scholarship program for anyone who wanted to go to college.

Chief Redfoot thought that a wonderful idea but did think Dad was being a little extreme in wanting to give extra credit for white Republican scalps. With Dad, you never can be certain. Now, if Mum had brought it up, I would know she was dead serious. Except with her, it would be Democrats.

I told them they were all wet; it should be lawyers. This got more laughter than it deserved.

In the middle of the meal, there was a phone call. It was for me. It was Empress Ping of China.

"Rick, I apologize for the interruption. I have been asked to appear before the United Nations and need a safe way to get there. China doesn't have any aircraft capable of making the trip safely. Could I borrow your airplane?"

"Most certainly, Your Imperial Highness."

"Rick, how many times must I tell you a simple Lady Ping will do?"

"At least you only tell me; Queen Elizabeth threatens to have my head."

"What a wonderful idea! I think I'm going to like her; we can compare notes on how to bedevil Lord Blackhoof."

Now, I know she knows my title, so she was trying to get a rise. She got one.

"I know you will, Daughter of Heaven and Virtuous Lady."

"Cut it out, or I will tell Chairman Deng you called him Chairman Dung."

"Ouch, you win. When do you need the plane?"

"I need to fly to New York, arriving by Thursday week."

"That works out well."

"I was afraid your girlfriend could have it scheduled. That even made it in the newspapers over here. The people are interested in the one who has saved China from starvation."

"Two things: It is you that saved your people, and second, Nina and I are no longer together."

"From the way you talked of her, I don't think you are the one that caused the parting."

"No, you will be able to read about it in the papers."

"Foolish girl! I don't think she knows what she has lost."

"She knows she has lost all the worldly benefits of being my girlfriend."

"She doesn't know it yet, but she has lost much more than that. A good person is hard to find."

"Thank you for that thought. Who should be contacted about your schedule?"

She gave me the name of her secretary and how to contact them.

When I returned to the table, there were raised eyebrows all around.

Mum asked, "Was that Empress Ping?"

"Yeah, she wants to borrow my airplane."

Chief Redfoot spoke up, "You certainly lead a different life, Rick."

"Yes, I do. Here I am having dinner with a real Indian chief."

This broke the ice that had formed on the table conversation. We all enjoyed our meal.

Chapter 26

Before I could get out of the house the next morning, I had a phone call from an old contact from *Variety*. They had caught wind of my breakup with Nina and wanted my side of it.

I told them what had transpired. They seemed to know more than I did. It seemed Nina had met the prince at a school dance. No one was sure how he got there. It was like he came with the express purpose of meeting her.

He was the heir to a little principality that now only existed on paper. It had been absorbed into Germany in 1876. He was poor and lived off his girlfriend. He has been known to steal from them—the lowest of the low Eurotrash.

After talking to the reporter, I was depressed about the events.

Well, he had certainly taken Nina in. She must have been flattered that a "real" prince was paying attention to her. Not much to say to that. Yeah, he came on to her, but she went to him and, from what I saw, actively went to him.

I can see now why the rich must be so careful. There is no one they can trust.

Then I started thinking of all the wonderful people I had supporting me, from John Jacobs to Todd Pearson to Jim Williamson, and then there were my drinking buddies at Oxford.

That's it, I thought. I need to go see my friends in Oxford and tie one on. No, that way led to danger; I wasn't going to end up an alcoholic like many in my family.

Instead of doing anything crazy, I saddled George and rode over to practice golf. I was looking to get into a contest with professional sharks. There could be no such thing as too much preparation.

While riding over to the Forestry Station, I had a thought and turned back to the house. It was a good time to call China.

I got through to Empress Ping's secretary. I told him that I had forgotten to offer the use of my suite in the Waldorf Astoria. He was most appreciative as he was trying to arrange rooms for her party today.

My suite was the largest they had, with three bedrooms, a dining room, a full kitchen, a living room, and a study. Each bedroom had a full bath, and there was a half bath for guest use.

They would still need more rooms, but we were both certain that the Waldorf would find other rooms for the rest of the party. I even told him about track 61 and how it could be used for discreet comings and goings.

He liked that idea because the reporters were already inundating them with requests.

We talked for a few minutes about their schedule. I was surprised to hear that there was no meeting scheduled with President Kennedy. I wondered what was behind that reasoning.

He was surprised when I told him that former President Hoover and General of the Army MacArthur lived there. The empress would be most interested in meeting both, MacArthur as a hero from World War II still having immense popularity in the Orient.

President Hoover could be a possible backdoor to the US government. I didn't say anything to that. I was in too deep as it was.

After making that call, I went to practice golf. John noted that it was good that I was putting today instead of driving the ball on the green. He exaggerates sometimes, but I got his point.

They were right about time healing wounds; I was now only thinking of Nina every two minutes, and I kept asking myself, why?

I never had an answer.

At least my putting settled down. John joked that he thought I was going to tee one up yesterday; he had never seen me so tense. He had observed me playing in some tight tournaments, and I appeared to have nerves of steel.

I didn't have nerves of steel, but I was good at not showing my fears and frustrations. I told him that Nina had two-timed me with some guy. He told me, "I'm sorry to hear that, but that is what separates a good golfer from a great one. A great one could set everything aside and concentrate.

"Even if an atom bomb detonated in the distance, they would still be able to successfully make that putt while waiting on the shock wave."

As I said before, he tends to exaggerate, but he wasn't wrong.

Maybe I'm not destined to be a great golfer, but I will go out with a bang this year.

After practice, cleaning up, and lunch, I went to the studio. It was nice of them to arrange my shooting schedule around my golf practice.

When I expressed that to Mr. Wayne, he told me, "It's an investment in future publicity. If you win any of the big ones, the movie will make a lot of money."

Today, they were filming a scene that was a cliché in Westerns. It was a runaway wagon. In this incident, it was the chuck wagon with the pretty Miss Molly on board.

She and I had to have many shots of us with her on the wagon and me on my horse. Her job was the hardest as she had to pretend that the wagon was being pulled at a high rate of speed by terrified horses, but the wagon was only gently rolling along.

I had similar shots, but I could move the horse at a faster pace, so it was easier to make it look like we were galloping. For fun on one pass in front of the camera, I did break out my ride in a gallop.

They caught it on camera, and it ended up being used in the movie, but the insurance people on set weren't happy.

Stuntmen were supposed to do all the dangerous scenes. I didn't realize that was considered dangerous. They should have seen me on George when he was feeling rambunctious.

Miss Fields and I got along okay, but there was no chemistry between us. We were destined to end up as friends, or so I thought at the time.

We waited for our next call in those folding high-backed chairs with our names on them. Heaven forbid that a common person sit on our thrones. I had to smile at the thought of Queen Elizabeth on one of these.

We bantered back and forth. We didn't have any friends in common to gossip about, so it was a nothing sort of conversation.

This went on until a studio runner brought me a note. The note was to call Ken O'Donnell at the White House as soon as possible.

I let the director know I had a call that had to be returned and needed to leave the set.

"It is the president of the United States or the death of a family member," he grouched.

"Got it in one," I said as I handed him the note.

"Yeah, you probably had your mother call."

"The countess would have sent someone."

"I keep forgetting you are one of those hoity-toity nobles."

"Well, hoity-toity or not, I have to return this call."

"Make it quick. We're going to need you shortly."

I rode with the studio runner in his golf cart back to the main office building, where I placed my call.

I was put right through.

"Rick, thanks for getting back to me quickly. We need you this Saturday night to attend a state dinner we are giving for Empress Ping."

"I wasn't aware that you had opened relations with her."

"We hadn't had a chance to open any back channels to make certain she would accept, so we were reluctant to approach her. We got lucky; she is staying at the Waldorf-Astoria and ran into President Hoover, and he called us."

I had to smirk at hearing that.

"I can make it, white tie?"

"We would prefer you in your British rig."

"Keeping a little distance, are we?"

"Yeah, nothing personal, but we don't want you to mess up our relations with her. If she takes any offense with you, we will point out your British connections and blame them. If all goes well, you are American as apple pie."

That was so blatant I had to laugh.

"And if you guys screw up, I can blame it on those upstart colonists."

"We are professionals at this. We won't mess up. Why, look at how we arranged back channels."

"Yeah, that is impressive."

"Bring a plus one. I know it is short notice after your breakup with Nina Monroe, but we need a balanced table. If you don't have anyone, we will get you one."

"I'll bring someone. You know this depends on the movie producer agreeing to my having the time off."

"We need her name as soon as possible for the list at the gate. I'll take care of the producer. Who is it?"

"John Wayne."

"We will have to bring the big gun in for that."

As for them providing me with a date, I shuddered to think what the politicians would saddle me with.

We settled the details. I would fly on Friday and stay at the Willard House as usual. On the way back to the set, I thought of someone I could invite to the dinner.

Chapter 27

Sitting down on my portable throne, I turned to Sally, "Do you have any plans for this weekend?"

She cautiously said, "Not really."

"Would you like to go to dinner Saturday night?"

You could tell she wrestled with the idea of going out with a kid. Luckily, I won.

"Okay, where are we going?"

"A State Dinner at the White House."

She looked at me as though I had sprouted another head.

"Are you serious?"

"Yes, that was the message I had; I have been asked, well, more directed, to come to a State Dinner for Empress Ping, and I need a plus one."

"Well, then, I'm afraid I will have to turn you down."

"Why?"

"Rick, I know you are an established actor with a good income, but I'm what is called a struggling actress, which means I'm dead broke and can't afford the clothes for this dinner."

"Oh, I hadn't thought of that. It's no problem. I will pay for everything."

She got a hard look, "And what do you think you will be buying?"

"Not that!! I mean, just the clothes; you will be doing me a great favor."

"Another problem is that I have no idea what to wear or where to buy it."

"That's easy. Come home to dinner with my family, and we will take care of it."

You could see she was about to reject the whole plan when John Wayne came up.

"Rick, I just got a call from JFK; he needs you at a dinner on Saturday so you will need Friday, Saturday, and Sunday off. He offered special tax concessions if we let you go, so it's okay."

I had been hoping a little that John would say no, but money and the president talk. At least this changed Sally's mind.

Since we were done with our parts for the day, Sally and I took off for Jackson House, and she followed me in her beater. It was so banged up I couldn't even figure out who made it.

We had to stop at the gatehouse, where the guards took her name and asked to see her driver's license. It might seem over the top, but we've had enough problems over the years, and we were being careful.

After entering the courtyard, I parked us out front instead of going behind to the garage as normal.

I wanted her to get the full effect of the house.

"Rick, this is more than any money you could make acting."

"You don't know?"

"Know what?"

"I'm what they call wealthy. I have several patents and own a large company."

"I've been trying so hard to break into acting I've let the rest of the world go by."

"I understand."

As we spoke, I opened the front door of the house, or I tried to, but the butler beat me to it.

"Lord Blackhoof, welcome home."

I could see Sally getting overwhelmed as she looked at the grand entrance. I was saved by a seven-year-old who came sliding down a banister.

"Rick, save me; Eddie is going to tickle me until I pee!"

"What have you done now?"

"I only tied his shoes together."

"How many shoes?"

"Six pairs."

"What will I find if I go to my room?"

As she took off running, she shouted over her shoulder, "I think it was twenty pairs."

I turned to Sally, "Welcome to our madhouse."

About that time, Mary came running back through, "Now Mum is after me!"

"Did you tie her shoes together?"

"No, I put pieces of newspaper in all the toes. There must have been a hundred of them."

As Mary disappeared into the coat room, Eddie came down the stairs. I didn't say anything but pointed to the coatroom.

Mum came in about that time. She stopped when she saw that I had a girl with me.

"Hello, Rick. Introduce me to your friend."

"Sally, this is my mum, Countess Jackson. Mum, this is Sally Fields, who is the leading lady in my movie."

They both made the proper noises while checking each other out.

"Mum, I have to go to Washington for a State Dinner for Empress Ping. Sally has agreed to be my plus one, but we need help with picking clothing and all that goes with it. I will be paying."

Mum took Sally by the hand, "We are going to have fun shopping, and Rick will pay!"

She led Sally by the hand into the reception where my mum's guest was sitting. I had no idea that Anna Romanov was visiting.

You could see Sally gulp when she realized who was sitting there. When Mum explained the mission, Anna declared herself in. It would be a ball. They would go out all day tomorrow, do lunch, go shopping, and then a spa.

I had to put a damper on it, "We have a movie we are shooting."

Anna said, "Nonsense! This is more important."

Since she knew everyone and everything going on in Hollywood, it was no surprise she dialed John Wayne's home number from memory.

"John, Anna. Sally won't be in tomorrow. Countess Jackson and I are taking her shopping."

She listened to the shouts on the other end.

"Not to worry; you have never kept a schedule, and yes, Rick is paying for everything."

After she hung up, I asked why he wanted to know if I was paying.

"If you weren't, it was the water trough."

I went to my room to change for dinner, leaving the women to plan how to spend my money.

As I took a shower, I realized I hadn't thought of Nina in an hour.

In the morning, I rode over and practiced my golf. I was feeling in the groove these days. The muscle memory was getting ingrained for the right sort of putting.

Sam had done a wonderful job in recreating the tricks of the various greens I would be putting on. Other than grass-type differences, I was getting dialed in.

Who was I kidding? There was also the weather that could change the way a green played, along with the time of day, pin placement, and probably a hundred other things, but I was getting as ready as possible.

I went to the studio and walked through a barroom fight that I was in. The fights were dangerous, not in the fight itself, but if someone went the wrong way when things were flying. I once went left when I was supposed to go right and about got knocked into next Sunday by a right hook. That right hook was sure a wrong hook for me.

I got home that evening at about the same time as the shopping crew. They were as thick as thieves. I could see Mum and Anna would corrupt that innocent Sally in no time at all.

Wednesday, we were both on the set. As fate would have it, there was nothing for us to do most of the day as other shots were being made. I think this was a time-out for us. They could have called and told us to stay home. Thursday was also quiet.

Friday morning, I took a limo to the airport, picking up Sally on the way. She had a ton of luggage with her. All her new purchases, I supposed.

As we boarded the aircraft, Harold took possession of everything. One small detail came out. I had forgotten to tell Sally about the plane.

She had thought we would be flying commercial and hoped for first class. She looked around in amazement. We had barely gotten into the plane when the pilot came on, "Lord Blackhoof, we are cleared to go; please buckle up."

After we were airborne, I had the head stewardess take her on a tour of the aircraft. I had given so many that it was boring. I spent my time reading a book on the pluses and minuses of the gold standard. I could see that no one could remain on the gold standard for many more years if they wanted their economies to grow.

Then, there would be a myriad of ills to follow, but they would be less than remaining with gold.

After her tour, Sally came and sat next to me in my private office.

"You are very rich, aren't you?"

"It is said that I'm the richest person in the world, but I don't know it for a fact."

"How did it happen?"

I proceeded to tell her my story, starting with hitchhiking to California that summer several years ago. It seemed like a lifetime, but it was only three years.

We had lunch in the conference room, where I continued my saga. We were starting our final approach into Friendship International (the airport between Washington and Baltimore since large jets were not permitted to use Washington National) when I brought her up to date with Nina.

"Rick, I like you, but you live life too fast for me. I would rather go slowly down the highway rather than be chased by everyone."

I hadn't even told her about my run-ins with the KGB.

We checked into a three-room suite at the Willard, one each for Sally, Harold, and me.

Chapter 28

Saturday was a busy day. Sally had to have her hair and nails done. Harold had me put on my mess dress uniform to make certain all was still correct. It was.

I would be wearing all the real medals along with my Order of the Garter sash and star and carrying my dress sword.

I looked like a German princeling from some cheap movie. German princeling made me think of one I would like to punch in the nose.

Which, in turn, made me think of Nina. I wondered what she would be doing now. Maybe I should call her? No way would I call that traitorous—

Even in my anger, I couldn't finish that thought.

As we were having breakfast in our room, the phone rang. It was the front desk. There was a message from the White House; should they bring it up?

The message was a request that I call Ken O'Donnell to arrange a meeting. I made the call, and we worked it around the time that Sally would be on her beauty trip, which was an hour from now until 5 p.m., all day. Mum and Anna had set it all up for her. I wondered what all could be done to the human body during that time. On second thought, I don't want to know.

I was escorted into the Oval Office, where Ken and both Kennedys were waiting.

Bobby started, "Jackson, you set us up."

"How?"

"You provided transportation, rooms at the Waldorf, and an introduction to Hoover. You left us no choice but to have this dinner."

"I didn't do any of that. A friend asked for a loan of my aircraft; I offered the suite and told her that Hoover and MacArthur were living there. I had no plan."

"God, she has spoken to MacArthur?"

"I have no idea. She expressed the desire to, but I don't know if they did."

"We wanted to go slow on recognizing China in case it all blows up. You forced our hand."

"If that's what you want to think. How do I benefit from that?"

"We will have to offer loans to build those damn ports of yours. By the way, how much does it take to install all the infrastructure to handle those containers?"

"I'm told, on the average, about ten million dollars."

"So, we are going to have to loan them at least fifty million dollars to save face, and you ask what benefit there is to you?"

"Again, that never entered my mind. You seem to think I'm an evil genius or something. I'm just a kid who has a lot of money and loaned their airplane to a friend."

At that, the president spoke up, "Maybe we are reading too much into this. Rick, you have to appreciate that we need to look at everything that happens and try to figure out how it will play out in the best interest of the United States.

"I spoke to Ike about it, and he told me that you don't think like that, that you probably reacted nicely to a request. Also, he told me that the empress and her advisors knew the probable outcome."

"While you aren't the devious one here, I'm darn certain the Chinese are. Please give some thought before you volunteer anything in the future to China or any other world power."

He said the last with a straight face. Who did he think I was?

"I will. Are you aware that the Chinese are now allowing private ownership of land under certain conditions?"

The president asked, "What conditions?"

"I'm not certain of the criteria, but they have allowed me to buy most of the old trade zone in Beijing."

"I didn't even know they had a trade zone in Beijing. I thought it was limited to three cantons."

"There wasn't that much trade done there. For both sides' convenience, they allowed Western buildings to be put up and leased out to diplomatic missions. Think of it more as embassy row."

"Now you own all these buildings?"

"Yes, there are only twenty or so, and of those, only three are habitable right now. I have had work started on upgrading them and refurbishing the others."

"I don't recommend that the US buys one. There is enough land left that I think you should buy part of it and build your embassy there."

"I suppose you own that land?"

"Yes, I do, and it is for sale."

Bobby curiously asked, "How many arms and legs are you asking?"

"I'm offering twenty-five acres to the United States for one dollar."

The president and his brother both spoke up at the same time, "What swamp is it located on?" and "We will take it."

"No swamp, good solid building land and sold."

"I'll make arrangements. I suggest you ask Chairman Deng as to which construction company to use, then have plenty of people there to ensure they don't have too many spy devices implanted in the building."

"We will do that."

"I also should share that the Chinese intend to develop a hard currency."

"How do you know that?"

"I was asked to quiz some experts on how to do it."

"Where are these experts from?"

"The London School of Economics."

"You are full of surprises, Mr. Jackson."

"Just the right place at the right time. I do have a vested interest in their successful opening of China."

"That's right, you are upgrading their ports."

"That, and they are into me for a hundred and fifty million dollars right now."

"I thought it was two-fifty."

"I forgave the first hundred."

"I think I know why the Chinese like you. Do you want to loan the US any?"

"Not particularly. You will just waste it on social projects to buy long-term votes."

"From that, I gather you would loan it to a Republican administration."

"No, they would waste it on unneeded construction projects for their donors."

"An equal opportunity cynic, I like that."

"I like to think I'm a realist."

"That you are, my boy, that you are."

That comment ended our meeting. I left on a much higher note than when I had entered.

I returned to the hotel and took a nap. When I woke, it was time to get cleaned up and dressed for the evening.

When I came out in full uniform, Sally, who was entering at the same time as I was, stopped dead. So did I. She is gorgeous in an innocent-looking way.

I told her so. She replied that she had never seen such a costume as I wore. Did I borrow it from the wardrobe department, and if so, why? People would know it was just a costume.

I thought Harold, who was standing there, would die.

"No, this is all real. I'm a colonel in the Coldstream Guards. All these medals are the real thing."

"Oh," she said in a suddenly small voice."

It was time to go, so I offered her my hand, and we descended to the lobby. There we were the center of attention. The papa-rats-eye were out in force. They crowded us to snap pictures.

Poor Sally was so small that they kept pushing her around to get better camera angles. Tired of all the jostling around, I swept her up into a princess carry and bulled my way through.

Our limo was waiting for the short drive to the White House. It was a presidential car driven by the Secret Service, so we didn't have to stop at a gate.

At the entrance, I was asked if I had my normal weapons. I told them no, only my sword. The agent laughed and said, "I don't think we will be too concerned about that."

I think he was being too sanguine about my sword; it was the real deal made by Wilkinson. With my height and reach, I could draw it and make a killing lunge at someone fifteen feet away.

I hoped I didn't have to tonight. The blood would ruin my uniform.

As with all events like this, there was a reception line. First, the president and first lady, then Empress Ping, with a translator standing slightly behind her.

I held out a hand and said, "Mr. President."

He interrupted me with, "Call me, John."

"Yes, sir, Mr. President."

He laughed at that. I introduced him and Jackie to Sally. I noticed he held her hand longer than needed. So did Jackie. I wondered what their marriage was like.

Next was Empress Ping.

She hugged me and had me introduce Sally.

"Sally, take good care of this young man. As you can see, he is worth a great deal to both of our countries."

"Rick, I would like to thank you for the use of the aircraft, your hotel suite, and introductions to General MacArthur and President Hoover.

"The president is going to be unbelievably valuable in our conversations with your country going forward. Speaking of countries, I would like to meet with Queen Elizabeth in the not-too-distant future. We would like to store gold with the Bank of England. Would you arrange that?"

"The gold or the Queen?"

"Both of them, if you would."

"My pleasure."

After that, we mingled for a while, mainly with the British ambassador, who wanted an update on things. I told him what I knew and let him know that I would also offer land for an embassy in Beijing to Her Majesty for one dollar.

"No, old boy, not the done thing; it must be sold to the Foreign Office."

"I could do that at full price, ten million dollars an acre."

He turned away and didn't speak to me again.

Our table was halfway down from the head table, so that was the last interesting conversation I had for the evening.

Chapter 29

There was the usual fawning over Lord Blackhoof at the dinner. What is it with Americans and nobility? They had a war to get rid of them, and now they can't get enough of them.

Sally stood quietly by my side. She held herself well as though she were the queen, and they were there to pay her homage.

I even mentioned that to her on the way back to the hotel. She let me know that she was miserable the whole evening. She wasn't comfortable with any of those snobs.

"You sure didn't show it."

"Of course not. I'm an actress."

"You gave a terrific performance."

"Thank you, and it is my last one for that audience. You will have to find another plus one. I find I prefer the cowboy types. I thought you were one, but you are only acting."

I was sorry to hear that on several levels.

When we got back to the hotel, we had a guest waiting in our room. The hotel had let her in. It was Empress Ping.

"Rick, it went well this evening, and I thank you. The Americans have given us more than we asked for. They have extended a line of credit of one hundred million dollars to us, which is much more than we need."

"Are you going to take it?"

"Silly boy. Of course, we are taking it. There is a loan I would like to start to pay off."

At times, I'm a little slow.

"What loan?"

She sighed and turned to Sally. "Sometimes, I forget how dense men can be.

"Your loan. After this, we will only owe you fifty million. I'm sure we can talk the French or Germans out of that so we can repay you completely."

Sally wasn't aware of this, so her eyes were wide.

She spoke up, "Rick, I need to marry you or run. I think I will run. This isn't my life."

Empress Ping changed the subject.

"I know you have to get back to California tomorrow. Can I ride with you, then continue to China?"

How can you say no to an empress?

The next day, before we left for the airport, I put in a call to London. I informed Mr. Norman that China wanted to proceed with shipping one thousand tons of gold to the Bank of England as a guarantee of good faith support for the yuan.

Also, the empress would like to arrange a meeting with Queen Elizabeth as soon as possible. Sally, who was standing right there, pretended to ignore it all. I think this is what they call culture shock. Thinking back to two years ago, I would have never dreamed of this life.

We had a pleasant trip to LA. The empress entertained Sally with stories of my dry-cleaning days. She even told of the KGB's attempts on me.

I doubted if the young lady would ever go anywhere with me but a movie set again in her life.

We had picked up the newspapers at the airport.

The front page of my favorite Inquiring Minds Want to Know was a picture of me carrying Sally through the hotel lobby.

My first reaction was that I had better call Nina and explain what had occurred. A moment later, I realized that I owed her no phone call, and this picture would show her that other girls would go for me.

I made the mistake of mentioning that to the ladies. They exchanged looks. The empress said, "He is still young."

Sally nodded.

We had started a new tradition at Jackson House. Our schedule was so jammed these days that we couldn't get together for everyone's birthday.

To make up for this, we would have a small party on the person's birthday with whoever was present in the house.

In the middle of June, we would have a grand party for all of us. Mum and Denny shared a birthdate, May 19th; she was born in 1920, and Denny in 1947. I knew how old she was because I had accidentally seen her passport once.

Well, maybe not a full accident. It was lying there open. I only had to turn one page to see her age. She was two years older than Dad. That was a shocker.

Mary was born on June 1st, 1954. Dad June 5th, 1922.

That left me on October 11th, 1944, and Eddie on December 12th, 1949. We also included Mrs. Hernandez and Ben, who were on July 3rd and September 23rd.

With so many of us, it is no wonder that I always had our birthdays mixed up.

The gifts on the real birthday were always small, sincere gifts; even when out of town, we each made certain that a gift was sent.

For the grand birthday party, we would go all out with gag gifts. Since I was now considered filthy rich, I was presented with a gold-plated, well, gold-painted horse trough to bath in.

Without any consultation with each other, Mary ended up with "Save the Aardvarks," "Save the Armadillos," and "Save the Plankton" T-shirts.

Denny gave Mum a gold-plated squirt gun. That was a big mistake as she promptly disappeared and filled it.

Mum got Dad a safari jacket with his name tag, followed by Great White Hunter. The jacket fabric had the cutest kittens imprinted. Oh, and it was pink.

These were just examples of the types of gifts given. Some that Mum, Dad, Mrs. Hernandez, and Ben gave each other they wouldn't let us see.

Mary had picked up one of the boxes and was asking, "What's a dil—" when it was snatched from her hands by a red-faced Mrs. Hernandez.

We had ice cream and cake, and there was a *piñata* for the kids. When they couldn't get it to break, they asked me to put on the blindfold and take a swing.

I should have realized something was up when it took so long to cover my eyes. It was twirled around. I thought I had kept track of where I was at.

I hadn't. It took me two wild swings to hit the "*piñata*." I didn't know you could make a water balloon that big and not have it burst from its weight.

I swore revenge.

I don't think anyone took me seriously as they were laughing so hard. Wait until next year.

I changed clothes and returned to the party. It had settled down. The adults were having coffee, so I joined them.

Ben asked me, "Rick, what are your plans for the future? Right now, you have golf, the movies, and your companies. What is the most important to you?"

"You don't mess around with the softballs, do you, Ben? I have been wondering that very thing recently. I love to play golf; I just don't want to do it professionally."

"I don't plan to enter any tournaments after this year's, but at the same time, there is nothing like the pressure of playing against the greatest in the world.

"Movies are getting to be old hat, and I mean old cowboy hat. There is no challenge in them anymore. I realize I'm a character actor; I play myself. "Death Wind has won critical acclaim, but it wasn't my acting that made it. It was the director's cutting that did it."

"I would love to do a spy movie as the lead, but I don't think that is in the cards. I think my movie days may be about over."

"As far as business, I have had some good ideas and been fortunate in being able to find good people to implement them. That said, I'm under no illusion that I'm ready to run anything larger than a lemonade stand.

"All that said, I don't know where I'm headed or what I want to do next. I plan to bump along and see what happens."

Mum and Dad were listening intently but had no comment.

Mrs. Hernandez asked if I had any plans for a singing career. I just glared at her. She was high on my revenge list.

Chapter 30

The next few weeks flew by and at a snail's pace. It is hard to explain. Each day was a repeat of the last: golf in the morning, on the set in the afternoon. They kept telling us we were going on location but never went.

I began to wonder if the entire movie would be done on the Warner Brothers lot with the fifteen head of cattle they had.

Things became clear later one Monday morning in April. The original ranch that was going to be our location had foot rot throughout their herd. We couldn't use them in the movie.

They looked all over the west to find a suitable place. Finally, in Texas near the Goodnight-Loving trail, they found a ranch.

We were given directions to the ranch. Buses were provided to those who needed a ride. I elected to fly my Cessna into the local airfield and rent a car.

It was a good thing that I worked with the studio on my travel arrangements instead of just taking off. There was no car rental agency at the airfield. The airfield was just that, a grass landing strip.

Knowing this, a car was driven up from Austin for me to use.

There was a local motel, and the studio had rented almost all the rooms. Several permanent residents would be staying.

My flight was uneventful. Boring would be a better description. There was some bumpy air but nothing to write home about.

They did have t-hangars, and I was able to rent one for my stay.

I checked into the hotel. When I gave my name, I was told I had a suite. Thinking that things weren't all bad, I went to my room. Their definition of a suite differed from mine. It was a large room with a built-in kitchenette and a small table to eat at.

I had slept in much worse places, and it would only be for a couple of weeks, so I wouldn't complain. If I did, the best I would get is a trailer hauled in. They weren't much better than this.

I drove out to the ranch we would be shooting at. That is when it got strange. According to the signs, the Triple R Bar Ranch was a dude ranch!

Maybe this was their offseason, and there wouldn't be any dudes around. Wrong. There were dudes everywhere. You could tell them by their outfits and the way they sat a horse.

Since I knew I was going to be on a working ranch, I had dressed appropriately. Boots, jeans, a white hat, and a plain shirt. Nothing fancy. All comfortable work clothes. Maybe my belt buckle was a little large, as it was one of my minor rodeo ones.

I drove up to the main house and parked my car in a large lot filled with what I supposed were dudes' cars.

As I was walking to the main office to check in, a female voice shouted, "Hey you."

I turned to face a beautiful young lady with blonde hair, blue eyes, fair skin, and large, well, you get it.

She was perfect.

"My saddle won't stay on my horse. What am I doing wrong?"

She had her horse on a lead. It was easy to see the problem as the saddle was almost upside down.

"It looks like you didn't cinch it tight enough. The horse played a trick on you by expanding its belly with a deep breath. You tighten the cinch, the horse lets out its breath, and there you go, loose saddle.

"Would you please show me how to do it right?"

"Yeah, no problem."

I got the saddle to the point of tightening the cinch. I told her to watch the horse's sides. Sure enough, its belly swelled up. If I had tightened it then, the saddle would be loose.

I kneed the horse in its side, not hard enough to hurt it, but enough that it let its breath out. That is when I quickly tightened the cinch.

The girl who had been watching me said, "Oh, I forgot that step. They did show us. Are you new here?"

"Just arriving."

"I thought so. I have been here two weeks. My name is Karen Klima. What's yours?

"Rick Jackson."

"Well, Rick, we have been told not to talk to the hired hands too much, but I do thank you for your help."

Tipping my hat, "My pleasure, ma'am."

This could be interesting.

She gave me a shy smile and turned to her horse.

I went on into the office. Since I had flown in, I was the first of the film crew there. The lady manning the office told me about their ranch.

It was a working ranch, and all the paying customers were expected to take part in events. There was a roundup going on to take cattle to market.

The normal procedure was to round them up, put them in a feedlot to fatten them for the market, and then haul them away by truck.

The studio was paying extra to move the cattle around so they could get their film. The dudes would be helping the ranch cowboys do the actual moving while we actors would pose for pictures. It wasn't expected that we could be of any use doing the work.

Once again, I thought, *This could be interesting.*

She told me, "At least you look the part. Can you ride a horse?"

I assured the office lady I could, but I'm not certain she bought it.

I asked, "Is there a local rodeo, or do you put one on here at the ranch?"

"There is one once a month at the fairgrounds. We take our customers over there on a bus to watch it. Would you like to sign up for that? It is this weekend."

"I think I will pass on the bus ride. If I go, I will arrange my transportation."

"Okay."

It was obvious she had written me off as a Hollywood fake. She knew I was here and would pass the word on to my bosses when they arrived. In the meantime, she suggested that I get out of the way of the working people.

She wasn't nasty about it; she just didn't have much use for us Hollywood layabouts. So I left, intending to go back to my luxury suite at the hotel.

"Hey, man."

What's with the hey man?

"You need to get to work before I fire you on your first day. Get over to the corral behind the barn and help with the branding and vaccinations."

"Yes, sir."

This could be interesting. Better than sitting in a hotel room counting the flowers on the wall as the song went.

Out back, it was controlled pandemonium. It was spring, and a lot of calves had dropped. They needed to be branded with the Triple R Bar brand and have a set of vaccinations. This required the calf to be caught, branded, and then fed into a chute where the shot could be administered.

It was evident they were having problems catching the calves. One cowboy was trying to teach the dudes how to do it. He looked very frustrated.

There were several horses saddled up, so I asked the frustrated cowpoke if I could use one.

"Please. This is killing me. I don't know who is stupider, the dudes or the calves. I always thought calves were smart for their station in life. I don't know about someone who wanted to be a dude cowboy."

It had been a while, but I hadn't lost the touch. Using a lariat and piggin strings held between my teeth, I was able to lasso and tie a calf down the first toss.

I wasn't setting any timed records doing it, but I wasn't a disgrace either, taking about eight seconds. This wasn't worthy of rodeo time, but it was a good working time.

After I had one tied down, a dude would run over with a hot iron and brand the calf. After that, he would untie the string while the rope remained around its neck, and I would back my horse up to keep tension on the rope and lead it to the chute for its vaccination.

Doing fifty calves can tire you out. I was a dusty, thirsty mess when we were finished. The real cowboy thanked me for the help and was glad to see the foreman had hired someone who knew what they were doing and wasn't afraid to work.

At that, I headed back towards my car. I needed a shower. I was almost there when I heard.

"Hey, man."

Now what?

"We are just checking in. Carry these bags to the registration area."

Now, I could explain my role, ignore the guy, or carry the bags. I chose to carry the bags. I have a sick sense of humor, you know.

He gave me a buck tip for carrying five bags. What a cheapskate.

Chapter 31

I went back to my hotel room, showered, and shaved. My body was tired. I wasn't used to real work like roping calves.

I lay down on the bed to rest a minute, and the next thing you know, I had an hour's nap. I flipped through both TV channels and didn't find anything I wanted to watch.

The brown-stained walls and wagon wheel lights may have been top-line Western decorations back in the day. Maybe around 1890 or so. I wasn't going to spend a whole evening here.

I had a good selection of clothes with me but thought it would be wise to keep in the working cowboy mode.

The motel was on the edge of town, but it wasn't a far walk to the town center as the whole main street was only ten or so blocks long.

It was past five o'clock, so the sidewalks had been rolled up. Not really, but all the stores were closed except for one bar. It had a sign saying "Eats", so I decided to chance it. That or go hungry, and I was starving.

Inside the bar, the Western motif of brown stained walls and wagon wheel lights was continued. That oddly made sense. How many decorators could this town support? There was the traditional bar with bar stools and about a dozen tables with chairs. Along one wall was a row of booths.

A jukebox was playing "North to Alaska". Three guys were sitting at the bar, all separately. One couple was in a booth, and that was it.

I went up to the bar and sat on a stool. The bartender quickly came over.

"Son, you don't look like you are twenty-one. You can't sit at the bar in Texas. Please move to a table."

"Yes, sir," I said as I started to move.

"Will I be allowed to order some food?"

"That we can do."

I moved over to the closest table, and he brought me a menu. After a glance, I ordered a cheeseburger and fries with a Coke. Hard to go wrong with that.

Just because the place smelled of stale beer and cigarette smoke didn't mean they couldn't make a mean cheeseburger and fries. They were just what the doctor ordered.

I had just finished my meal and paid when three guys came in. They were dressed like townies, as opposed to cowboys. They had on khaki pants and polo shirts.

"Hey, look, guys, a cowboy has come to town."

I wasn't looking for trouble, so I tipped the brim of my hat and attempted to walk around them. The biggest one of them held out an arm to stop me.

"Guys, I'm not looking for trouble. I just want to go get some sleep."

"Well, trouble has found you. We told you cowboys to stay out of our bar."

The bartender spoke up, "No fighting in here; take it outside."

Well, there went a chance for help. I didn't see any way out of this, so I started for the door. My new friends followed me. I had a moment to plan as we headed out.

As soon as I cleared the door, I swung to my right up against the bars on the front window. Now, they couldn't come at me from the back. From the front and two sides were bad enough.

As they came through the doorway, they were bunched up with the big guy in front and at the center of them. The one lesson from unarmed combat I remember was when you are outnumbered, take them out as fast as you can.

I didn't give any warning or fancy speeches. I just lashed out with my boot into the side of the big guy's knee. As he was going down, he grabbed the guy on his left to try to stay up. This threw that guy off balance.

I used this slight edge to slam a right hook into the right-side guy's nose. This resulted in a gush of blood. I then turned to the big guy, but he was down and holding his knee. He was out of the fight.

I grabbed the front of the shirt of the bloody-nosed guy who was still holding his nose and swung him into the last one standing. This knocked them both off their balance.

A kick to the side of the head settled the last guy down. The bloody nose guy was now coming out of his stun, so I hit him in the solar plexus and then another right as he bent over.

Fight over. Not pretty, not sporting, but I was standing, and they weren't.

I went back inside the bar and told the bartender, "You'd better call the cops. There's some trash on the sidewalk that needs cleaning up."

I went back to the hotel to get a night's sleep. I was about to get undressed when there was a pounding on the door. It was the local cop and, from the looks of him, a hastily deputized bartender.

"This him, Bud?"

"Yep, he's the one that busted your son's kneecap."

The cop, whose uniform looked like he had spilled his dinner down it, had his pistol out. I knew I could take both guys; I mean, their bellies hung down over their belts. It would do me no good as it would lead to deeper problems.

I submitted to being handcuffed and placed in the back of a 1951 Crown Vic that must have had one hundred thousand bad miles on it.

I was unloaded and put into the drunk tank. I was told I would be booked in the morning. Thinking what a fine mess this was, I did the only sensible thing and got a night's sleep. I won't say it was a good night, but at least no one else was in with me.

In the morning, after using the hole they called a toilet, I was led out to be fingerprinted and a mug shot taken. I asked if I could make a phone call. I was told that would be later.

Next, I was taken to a small courtroom where a wizened old man in black robes presided.

"Is this the guy, Caleb?'

"Yep, Uncle Joe, it's him that busted up little Joe's knee. I reckon he should do a couple of years hard time as an adult."

The judge pounded his gavel.

"So be it, two years in the state penitentiary."

Things weren't looking too good. I could get lost in the system.

"Your Honor, may I have a word?"

An unexpected voice came from the back. This was as good as it gets, John Wayne to the rescue.

"And who are you?"

"Who the hell do you think I am?"

That's shy and bashful John. The policeman turned and faced John.

"What the hell? Are you John Wayne?"

"Yes, I am, and why are you trying to railroad the lead star in my movie?"

"Huh?"

"Lead star is what I said; from what I understand from the people that were in the bar, three guys jumped Ricky, and he took care of them."

"That's not what my boy said."

"Did you talk to the other people?"

"No."

"Well, I suggest you do, or Rick here is going to own this flea-bitten town for false arrest, though why he would want it, I don't know."

Suddenly, things changed in the courtroom. The judge told the cop to get his facts straight and, until then, let me go.

I was let go. I had to ask Mr. Wayne how he knew of my problem.

"The cab driver that picked me up at my plane was telling me about the big fight last night. He described you well enough that I knew it had to be you.

How did he describe me?

"Real tall, mean-looking SOB."

I never thought of myself that way. I knew I was tall, but mean-looking?

At the look I had on my face, John started laughing.

"What he said was a tall kid who knew unarmed combat. He was a former Marine, and from what he saw, you had that training and then some."

"He was in a booth with his girlfriend and saw it all. He hates the three guys who are the town bullies, so he was glad to see them get their comeuppance."

"Thanks for coming to my rescue, John."

"No problem, Pilgrim," he drawled.

"I have some other news that might not be so welcome. We've had some equipment problems so that we won't be bringing the rest of the cast and crew down till Friday morning. I've got some business in Dallas with the Ewings, but you need to decide whether to fly home and back again before Friday or just stay here."

I told him I would be staying. "It looks like I have a job."

"Doing what?" he asked.

"Well," I replied. "They thought I was a new hand yesterday, and I spent the afternoon roping calves. I enjoyed it, so since I'm stuck, I might as well keep at it."

He thought that was funny and told me to go for it.

Chapter 32

I returned to my hotel room and took a long, hot shower. After that, I packed a bag with three days' change of clothing and my shaving kit.

I drove out to the ranch. As I thought might happen as I was parking my rental, the foreman came up to me.

"Where have you been?"

"You'll hear about it sooner or later. I spent the night in jail."

"What for?"

"You know the bar that stays open late, well past six o'clock?"

"Ah. You didn't run into the cop's son, did you?"

"Yep."

"You don't look bad. What did they do, stove up your ribs?"

"No, it was the other way around. Little Joe has a busted-up knee. His friends got off with a bloody nose, and probably each of them has a slight concussion."

"Well, hot damn. They have been giving the guys here a tough time. I'm glad to see them get what they deserve. In the meantime, I have a different job for you today."

"What's that?"

"The dudes expect us to break our horses the old-fashioned way by riding them till they stop bucking. We keep a few incorrigible horses that have been retired from the rodeo circuit to show off. Since you're the new guy and seem fit, you get to ride them today."

"I get to ride rodeo bucking broncos that won't let anyone ride them and pretend I'm breaking them?"

"Yeah, you only must do two in the morning and two in the afternoon. That way, all the dudes get to see a show."

"Did you tell me how much I'm getting paid?"

"The same fifty a week as the other guys; they all have paid their dues."

"Okay, boss. What time do I start?"

"If you head on over to the corral, it will be just about right."

I went over to one of the corrals behind the barns, where a crowd was gathering. One of the older cowboys waved me over.

"You do any rodeo riding?"

"Not horses."

"If you can stay on board for eight seconds, you are good. We tell the crowd that the horse needs to be ridden like that multiple times for them to get the message. Some horses take longer than others. Why, Diablo has been ridden hundreds of times and still don't get it."

I could see this was going to be a tough day. He took me over and showed me the equipment; the saddle had free-swinging stirrups and no horn. The horse would have a leather halter attached to a cotton braided rein.

The old cowboy told me to find a rhythm by spurring forwards and backward with my feet in a sweeping motion from the flank. That part I got from bull riding.

They had Diablo in a chute. As I got up on the rail, I swear the horse turned and winked at me as if he were in on the deception.

The cowboy turned to me and asked, "What's your name, son?"

"Rick Jackson."

He then stood high on the rail and told the crowd, "Old Diablo is going to be saddle broke today by none other than our own Rick Jackson."

I was handed a pair of leather gloves, and I wound the reins tight around my left hand. I hoped I made it past the first buck.

Then, just like that, Diablo exploded out of the chute. He went high and came down stiff-legged, which was a new one on me; thankfully, I was braced well and hung on.

After that, it was the more traditional bucking. I got lucky and fell into his rhythm quickly. He bounced me around up and down. I hung on like crazy while swinging my right arm up and down to keep my balance.

After about a year of this, a horn sounded, and another rider came up beside Diablo. I grabbed the rider and jumped to the ground. I had lasted eight whole seconds on the horse!

My cowboy mentor came up and handed me my hat, which had gone flying.

"Not bad; you would have been disqualified in the rodeo, but not a bad ride at all."

"Why would I have been disqualified?" I knew full well why but was keeping to my image.

"Your hat came off."

"What?"

"Yeah, the sissies today pin or glue their hats on, so they don't lose them. It's an image thing.

"I saw Bill Pickett when I was a kid. Now he lost his hat every time, but it didn't hurt his image none."

No, I thought, anyone willing to bulldog a bull by biting its lip wouldn't have an image problem.

Anyway, I dusted myself and waved to the crowd. That cute blonde from yesterday was up front and waved back. I wondered if she would like to take a walk and look at the stars tonight.

In half an hour, I had to do it again. This horse was well on its way to being broken because it was bucking at first, then ran a few circles around the corral and stopped.

My spokesman told the crowd, "Rick's been working with this horse for a while, and he is about ready for regular ranch work. If you're lucky, maybe one of you dudes will get him tomorrow!"

When the iron triangle started ringing for lunch, I was first in line. I was starving. By accident, I'm sure the blonde girl was right behind me, so it was natural that Karen and I ate together.

I found out that she was a senior in high school and that this week was their spring break. She didn't want to come here, but her parents insisted. Now, it didn't look so bad.

I managed not to say much about myself by showing interest in her. That worked well. Getting my nerve up, I asked her if she would like to take a walk tonight to watch the stars.

She giggled and asked if that was the Western version of submarine races. I admitted it was.

As she was staying in a cabin with her parents, she would need permission to be out with some of the other kids.

We went our separate ways after lunch. The foreman hunted me up and told me I did a good job riding today. I should consider rodeo riding. That was when he glanced down at my belt buckle.

"I may have spoken too soon. This isn't your first rodeo, is it?"

"No, sir."

"Well, good job. Now I have to say something not so good. We don't mix cowboys with dude girls. Bad for business, you understand?"

"Yes, sir."

Damn! I had a choice: to tell him who I was or not to go walking with Karen. That was an easy decision.

"If I were one of your cowboys, I wouldn't go walking with any of the girls, but I'm not on your payroll."

"Tarnation boy; what are you telling me?"

I held out my hand to shake and said, "Let's start over. I'm Rick Jackson. I'm in the movie that starts filming here on Friday."

He got red-faced, then started laughing.

"You're one of those actor fellows that Miss Nellie in the office says are all hat and no cattle."

"That's me."

"This is wonderful. That old biddy thinks she knows everything."

"I didn't defend my title, but I was the World Champion Bull Rider in the Youth Division several years ago. That is where this buckle came from."

The foreman settled down from his laughing. He got a funny look on his face.

"My wife reads all those scandalous newspapers and magazines, and now I know why you look familiar. I'm going to look you up tonight while you are out walking."

"After you read them, please give me a chance to defend myself."

After dinner that night, I met Karen near the campfire they had every evening. We stayed for the sing-along and then went for a walk.

"Rick, you sing fairly well if you don't try to get loud. I was impressed you knew the words to "Rock and Roll Cowboy". No one listens to it anymore."

"Probably a good thing; the singer is terrible."

"He's not that bad. I can't remember his name, but he isn't terrible.

For the record, I did point out some of the constellations. Of course, to see them, we had to lie on the ground. Fortunately, I thought of bringing a blanket. That's all you need to know about our walk.

The next morning, the foreman joined me at breakfast.

"Movie star, inventor, British baron, colonel in the Coldstream Guards, pilot, owner of one of the richest companies in the world. Why are you here roping calves and riding broncs?"

"Nothing better to do this week?"

"That works for me. How are you with a gun?"

"Fair."

"We usually do a pistol and rifle shooting demonstration. You up to that?"

"Sure."

"Then there is the Old West shootout on our main street."

"As long as we don't use live bullets."

"Nah, we have a couple of those special Hollywood guns that won't even take live ammo."

"I'm up for it. Who am I shooting it out with?"

"Billy the Kid, of course."

"Who wins?"

"This time, you do. We alternate every week."

"Sounds like fun."

Chapter 33

The shooting demonstration was on a special target range. It was special in the targets used. The backstop and bench rests were standard. Sitting out in the hot Texas sun like they were, the bench rests were weathered, and boy, did they have splinters.

I learned that the hard way.

The special targets were cutouts of buffalo and mountain lions. To add some spice to the range, they had a bandit and a mask, all with six guns posed and rolled out by a mechanical device.

I thought it was random until I saw one of the cowboy onlookers push a button. He could move it out and leave it or move it back immediately. He was leaving it out for the kids and pulling it back quickly for the adults.

The more obnoxious the adult was, the less time the target was available.

The weapons being demonstrated were the Colt Peacemaker with wood grips which was the Gun that Won the West and a Winchester lever-action rifle.

I had shot these types of weapons in my movies, both pretend and for real, so I was comfortable with my accuracy.

It was a good thing because that clown pushing the button was giving me as short of time on the bandit target as possible.

It still was enough as I managed to hit center mass every time it came out. That was another thing. The dudes would get one chance, and it would be their last shot after shooting at all the other targets.

I had the bandit every other shot. Since the guy didn't know that I was experienced, I think he was trying to show me up. Show me up he did, but in a good way.

I had the first shooting session and the last one. The first to show how it should be done, and the last to show how it was done.

The first was slow and methodical, with safety in mind. This was to teach the dudes what they should be doing. For the most part, they followed instructions well.

I only had to grab the rifle once as an eight-year-old turned with the weapon and ended up pointing it at his dad, who was telling him to shoot better. Dad shut up after that.

The last time I was up, I shot for effect. I fired at the targets as fast as I could while the bandit kept rolling in and out. The gunfire sounded continuous. I even hit the targets.

I did it in about a tenth of the time of my first round. When I finished, there was silence, then a round of applause.

The guy rolling the bandit target back and forth looked familiar. Then it dawned on me he had to be related to the policeman from town. I asked about him and found out he was Little Joe's younger brother.

The younger brother picked up the live weapons and ammunition to return them to the main house to be locked up as we moved over to Main Street.

The crowd was told that Billy the Kid was in town and wanted a word with me.

A man with a big sheriff's badge deputized me as I was the only one who could stand up to Billy the Kid. I was handed a holster with a Colt, except this one had ivory grips. I double-checked, and it was a movie set pistol.

It took special cartridges, which made a loud bang, and that was it. Real cartridges wouldn't fit in this pistol.

Billy the Kid finally showed up and walked into the center of the road of our main street. I followed suit. We were only about twenty feet apart. The dudes were lining the street on both sides. The younger brother was playing Billy.

Just as I thought we were getting ready to have the shootout, the foreman stepped up. In a loud voice, he announced to the crowd.

"Today we have a special treat for you: a movie will start filming here on Friday. Its star, Richard Jackson, is here early. You have seen him rope calves and ride broncos, and he taught you how to shoot."

"Now, this honorary Texas Ranger and real US Marshal will show us the fast draw."

I had been in enough publicity moments with the Ricky Jackson Circus that I didn't think anything would embarrass me anymore. I waved at the crowd.

The foreman continued, "The cowardly Billy the Kid is about to get his comeuppance. At that, he pointed at Little Joe's younger brother. The young man turned to the crowd, took his hat off, and made a bow.

That is when I noticed his Colt with the wooden grips. He had a live weapon. The thought flashed through my mind. He was going to shoot me down.

These thoughts didn't interfere with my reaction. I pulled my useless Colt and reversed my grip, so I was holding it by the barrel.

He had just straightened up from his bow, so I had a very slight advantage. He went to draw his pistol when I let my gun fly like I was throwing a tomahawk. It didn't have a good balance like those we played with on the stuntmen's set, but it was rotating in the air towards him.

While it was flying towards him, I charged, zigzagging slightly to throw him off target. He did flinch away from the flying pistol, which missed him but made him miss his first shot. I dodged to the left as he tried to aim at me.

Most people don't understand how hard it is to hit someone with a handgun while under pressure. His second shot went high.

By this time, the crowd had started to scream and move. Before he could get a third shot off, I hit him like a ton of bricks, well, more like a 6-foot-five-inch guy weighing 215 pounds running as fast as he could.

He went down hard.

The foreman rushed up, and I pointed to the handgun that the kid had dropped. The foreman gave an "Oh shit" as he took possession of the pistol. He emptied the remaining bullets from the pistol, showing me they were live ammunition.

The kid who had been lying on the ground wheezing asked why I had tackled him. I asked, in turn, why he was using a real pistol.

He tried denying that he knew it was real. This was disproven by a check; the other weapons were not at the house. A search found the rifle, one live pistol, and one stunt pistol under a bush near the front porch.

Finding those weapons took the better part of an hour. In the meantime, the county sheriff had been called. A deputy pulled in right after the weapons stash was discovered.

The deputy took a first cut of what happened, cuffed the kid, and placed him in the back of his cruiser.

He then separated us and some of the dudes who had hung around. He started taking statements. Other deputies pulled up and roped off the crime scene and assisted in getting the story from each person present.

They quickly confirmed that the kid had been firing live bullets at me.

One of the deputies spent time with the kid, trying to get him to talk. He came over to us.

"The kid has signed a confession, and yes, I made sure he understood that he could have a lawyer. He declined; he just wants it over with."

I had to ask, "How did he think he could get away with it."

"He didn't. His dad told him that if he could get away in the confusion and back to town, he would get him into Mexico."

"His dad is in on it."

"Yeah, two deputies are picking him up as we speak. We've known he is bad news for a long time but could never pin anything on him."

Karen Klima and her parents were among those still standing around, so I went over to see how they were doing.

"You folks okay?"

Her dad answered, "Yes, we are; this will be some vacation to talk about. More importantly, how are you doing?"

"I'm okay. This sort of thing happens too often in my life."

Her mother spoke up, "I've read about you in the *Inquirer*. So, it's all true?"

"Very little of that is true. The true stories are much worse."

Dad spoke up, "One thing for certain: I'm not going to let my daughter go walking with you again; it's too dangerous."

"Daddy!"

"Karen, we are going home in the morning, so there won't be any more chances."

"What about tonight?"

Nobody had asked my opinion, and I wasn't about to step into this family mess.

His wife Carol spoke up, "Oh Ed, let them go for a walk tonight; as you said, we are going home in the morning, and this will give Karen some story to tell back at school. Shooting, a movie star, what a vacation."

I think the mother would have gone walking with me if I asked her.

Karen and I did go walking. I did have a blanket, and the rest is none of your business.

Chapter 34

The next day, Thursday, the actors and crew started coming in. Word of my week spread quickly, so I had to answer many questions. It got so bad that I told everyone that I would give a statement at lunch and answer any questions then.

Lunch for the film bunch was set up near a field canteen that had been arranged earlier. To my surprise, not only were the cast and crew there, but also many of the ranch guests and maybe even some working hands.

The outsiders didn't get in the lunch line; it was obvious that they were there to hear my statement. Wanting to get it over with, I stood up on top of one of the picnic tables that had been set up.

It didn't take long for everyone to settle down and let me talk.

"You have heard some tales about my week here. They probably have been exaggerated beyond belief."

I then proceeded to give a synopsis of my week and then opened it up for questions.

The first one took me by surprise.

"Is the ranch going to pay you for all the work you did for them?"

"I never thought of it. Probably not. I didn't ask to be paid."

The foreman, a bit of a showman and certainly a good publicist, spoke up, "We will pay him the standard pay for a cowhand for one week. That works out to about twelve dollars and fifty cents; stop by later, Rick, to get paid."

Now, that was probably the pay rate in 1890. It didn't matter as one cowhand had to shout, "Boss, why does he get more than us."

"Coz, he works, and you don't!"

His fellow cowhands pushed and shoved a little to show that he had been put in his place.

The rest of the questions were more in line with, "Were you scared?"

"Everything happened so quickly that I didn't have time to be scared until it was over, and then I shook like a leaf."

I fibbed; I didn't shake because my body had become used to coming off adrenaline highs. I didn't want to go there.

Then there were the "I heard you broke up with your girlfriend. What happened?"

"You will have to ask her."

"Will the movie need any extras here at the ranch?"

"You will need to talk to casting about that. They usually put out a call if they need someone."

At about this time, a deputy sheriff pulled up in his cruiser. Since he had his lights and siren going when he stopped in a cloud of dust, it couldn't be good news.

He got on his loudspeaker. "Everybody, please try to calm down."

The only reason they acted excited and started talking a mile a minute was his grand entrance.

"I need to make everyone aware we have three suspects on the loose, and they are considered armed and dangerous."

It didn't take a rocket scientist to figure out it was that cop and his two sons.

"We will have a car parked at your front gate, but I wanted to warn you as there are many ways onto this ranch. We don't know if they are out for revenge or are in the process of fleeing the country. Be alert and contact the Sheriff's Department if you see them. Do not try to handle them yourself."

He looked right at me when he said that. I don't know why. That broke up the question-and-answer session that had lasted about an hour.

I had taken to wearing my shoulder holster with my new Walther P38. It had a lot more stopping power than the Colt 38 I had been carrying and would not change the hang of my suit coats.

The foreman approached me and asked if I would wear one of the real Colt 45s. It would look more in tune with the theme of the ranch. Since it carried a modern load, it had even more stopping power.

It made sense to me, so I strapped on a holster. I thought about pinning my US Marshal's badge to my shirt, but that would have been over the top.

It all turned out for naught as the cop and his sons were found shot to death in the desert near the border. It was thought they had a falling out with the coyote, the guide, who was leading them across.

I bet that it was the smart mouth of Little Joe that brought their end about. We would never know.

One thing it did was save me the bother of testifying at a trial.

My movie workday on location consisted of riding at a fair pace around the twenty-five-hundred-acre ranch. I was followed by a truck with stabilized cameras. Since most of my job on the trail drive was to deliver messages to each of the ten herds we were moving, they needed lots of footage of me riding in different areas.

I will tell you it is hot, dusty, dirty work. Now I know why cowboys wore a bandana around their necks. It wasn't just for holding up banks and trains.

If you didn't wear one on the trail, you would choke. If you didn't wear one when coming to the dust cloud of a moving herd, you would suffocate.

At one point, there I was, crossing a small stream, and I had had enough. I brought my mount, no idea what his name was, to a halt. I dismounted and let him drink his fill while I soaked my bandana in the water and then wrung it out over my head. I did this several times.

I finally said the heck with it, stripped down to my union suit, and sat in the water. After splashing for a while, I had cooled off and didn't pinch in unmentionable places.

Feeling much refreshed, I got dressed and went back to work. What I didn't know was that the cameras kept running. Part of the scene made it into the movie. The editors thought it made things more realistic.

I know it made me feel better. That evening, I limped a little from saddle sores, but it wasn't as bad as if I hadn't done any riding.

There were still guests at the ranch, and many of them had been hired as extras for the movie. It was a hoot listening to them talk about their part in the movie. I didn't have the heart to mention that most of them would end up on the cutting room floor. I noticed none of the crew said anything either.

One bit actor had a big mouth telling them that he would be in the movie, but they only had a slim chance of making it. I noticed an editor shaking his head. I wouldn't bet on that bit actor making the final cut.

John Wayne didn't have any filming today, so he hadn't been on the set. He did fly in and have dinner with us as he had an early morning call. He hunted me up.

"Rick, how are things on the international scene? Are you going to be able to keep on schedule?"

"As far as I know, Mr. Wayne."

"Dang it, Rick, how many times must I tell you it's John!"

"Uh, a few more?"

"Ah, forget it. How are you getting along with Sally?"

"Fine. She was overwhelmed with that trip to DC, but we will work together with no problems."

"Glad to hear that. I heard that she was freaking out later about the situations you put her in."

"I didn't think it was that bad."

"Only a US president and an empress. Nah, why should that upset anyone?"

"Exactly."

He looked at me strangely for a moment.

"You don't get it, do you?"

"Get what?"

"That most people are overwhelmed by meeting high-ranking people."

"I guess I have been around so many of them that I realize that they all are just normal people in an abnormal situation."

"Well, I know one abnormal person who thinks he is in normal situations but never is."

I did catch onto that one but decided to let it go. Maybe I was abnormal. If that were the case, I would just have to fake being normal. What is normal?

"Change of subject, Rick. I was told that you entered the local rodeo as a bull rider. It has been a while; do you think you are up to it?"

"I will find out quickly."

"True."

"I don't intend to try any crazy stunts. A solid ride is all I'm going for. If I don't win, it's okay."

"No, it's not okay. You are the star of this movie, and your ride will be reported. Win, and get us some good publicity."

"Yes, sir, John."

He wandered away, muttering about damn teenagers.

I called it a night and drove back to my hotel room. There, I cleaned my pistol as I was sure it was full of dust from the day. These guns were rugged, but the last thing I needed was a misfire. On that dreadful thought, I did go to bed.

Chapter 35

Saturday started fine and continued that way. I had a hearty breakfast with a lot of coffee, as there was no hurry to be anywhere.

There was no shooting schedule. Since most of the crew was still getting organized, not even all the actors or actresses were on set. I didn't think Sally was due until Monday.

Chief Redfoot was there. It wasn't that far of a drive from his home in Oklahoma. As usual, he was concerned with how the Indians would be portrayed.

At this time in history in which the story was set, not only were there many different tribes but also another difference, those that had moved from the east and what we called the Plains Indians.

The Plains Indians were still fighting a losing battle against the encroachment of the white settlers.

The Indians from the east had already lost that battle. Many were bitter and beaten down, but others had learned the white man's ways with the best of them and were ready to deal.

Those who had adjusted to the white culture drifted from the tribal settings. They realized that they had to blend as much as possible and that living on a reservation wasn't the way to do it.

In particular, he was concerned about how the town of Shawnee would be portrayed as its main population in the film would be Shawnee. They had moved from settled Ohio on their terms in real life, and he didn't want them shown in the film as savages.

It surprised me that he considered the Plains Indians of the time savages, but it shouldn't have. From his modern point of view, they were living like savages, so they must be savages. If it walks like a duck, etc.

The story writers he was talking to didn't disagree with his request, but he had to appreciate what they needed from a story point of view.

"What do you need?"

The lead writer told him, "When the cowboys come into town, Rick meets a young Shawnee girl and finds her attractive, and they go walking together. We need that for two reasons. First, it gives Molly a reason to realize that she is jealous of the girl. The other reason is that the local boys will want to warn you off.

"This gives us two tension points in the story."

The chief spoke up, "I don't see the problem. Instead of living in a teepee, which we Shawnee never did, and meeting her at a watering hole, he meets her in her father's mercantile store."

"As far as the jealous young men who want to warn Rick off, teenagers are teenagers no matter where you find them."

One of the other writers said, "If we play it that way, she can be more sophisticated than Rick's character. In the end, she can dump him because she wants to go to college in the east."

The lead writer asked, "Who would believe that an Indian woman would get into much less graduate from an Eastern school?"

The chief didn't let that stand, "My great-great-grandmother, who would have been the right age at that time, went to and graduated from the University of Edinburgh."

There were some visible gulps around the circle as the chief was now twirling his tomahawk that had been in his belt.

Suddenly, he let out a belly laugh and, with a terrible Scottish accent, said, "Gotcha."

I was impressed with how he handled those guys.

They started building on the storyline. It looked like the cattle drive might spend a week in Shawnee, which would never happen, but they were having fun discussing possibilities.

After that, I wandered over to where the stuntmen were hanging out. As expected, you couldn't have a cattle drive without a stampede. They were arguing about how they would make it look like they were in danger from the moving cattle when they were safe and sound.

Someone said, "There's Jackson. He's been in a stampede. How did you do it?"

"Hung on for dear life; I was never safe and sound; I don't recommend it."

That led to some tall tales of previous Westerns and how the issue was addressed. At one time in the 1920s and 30s, they would have got a bunch of cows together and fired guns until they got moving, filming all the time.

There were disgraceful stories of horses being driven over cliffs to shoot a scene. Thankfully, those days were over.

Now, we had to be creative. The cattle would be herded into place with trucks. The cowboys would be filmed separately and would never be close to the moving herd. The stuntman that would take my place would ride with the cattle until they got moving fast, and then he would slow down as they passed.

His horse would be jostled enough by the passing cattle that it would look dramatic from a distance but be fairly safe. Nothing in this business is completely safe.

I didn't understand why they wouldn't let me ride as I was the only one there with real-world experience. Yeah, I know, insurance.

The conversation turned to the rodeo later this afternoon. It wasn't generally known that I had entered the bull riding event.

They kidded each other about how they should enter and show the locals a thing or two. I thought that would work out differently than they thought. I knew the sort of guy who entered these small-town events.

They seldom made it to the big time, but that didn't mean they weren't any good. They had years of experience doing this, whereas the stuntmen could do all the events but hadn't done it for years.

Another factor is the stuntmen were professionals and thought about life and limb. The local guys didn't. They were all male hormones, wrapped as tight as a stick of dynamite. I wonder what that said about me.

I kept my mouth shut as I didn't want to start a big debate about experience over youth. What they didn't seem to understand was that these fifteen and sixteen-year-olds had probably been entering these events since they were nine.

On top of that, they probably were taught at Daddy's knee starting at age three. City kids had the whiffle ball teed up for them. These kids had their pony.

Anyway, some smart mouth knew I had entered and asked how I thought I would do.

"I think I will be able to hang on for the eight seconds. How good of a ride it will be is a different story. If it is a good bull, and by that, I mean an active one that hates to be ridden, it will be a plus. If it is an old, tired one, then it will be as adventuresome as a rocking chair."

"How often have you had one like that?"

"Well, never."

"So, what else will affect your score.?"

"How well I can get the bull to up its game while I try to make it look easy."

"I saw a film of the World Championships and how you flipped over the horns and back."

"That was a once-in-a-lifetime accident. I would never think of trying to repeat it."

"Then what are you going to do?"

"Hope for a good ride, kick the heck out of it, and hang on."

"You sound like a man with a plan."

"If you can call that a plan."

I ate a light lunch and headed to the fairgrounds. Once there, I checked in. I had forgotten that I was wearing a Colt Peacemaker. Since this was Texas, they didn't get excited about it but did remind me that weapons weren't allowed on the fairgrounds.

I had to walk back to the car and lock the holster and weapon in the trunk. I was glad I went through that exercise because it reminded me of something I had meant to do. I took the opportunity to use the clips inside my hat to attach them to my hair.

Hopefully, I wouldn't lose the Resistol on the ride. If nothing else, I wanted to look good. Once I was checked in and had my contestant number tied onto the front and back of my shirt, I walked the area.

I had a chance to see the bulls that were to be ridden. They were all good ones, and they were also all from the Easterly Ranch. My friend and mentor, Clint Easterly, was there. It was like an old home week for me.

He didn't know I was in the area, much less entering the rodeo. We spent a good half hour catching up on things. He and his wife had followed me in the newspapers.

He said it had become a local sport back at home to guess what I would be up to next. No one ever came close; it was always a step or two above their guesses. He liked the Brigitte Bardot rescue, which was the most fun thing. My rescue of those boys in the flooded river was a fine thing.

It was getting time to move the bulls up to be ridden. He told me that they were all good rides, but I should hope I didn't get the Big Guy. He was plain mean. He pointed the bull out. I could see how he got his name.

It didn't surprise me when I drew Big Guy as my ride. A couple of the other riders told me, "Better you than me; that bull has a reputation. He has only been ridden two out of his last ten tries."

This was good and bad. Good in the sense I would be able to showcase my talent. Bad in the sense that the bull could showcase his talent.

Chapter 36

The announcer spent a couple of minutes explaining my bull riding history. He was sarcastic about it, as though my being a movie star had somehow given me the wins.

The ride was the longest eight seconds of my life. Not even jumping between the horns at the championships was as hard. Every jump the bull made, I thought it would be my last. Not the last jump, the last day on earth.

When the horn sounded to end my eight seconds, I could feel gravity pulling me backward from his last buck. I went with it; I was forced backward until I did a backflip off the bull.

I saw a hoof fly past my head. I landed on my feet, facing the bull who had turned to circle me. From the force of my landing, I had to run to keep from falling on my face, which also had me running away from the bull. This was a good direction, so I kept going. I made it to the fence and jumped for the top rail.

It was a good thing I did because that bull was mad at me. He tried to gore me as I climbed to safety. I decided my bull riding days were over.

After a successful ride like that, I won hands down. The local riders were gracious in their congratulations. They had never thought I could ride like that.

The announcer came on and told us he had bet a friend that I couldn't make the time. If I did, he would eat his hat. Did anyone have some salt and pepper with them?

I won the one hundred dollars first prize and another belt buckle. This one wasn't as nice as the one I was wearing. I would probably donate it to one of Mary's or Mum's charity auctions as I did with those I won previously.

There was a square dance after the rodeo rides were completed. I attended and danced to almost every reel. I had learned previously in one of my other Westerns. It was fun. The girls were nice, but I didn't have a chance to ask any to go walking.

Mr. Wayne hunted me up before the end of the festivities.

"Good job, Rick. I thought you had met your match with that one. Easterly told me all about him."

"As Wellington said, 'It was a close-run thing.'"

"How did you get the nerve for that dismount? We caught it on film, and it will make the movie for sure. Also, the newsreels, the publicity tour, and the trailer. It was fantastic."

"Blame it on Sir Isaac."

"Sir Isaac?"

"Gravity. I didn't plan it but went with the flow. I knew that I couldn't stay on, so I went in the easiest direction, downhill. The landing was plain luck."

"You seem to have a lot of that. I'm glad you didn't get hurt."

"Thanks. What is our schedule for next week? I looked, but it wasn't posted."

"You have the week off. We are doing inside scenes back at the studio."

"That's good news. I'm going to see if I can get some golf in at Augusta."

"Good luck with that."

"They seem to be cooperative, that and President Eisenhower is usually my partner."

"That will work. See you in a couple of weeks."

"Okay. If you need me, leave a call at Jackson House. I check in there every day."

At that, I headed back to my luxury suite at the hotel, wagon wheel lights and all. The first thing I did in my room was place a call through the front desk to Hastings Aviation to ask them to pick me up tomorrow in Dallas. Also, to arrange for a ferry pilot for my Cessna back to California.

We talked about timing. It turned out to be a bad idea. The crew had just returned from China and were taking downtime at home in Oxford. It made no sense for them to fly from Oxford to Dallas, then drop me off in Atlanta, then return to England.

Instead, they arranged a charter flight from Dallas to Augusta and a ferry pilot for the Cessna. That worked for me. No sense in stressing the flight crew for no good reason. Someday, I may have to do that, but not this trip.

Next, I called President Eisenhower at his farm in Gettysburg. It was getting a little late, but I took a chance. Ike came to the phone. When I told him I had a week off and wanted to get some practice in at Augusta, he thought it was a wonderful idea. It was a shame he had commitments and couldn't join me.

He would make some phone calls and make certain a full member accompanied me so I would be allowed to play. I told him I would be in transit the next day but that he could leave a message at Jackson House.

Then I called John Jacobs and asked him to meet me in Augusta the next night. Also, would he arrange a car and two hotel rooms? Of course, I expected him to fly first class. If there were no commercial flights, he was to call Jim Williamson and ask for a charter to be arranged.

My last call was to home to let Mum and Dad know my plans and expected phone calls. Dad told me that it had been over the wire that I had a spectacular bull ride, and that film would be provided.

I told him it was more luck than anything that I did as well as I did and ended up on my feet. He suggested sending a copy to the LA school board to demonstrate that I understood gravity. We had a chuckle but didn't follow up.

The next morning, I was up early, as usual, for my run and other exercises. I was stiff in places I didn't know I had. I was able to work it out, but I could tell I had been doing some things that I wasn't used to. This just reconfirmed my thought that I was done with bull riding. I was going to take up something less dangerous, like parachute jumping.

I checked out of my hotel and drove to where my Cessna was parked. After arranging for the rental car to be returned, I checked the fuel and oil filters to make certain no water had accumulated, had the aircraft fueled up, and then flew to Dallas. Oh yes, I did look to see if anything had fallen off the plane while it was sitting there.

Nothing had. The tires weren't soft. One almost broke my toe when I kicked it too hard. All the control bits that needed to wiggle wiggled in the right directions. I was good to go.

There was no control tower, so it was visual flight rules and every man for himself as I took off.

After that excitement, with my head on a swivel, I settled in for the flight to Dallas. I listened to commercial-traffic radio conversations. Nothing was going on weather-wise that was any concern. The trip went well.

It was a pleasure dealing with the Love Field air traffic control people. They had their act together.

I landed on the private aviation side of the field, where I met my ferry pilot. I handed the flight log and cabin keys over to the young lady who was taking my plane back to California.

She had a Jeppesen case full of maps for her proposed routes. She came prepared. I showed her the Forest Service airfield on her maps. She didn't think she would have any problems finding it, I-10, then 101 to the Santa Monica, and look for the airfield. She would use IFR, "I follow roads," which gave me a chuckle.

It was a good thing the airfield had a radio beacon for her to home in on. I can't say she filled me with confidence, but she did get the plane home with no problems.

I had a charter flight being run by Trans-Texas. I think the pilots thought they were riding a bronc in the rodeo. It was a rough flight.

But then I was like all pilots, critical of anyone at the controls if it wasn't me.

What was interesting about it was that the flight was in a Grumman Gulfstream, a new turboprop business aircraft with Rolls Royce engines driving big propellers. It wasn't as fast or comfortable as my 707, but it was a hell of a lot cheaper and almost as good for shorter flights and smaller airports. I'd have to think about getting one for traveling around the States.

Bumpy flight or not, we made it into Augusta just as they turned the field lights on. John was waiting for me in a rental car. He had ended up flying in on a charter earlier today.

Our hotel was a run-of-the-mill Ramada, which put its head and shoulders above my hotel in Texas and its luxury suite, wagon wheel lights notwithstanding.

As John drove us to the hotel, he told me he had made an interesting discovery about the way hole positions were chosen for the Masters. This could be big if his findings were correct. He told me that it was complicated and that we should wait until the morning to go over it. That made sense to me, so we arrived at the hotel and went to our rooms. I didn't even remember climbing into bed.

Chapter 37

John and I met for breakfast. He looked tired.

"John, you don't look like you slept very well."

"I didn't. I never sleep well the first few nights in a new bed."

"That has to be hard with what I have you doing."

"It can be, but it is worth it. My wife and I talked about this the other day. You have given me a chance to get ahead. It looked like I was just going to be a caddie and make a mediocre living."

"Instead, we have a chance to do very well. It is worth a few rough mornings. However, you look like you are ready to face the world."

"You should try getting up at 5 a.m. every morning to do a workout and then finish up with a five-mile run; that and a shower make you ready for anything."

"You lost me at 5 a.m."

"To each his own. I used to want to sleep in every day, but once I got into this routine, I loved it."

We ordered our breakfasts along with a pot of coffee, which was one thing we shared. While we waited for our food, I asked, "What did you discover that has you so excited?"

"Did you know that *Golf Today* has their reporters keep records on every shot made in the tournaments that they report on?"

"I didn't."

"They never know what shots will determine the winner, so they keep track of clubs, distance, weather, time of day, results of the shot, all that.

"When they write the story, they can pick out the shot that sets it all up for the winner. It makes them look like the super reporters of golf, knowing which shot set things up."

"Like Monday morning quarterbacking."

"You got it."

"So where does this lead us?"

"I had a thought, so I made some phone calls. I got after-hours access to their morgue."

"Their morgue? Do they store dead golfers or what?"

"Funny. A magazine or newspaper morgue is where they store dead stories, hence the morgue. It is also their library."

Talk about feeling dumb for a moment.

"What did you find?"

"Confirmation of my theory. I have been working on this for almost a year. It was a lot of data to wade through."

"What did you find?"

"Let me set the scene a little. What surprises can a greenskeeper play on a golfer during a tournament."

"That's easy, pin placement."

"How do they decide that?"

"I don't know, random draw?"

"Not at Augusta they don't."

"How do they do it then?"

"They analyze the player entry field for its strengths and weaknesses. They want to make the course as challenging as possible."

"I get that."

"If the entered players are good at chipping to the pin, they will place the pin accordingly. If they are good at pitch and run, it will go elsewhere."

"So, they are playing to the weakness of the field. They can't tell how any individual golfer will do on any shot, but they can tell the average of the field."

"John, this is huge. If you know the entered players, you can analyze their weaknesses and thus predict pin placement. Then you can emphasize that in your practice."

"You got it, Rick. The entry list for this year has been posted, and I can predict with an eighty-five percent accuracy the pin positions that will be used."

"When did you become such a statistician?"

"I'm not; my wife is. She teaches statistics at UCLA. She had a lot of help. As I told you, it took a lot of number crunching. She gave it out as a series of class assignments. She broke it up into separate groupings or modules, as she calls them, so no one could figure out that it was about golf."

"Somehow, I will figure out a way to repay her."

"Win. That will set me up to make a lot of money."

Our food arrived about that time, so we went silent as we chowed down.

"John, what if a golfer was notoriously bad at a given shot, and the greenskeeper hated him?"

"He would have a bad day."

"What if the greenskeeper wanted to make money at it and sold the information to gamblers?"

"Rick, one step further. What if he set the course up at the gambler's request?"

"He better hope the mob never finds out. Unless it is the mob doing the setup. Did you look at the other courses?"

"Yes, and they seem to be random, just trying to make the round exciting. Difficult placements, but not to any discernible pattern in the relationship of the field. My wife used terms like inferential and null hypothesis and a bunch of other stuff, but she concluded there was no relationship between the field of golfers and pin placement."

"She got into it and found there were some feuds between a few players and greenskeepers, but there was no evidence that it predicted pin placement."

"So, if anything is going on, it is only at Augusta."

"Yeah, but what are you going to do? Call the mob and ask if they are trying to tilt the field at Augusta?"

"Uh, no."

"That wasn't convincing."

"I don't know anyone in the mob."

I didn't tell him that Mum and Dad did...oh, and Popeye. I decided I would find out where Popeye was and ask him if he had ever heard anything. Mum and Dad discouraged me from talking to Mr. Lucky and his crew.

We drove out to the clubhouse for our ten o'clock tee time. I was playing with a full member, Dr. John Worthington. Why is it always a doctor?

We each had a caddie assigned, plus John could walk the course with me. I noticed on the practice green a couple of other players who would be in the tournament. This was serious business.

After warming up on the driving range and putting in a few, we were up. I wasn't playing for the score; I was playing to learn the course.

My constant practice was paying off. I was placing the ball where I wanted it on almost every shot. There were a few odd rolls and bounces, as to be expected, but I was hitting well for both distance and accuracy.

John was taking notes by the page full on every hole. He had a running conversation with our caddie. They would even consult with the doctor's caddy on occasion. Try that in tournament play!

Doctor Worthington was a nice guy, and we had one of those pleasant, nothing conversations guys can have.

He was almost a professional-level player, so it was easy to compliment him on good shots. He returned the favor. That was unusual for me; I normally was with a tense win-at-any-cost type of person. He made the round relaxing and fun.

We took a break for a quick lunch at the turn. There, he asked me if I had thought of turning pro. Instead of my usual smart answer, I told him the truth.

"I don't need the money."

"That's right. You have an acting career."

"Funny you should say that. I'm thinking about giving that up today."

"Then how will you live? It may seem like you have enough money now if you have a million dollars, but it won't last your lifetime."

"I realize that, like most people, you have never heard of Jackson Enterprises."

"Oh, but I have. My broker was telling me about them just the other day."

"What did he have to say?"

"They are making a fortune with the new shipping containers and handling systems. He urged me to get in on it before it was too late."

"How can you do that? To my knowledge, they aren't a public company."

"There is a fund established to use every legal method to force them to go public."

He got a funny look. "Rick Jackson? Are your parents the owners?"

"No, I am—lock, stock, and barrel. I would advise you to stay away from that fund. It will not end well for them."

His golf game went all to pieces on the back nine. As we finished up and were totaling our scorecards, he spoke up.

"Rick, I spoke out of turn. I wasn't told to keep that fund a secret, but the more I think about it, the more I'm glad I said something to you. I wish you well in both the Masters and in the attempted takeover."

"Thank you. I will have to find out who is putting this fund together. I'm not certain what tactics they will try, but I will warn my people."

That gave me a lot to think about. I shared the conversation with John on our ride back to the hotel.

"That's way above my pay grade. Who can you talk to about this?'

"It depends on who is organizing this effort."

"You know the president and the Queen of England. That should help."

"I hope I don't have to get them involved. If I do, it is because the Soviets are behind it."

"You sure know some fun people."

Chapter 38

Rather than calling the Queen or president, I placed a call to Popeye. Well, I placed a call to Jackson Transportation, who told me that Popeye was in our office in Buenos Aires.

I then placed an international person-to-person call. The operator called me back when Popeye's office was on the line; they couldn't get Popeye, so they wanted to know if I wanted to talk to anyone at the office. I told them yes.

Once the call was placed, it rang a bunch of times until someone answered in Spanish. I asked for Popeye.

In Spanish, I was told, "He is down at the docks. Do you want to leave a message?"

"Yes, please."

I left my name and number and told him to call whenever he got in. There wasn't that much time difference between us. They were two hours ahead, so it shouldn't be that late before he called.

John and I had dinner and returned to our rooms. As I walked into mine, the phone was ringing; it was Popeye.

"Rick, what's up?"

"I have a strange question for you."

"Shoot."

"Have you ever heard of the mob fixing any of the major golf tournaments?"

"Now that is strange. Does this have anything to do with you playing in the big ones this year?"

"It might; I need to know what I might be facing."

"How could they even begin to fix a tournament without intimidating half the field? I haven't read of any major golfers having both legs broken."

"No, it is much more sophisticated than that."

I proceeded to explain how the Masters had a pattern associated with the pin placements and that this could be used to influence the average outcome.

"Rick, that would work for the Vegas crowd. They know more about statistics than most university professors. That is how they know to bring the eye in the sky and their other equipment in to look for how the cheating is being done and by whom."

"I thought it was the cameras that caught them."

"Yeah, but you can't have that many cameras. For example, on any given table, they can tell you the average amount bet, hands dealt, and payouts given on any given time block of the day. They have statisticians who build the database over time and then check to see if any table varies by an acceptable amount.

"If it does, they start watching it. With them, it's all a numbers game. They would love this deal with Augusta. I will ask around to see if anyone has heard of anything like that."

"Okay, but be careful. I don't want to start a new growth industry on the pro tournaments."

"I will, though it sounds interesting. The bad part is these guys are not above moving the odds by breaking a leg or two."

"I'm sorry I asked. Please be careful."

"I will. Sybil would kill me if I got you in trouble."

"How is Aunt Sybil anyway?"

"She's great. She is with me on this trip, and we are entering and winning tango contests. She is as good as the old *Liberia*'s first mate."

"Wow, he sure could tango. What happened to him?"

"He's still on the ship as the captain now. He works for you."

"Hmm, I can still remember my time as a polliwog on my equator crossing. I may have to arrange a special trip for him."

"Ah, Rick, it was just clean fun."

"Terrible-tasting fun is what I remember; besides, you may want to go on this trip."

"Where?"

"I have been thinking about the international dateline and the equator at the sacred hour of the fall equinox."

"Count me in. The Order of the Purple Porpoise is the rarest of them all, which makes crossing the line seem like nothing. Few alive have done it. I would love those bragging rights."

"I'll make it happen."

Keeping that in mind, I placed a call to the Scottish Lines office. I forgot the time difference. I left a message with the evening staff that I would like a call tomorrow at my breakfast time here at this hotel.

My last call was to Jim Williamson in my California office.

"Jim, this is Rick. I have picked up a disturbing rumor."

"What's that?"

"A fund is being put together to force Jackson Enterprises to go public by any means possible."

"There are offers all the time, and there have been articles published about how we should do that."

"What are the benefits?"

"For you, none. You lose control of your company, taking what seems a huge chunk of money, which would turn out to be a pittance against future earnings. In turn, the investors would get rich, and the people who made the deal happen filthy rich."

"What's the upside for me?"

"None; the only people who go public are those who need to raise a lot of cash so they can fund their growth. You have the cash, at least if you didn't keep giving it to the Chinese, and growth has been exponential. We are trying to keep it under control."

"Could you start an investigation to see if this is real, and if so, who is behind it?"

"Do you have any ideas?"

"An investments group trying to get rich or a nation actor like the Soviets trying to break me."

"Let's hope for the investment group. I will have to hire a firm that specializes in takeover investigations."

"Spend whatever it takes. I want to head this off. I don't want to lose the company, and I don't want to start a war with the USSR."

"At least you don't think small."

After that, I was so worked up that I went out for a run. It was just dusk, and I made certain to wear a bright jacket as I had to run along a road.

I only had to jump for my life from one pickup truck, so I counted it as a win. After a few miles, the adrenaline wore off, so I turned back and turned in for the night.

The next morning, I updated John on my phone call to Popeye. He was vaguely aware that Popeye was a relative and that he did something in construction, but that was it.

I explained he was my uncle and that his job was to keep the work going on all our projects around the world. He was a very hands-on person, I told John. I must say that John is quick on the uptake as he now understood that Popeye may be the guy who would know some underworld people.

I didn't tell him that as a last resort, I would call Mum; she knew the Don of Dons, and I'm not talking about Oxford.

On that cheerful note, we went back to the course and played my last round here, at least for a while. In the pro shop, I was asked if I could take a few minutes to talk to the president of the club. Of course, I could.

I was introduced, and we went into the restaurant, which wasn't open yet; it only served lunch and dinner. Breakfast was in a small café. It didn't seem to make a difference as we were seated at a table and served coffee immediately. I turned down the offer of food as I had just eaten.

"Rick, may I call you Rick?"

"Certainly, I prefer that. There are too many other things people call me."

"I didn't know if you preferred your British titles."

"That only works in England or one of the Commonwealth nations. Here it is Rick, or Richard if you want to be formal, or Richard Edward Jackson if Mum's mad."

"Funny how that works. I can still hear my dear departed mother saying my name like that. It made things serious right away."

"Yes, it does. You wanted to speak to me?"

"To be blunt, Rick, we would like you to become a full member here rather than just an associate."

"What brings this on?"

"Your prominence in the golfing world while maintaining amateur status, your ability to afford the tariffs, and that some very high-profile people have recommended you."

President Eisenhower immediately came to mind.

"When would this happen?"

"Well, this is where it gets extremely sensitive. New members are only brought in when a present member dies or is asked to leave. Unfortunately, we have three members on their deathbeds right now."

"I'm sorry to hear that."

"So are we. Beyond losing good friends, the maneuvering to join has already started. Membership is by invitation only, and if you ask to join or even hint at it, you will never be let in.

"That doesn't seem to stop people, so we are always looking for the type of people we want in. You come under the heading of young blood. We are thinking of the long-term good of the club."

"If asked, I would join, but if I'm not asked, that is also okay."

"Exactly. This will not happen before this year's Masters, but we will keep you on our list."

"Thank you. I appreciate the honor."

I did appreciate it, but I seemed to be getting more cynical all the time. Who would benefit from this association the most, me or them? Ah, what the heck. It was always a good thing to have a nice course to play on.

I should have asked if they were reciprocal with any other clubhouses. That might have been considered tacky.

Chapter 39

One thing both John and I noticed once more was that the hole placements were nothing like we predicted they would be at the start of the tournament.

They would be moved daily during the tournament, but we had a predicted pattern for all the hole placements that fit the average of the field of players. It was so convoluted that it was of no surprise that no one had ever suspected a pattern being used.

Also, the hole placements would have to meet the rule: According to Rule 15-3, the most important factor when deciding where to place a hole is "good judgment in deciding what will give fair results." The USGA also admonishes tournament officials not to be "tricky" when choosing hole locations.

Toward those objectives, Rule 15-3 advises officials to examine the green's design and to consider the type of approach shot required. Officials should consider the length of the likely approach shot and should allow sufficient putting distance around the hole. For example, the hole will typically be placed farther from the edge of the green when the expected approach shot requires a long iron rather than a more lofted club.

Weather conditions are also factored in. For example, greens will hold an approach better when they're wet. More specifically, Rule 15-3(ii) recommends that holes should be placed "at least four paces from any edge of the putting green" and even farther if there's a sand trap near the edge or if the area surrounding the green's edge slopes downward.

The USGA suggests that at least a 2-foot radius surrounding the hole "should be as nearly level as possible and of uniform grade." The hole shouldn't be placed on a steep slope on which a missed putt from above the hole will roll a long distance past the cup. "A player above the hole should be able to stop the ball at the hole," according to Rule 15-3(iii).

Additionally, the hole shouldn't be located on a former hole's spot until the old location has healed completely.

Rule 15-3(vi) recommends that officials use a balanced selection of hole locations "for the entire course concerning left, right, central, front and back positions."

Officials also change some hole locations between rounds to force golfers to hit a different shot into the green. They try not to have the players hit the same shot or even use the same club. This is where it can get dangerous; by deciding on a different shot, they can play to the strengths or weaknesses of a group of players and still be within the rules.

The USGA also advises tournament officials to maintain a consistent degree of difficulty throughout the event. Rule 15-3(vii) rejects the idea of making a course progressively more difficult each day, calling such a plan "fallacious."

We got this information from an article in *Golfweek* by M.L. Rose.

The rule book covered every possibility but that of someone taking the players into account. It would only affect the average outcome, not an individual outcome, but that was the sort of edge the professional gamblers were looking for.

There was a note handed to me at the 9th hole turn to call Popeye. I did it. Fortunately, the foursome behind us agreed to switch places so I could make the call.

"Rick, thanks for getting back to me. I think my questions opened a hornet's nest. No one knows of anything crooked going on in golf except one well-known guy that will blow a tournament for a good payday."

"Other than that, they want to know how it can be done. I told them I had no idea, that the question was asked of me if it could be done, not that someone knew how."

"That said, these guys are going to put it together that you are the golfer in the family. What should I do?"

"Nothing. We can pull its teeth in the next two months."

"How?"

"An article in *Golfweek* talking about how it might be done will be enough of a spotlight to prevent it from happening. There is only one course where it might be possible, and we do not have any indications that anything has gone on other than trying to make it more interesting for the spectators."

"Well, watch yourself; some wise guys may come knocking at your door."

"That's why I carry a P38."

"And they may have a Thompson. Don't be complacent."

"I won't, and thanks for the heads up."

My play on the back nine was barely adequate.

We finished up and returned to the hotel, where another phone call was waiting, this time from Jim Williamson.

"Jim, did you find anything out?"

"Yes, I did. There is a group being formed to try to force you to go public. I haven't been able to identify all the major players yet, but it seems to be homegrown."

"That is good news, I guess; it's not like the Soviet government."

"It is a publicly traded investment bank. Now, they are selling Game Co. short to drive its price down so they can take control and loot the company. And of course, make a lot of money from the short alone.

They have announced their next objective is to take Jackson Enterprises public. The major investors are a bunch of moneymen and politicians."

"Which politicians?"

"They seem to be from both parties and all over the states, anyone wanting a fast buck. A local broker shared an information letter the investment bank sent out stating that they needed the help of anyone with political influence to make it hard for us to do business. Thus, encouraging us to go public to relieve the pressure."

"Jim, I can't let this go on. Write up a press release that Jackson Enterprises is expanding its operations."

"Where?"

"England and Germany for production; the European headquarters will be in England. This way, a lot of employment will go to Germany, but most of the corporate taxes to England.

"I will call the Germans and the Queen to see when and where. I will get back to you within the next twenty-four hours."

"One other thing, buy Game Co. stock to keep the price up."

"My pleasure."

It was too late in the day to make phone calls to Europe, so I turned in early and made them in the morning after my usual routine.

My first call was to the office of the German Federal President in Bonn. When I got through and explained who I was, I was put through to a senior staffer.

I told him about the federal president asking if I would consider putting a factory in Germany with at least a thousand jobs. I went on to tell him I was ready to make five thousand jobs in Germany with a shipyard in the Hamburg area.

This got me on the line with Mr. President quickly.

"Herr Jackson, what has prompted this decision?"

"I have found that it will become more difficult to do business in the States shortly. An expansion has been in the works. This news just moved up the decision cycle."

"I see; if you spread out, it will lessen the amount of pressure that can be brought."

"Correct. I will have Mr. Goodson contact whoever you want to make it formal, plus any concessions you would care to make would be appreciated but not a requirement."

"Herr Jackson, you are certainly different in your business approach. We have heard about your dealings with the Chinese. You are an interesting person. May I ask who has or will be trying to make it difficult for you?"

I gave him the name of the investment bank and how they were selling Game Co. short.

"I will instruct my broker to buy Game Co."

"That is wonderful. I also must tell you I will be opening operations in England and have a headquarters there."

"I understand. It is your heritage."

My last call was to Mr. Norman. I explained the investment bank and its objective. He liked the steps I was taking. He thought the new jobs would be a shot in the arm for the English economy, which was still recovering from the war.

I asked him where the Queen thought I should place my factories. Of course, the headquarters would be in London.

He told me they would get back to me on that. It appeared that some politicians who favored the Queen's approach would find their seats a little safer, while others might become nervous.

Again, I told him that Todd Goodson would contact their designated person. This time, I asked for no concessions, nor were any offered. I think I just robbed a dog for the Queen.

He also wanted to know who was behind this. When I gave him the investment bank's name and about them and Game Co., he wrote it down. I asked if he was going to buy Game Co., and he told me no, he was going to find out who was behind the bank's decision so they could watch for tricks like that in England.

After those phone calls, John and I headed out to the airport to catch our flight back to LA. It had certainly been an interesting trip, and I even got some golf in. It was a good week all around.

Chapter 40

We arrived in LA in time to fight the rush hour, or at least for our limo driver to deal with the heavy traffic. Construction was going on all along the way home. California's answer to congestion seemed to be more freeways.

What would they do when there was no land left to pave? Anyway, that wasn't my worry, at least today.

John had left his car at our house, so he moved his bags from the limo to his vehicle. I did help him. He drove away, and I realized that there was no one to help me with my bags. I thought I was supposed to be an important person.

Denny came out the door at that time, so I asked him to help. He wanted to know how much I would pay him. So much for brotherly love.

I managed to lug my stuff into my room. I was moaning to be moaning. It wasn't that much.

Mum was in her office doing her charity stuff, that or playing solitaire. I didn't ask. Dad was still at work, so I went through my accumulated mail. There were invitations to various Hollywood events, many of them already past.

There was one hand-addressed letter to me. It was from Nina. I debated just tossing it in the fire but decided to read it.

There were no surprises, she was deeply sorry, she didn't know why she did it, could we kiss and make up?

My first reaction was Yes! Then I thought, No! I wondered where that Yes! had come from.

Did I still have feelings for her? My mind said no; my heart said otherwise. What a stupid mess, Nina. Why did you have to do this to us?

I thought about calling her and decided not to. I would let this issue sit for a while and see how I felt. There was no hurry. I wasn't going to run off with some other girl. If she found another guy, that settled our relationship for all time.

Mum found me with the letter in hand. She didn't say a word though the envelope was lying in plain sight so she could see who it was from.

"Rick, I had the strangest phone call from Carl Gambino. I'm to tell you that golf is a game for gentlemen and not to be messed with. Also, there isn't enough money in it to make it worthwhile."

Mr. Lucky died recently and was succeeded as head of the Commission by Carl Gambino. Mum knew all the big-time gangsters.

"Rick, what is all this about?"

"Got half an hour?"

"Yes."

We went to her office and closed the door. I then related John's findings and our speculation about what could be done with them."

"You should have left well enough alone, but that ship has sailed. What are you going to do now?"

I told her about the article John was going to write for *Golfweek*.

"And what do you think it will do for Augusta?"

"I hadn't thought that through. They have asked me if I wanted a full membership, and I told them yes."

"If that article is printed, write that goodbye.

"So you could have John write two articles, one describing the statistical findings in general. That should put the PGA on notice they have a potential problem.

"Then, have him write the article as first proposed but only send it to the president of the board at Augusta. Let them know that I don't want to damage the club's reputation, but they might have an internal problem.

"Then I would come up with a nice gift for John and his wife."

"What sort of a gift?"

"She teaches at UCLA; make an endowment in her name. That will help her career tremendously, and she would not be directly connected to the articles."

"Mum, you should have been a troubleshooter of some sort."

She smirked as she said, "Well, I was a troubleshooter. I shot trouble."

"In Morocco?"

"Now, off with you; it's time to clean up for dinner."

I will find out one day what she did there.

As I was getting dressed in my room, I had the radio on. Dennis Lawson was reporting on changes occurring at the large transportation company, Jackson Enterprises.

It seems the company is going international, with production in Germany and England, plus a European headquarters in England.

Dennis speculated this was to serve notice to the US government that there was a limit to the taxes they kept piling onto the company. With a new headquarters and overseas production, they would be able to move operations out of the US if needed. He hoped it wouldn't come to that.

In unrelated news, he reported that an investment bank in New York City was in dire trouble. They had been short-selling Game Co. stock, and instead of falling as predicted, it was rising.

It had massive support from overseas, particularly in England. If there was any more bad news for this bank, its value could go down to zero.

I called my broker in England where the transactions were taking place and told him to buy more Game Co. stock and also that I had heard more bad news was coming out in the form of the Jackson Enterprises announcements.

I no sooner hung up than my private line in my room rang. It was Bobby Kennedy.

"Jackson, what are you trying to do to us?"

"What do you mean?"

"Moving your operations."

"I'm not moving anything at this time. We have to expand, and I thought it best to do it overseas. It spreads the risks of losses from hurricanes and such."

"They don't have hurricanes in Pittsburgh!"

"You know what I mean, things like tornadoes or tax-hungry governments."

"Do you realize that you are destroying the fortunes of hundreds of people in the investment bank?"

"You mean that bank that was trying to steal my company from me?"

"They wanted to make it more profitable."

"Profitable by selling off all the divisions to pay for the takeover, forcing me off the board, and then plundering the remainder of the company."

"That wasn't our plan at all."

"Your plan?"

"I misspoke, the bank's plan."

I replied, "Of course."

"So, are you going to call your dogs off?"

"Are you going to call yours off?"

"It's not my call. Some big money is behind this."

"Care to share?"

"I can't, Rick. This time, I'm only the messenger."

"Can you tell me this; is there any foreign government involvement?"

"Not to my knowledge."

"That bank has to go; tell your friends, whoever they are, that I'm going to take it down and that they should stop throwing good money after bad."

"I will, but I don't think it will do any good."

"It is going to be a bloodbath financially. If you have anything in it, bail out before you lose everything."

"Do you think you have enough money to outlast the Rockefellers or the DuPonts?"

"We will see."

I knew I didn't, but I bet England, Germany, and China did.

I went down to dinner. It was too late to call England and Germany. I would call China after dinner.

At dinner, the talk was about Denny's new photo franchise. He had opened a studio in San Diego. I asked how he was going to oversee it. He told me that he had created a team with Dad's help to provide technical support, advertising, and financial oversight.

It sounded like a good plan. I'm proud of my younger brother, even if he won't help carry my bags.

Mary had all sorts of questions for him. Was he open to outside investment in the overall operation? Would he sell territories? Had he thought of footstools to make little girls look taller?"

His answer to all was no, but he would think about the footstools.

Dad told me that he and a group in Switzerland associated with his bank were buying Game Co.

I brought the family up to date but only alluded to my call from Bobby Kennedy. I could hear Mary at school, or I would rather not.

Both parents agreed that pressure had to be applied until the bank collapsed. It would prevent problems in the future, especially if it became known that I had led the effort to take them down.

"How will people know that I'm the prime mover."

"I think Dennis Lawson would like an exclusive."

"Ah, perfect. Warning to the world while building up our people. I love it."

I made my call to Chairman Deng's office in China. He wasn't available, but the assistant who answered my call had a lot of questions and took notes. He read them back to ensure he got them correct.

Communists or not, the Chinese loved to make money, especially from that filthy capitalist—his words, not mine. I wanted to ask him if we were the filthy capitalists in the scenario and what it made him but left well enough alone.

My last call of the day was to John to ask him to do two articles. I explained the rationale behind them, and he agreed. I also explained that his wife would benefit from an endowment being created in her name.

It was one of the few times John was speechless.

I would have to remember to call the bursar at UCLA tomorrow to start the process.

Chapter 41

After my morning routine and breakfast, I did remember to call UCLA and leave a message that I would like to talk to the bursar about an endowment.

I forgot that they keep later hours than most of the world.

I received a call as I was getting ready to leave the house. It was ten o'clock on the East Coast, and the markets had opened. Once more, it was Bobby Kennedy.

"Jackson, you have to call your dogs off; the bank's losses just topped a billion; at this rate, it will be bust before the day is over."

"They should have thought about that before they decided to make a run at my company."

"Unless you stop buying Game Co., we will bring the full power of the United States government down on you."

"Did you hear that we are opening up production and a headquarters overseas? If I must, I will move everything out of the United States. Now, here is my counter-proposal. Don't support that bank. They are going down. Have everyone withdraw their money."

"They won't do it; they want all their money back."

"Okay."

"Okay, what?"

"Okay, I will prepare to break their bank and move my operations out of the country."

"You can't do that. Think of the loss of American jobs."

"Somehow, I'm not sure that you care about American jobs or your friends wouldn't play so fast and loose with them."

"That was when we didn't think we could lose."

"So, it's we now?"

"You know what I mean. I'm just the messenger."

"Well, take this message back. It is a war to the knife."

An unhappy Kennedy hung up the phone. I suspect he almost broke the handset when he slammed it down.

I did place calls to Germany and England. The Germans were completely on board with buying Game Co. stock. This would force the bank to make good on its short position, and they would make a bundle. They had made a couple of hundred million already.

Mr. Norman was still thinking about what to do. I told him to call the London School of Economics and take their advice.

After an hour on the phone, I was ready for some activity, so I headed over to the practice range.

I found John and Sam in a deep conversation. They had a series of drawings in front of them. They were hand-drawn sketches of the holes in Augusta that I had problems putting.

They seemed to have things well in hand, so I fell into my practice routine. Putt a couple of hundred balls, then go to the driving range to work my way through all my clubs.

At the lunch break, they explained what they were doing. It was as I thought. They were now laying out those specific putts I had problems with on the green. They would be virtually identical. You could call this virtual reality. That was a catchy term.

It seems diminishing returns had set in. I wasn't even getting a tenth of a percent improvement after my time practicing. At the same time, I felt like I was doing the best of my life. I now would try to stay at this level for the tournaments.

Based on that scientific analysis of my game, I decided to take the afternoon off. Mounting George, I rode back to Jackson House to find a minor uproar going on.

It seems my little sister had managed to pass a message from my mum to the broker who handled Mary's accounts. How she did that no one knew. She had listened at dinner about that investment bank. She didn't like them picking on me, so she bought Game Co. stock, several million shares.

By the time the broker, soon to be ex-broker, I think, thought to confirm things with Mum, Mary had made ten million dollars. Mum cashed Mary out immediately.

With that sort of money floating around, I wondered what my one hundred million in buying had done. I made a phone call and about choked. When I could speak, I told them to sell at the current price.

Mary had made ten million, and I had made close to a billion. I was on and off the phone for the next two hours as they liquidated my positions. Before the final bell rang on Wall Street, the bank's value had gone down to zero.

The bank managers had tried all day to have trading suspended, but the governing body told them they couldn't because foreign national banks were involved, and they had to play it straight.

That didn't make me feel warm and fuzzy. If my overseas friends hadn't chosen to play, I could have lost everything. Well, a bunch of money.

There was also no doubt now that I was the wealthiest known individual in the world. I still felt that there was a thousand-year-old vampire out there somewhere that was worth a lot more.

All the buying and selling had been done through my office in London with an English broker as a UK citizen. I did this upon advice as the British short-term gains tax rate is 15% while the US was 25%. There would be some screaming in Washington when they figured that out.

There would be a toast or two in Threadneedle Street. For me, it would mean a difference of one hundred and fifty million in taxes or two hundred and fifty million. It didn't take long to make that decision.

It would probably make me the highest ratepayer in England. Wait until the tabloids found that out. Maybe I should be applying for a position at McMurdo Station now.

At dinner, the table talk was of the day's trading. To say Denny and Eddie were jealous of Mary would be an understatement. I asked them why they didn't care about the money I had made, and I was told they expected it of me and that it was so much it wasn't real.

Mary didn't know how to act. She asked Mum how much she would be allowed to have.

"Nothing until you are twenty-one."

"But that won't be for another million years," she wailed.

"It will only be another fourteen years, and what would you do with all that money anyway?"

"I could buy ice cream for everyone at school. Then new shoes with what was left over."

It was not very polite of Dad to laugh at his daughter as he did. I hid my laughter behind a raised hand. Parents these days!

"On a more serious note, Rick, do you have any plans?"

"Not thought through. The money will all be in England, and I probably should invest a lot of it there. Also, I would like to buy land in Australia, a lot of land."

"You can't go wrong buying land. Any other thoughts?"

"A banana split?"

"Sounds like a well-thought-out financial effort. Maybe you could treat the whole family."

That's what we did. We all crowded into a Crown Vic that Dad used for less advertised trips and went down to Dairy Queen. We all had banana splits.

They had a deal going. They had bunches of bananas. You would pick the banana you wanted, and it would have a number from 1 to 49 cents. That is what you paid. The normal price was 30 cents.

It cost me two dollars and fifteen cents. If I had paid the normal price, it would have been a buck and a half. That hurt.

I know, but this was real; all that other money didn't seem real yet.

There was a phone message waiting at home. Please call this number. There was no name. I usually wouldn't return a call like that because of my movie status. In the business, you get weird calls all the time.

Since this was an unusual day, I dialed the number. A raw voice on the other end asked, "Is this Jackson?"

"Yes, it is. Who is this?"

"It doesn't matter. You are a dead man walking. You cost me a lot of money today, and tomorrow, you and your family will pay."

At that, the phone clicked, and he hung up. I immediately told my parents about the call. Dad called security at the front gate to alert them of possible intrusions. They were also to double the number of guards on duty until further notice.

After discussion, it was decided the whole family would stay in tomorrow. The guy probably wasn't being literal in his statement, but it wouldn't hurt to be cautious.

The next day, we hung out as a family and had a game fest—everything from Old Maids for Mary to a blood-thirsty game of Monopoly. Mrs. Hernandez cleaned up. I was glad we weren't playing for real money.

Late in the afternoon, there was the sound of gunfire at the front gate. It sounded like World War II, but it probably was only a couple of dozen shots.

We got a phone call from the guard station. A man had tried to ram his way through the front gate and got killed for his effort. A check of his car found a Thompson submachine gun and two hand grenades. This guy was serious. Since he was dead, we couldn't determine if he was the one who called.

The sheriff showed up and took over the crime scene. He cleared our people as soon as he saw the guy's weapons.

Later, we would find that he had lost two million dollars in the investment bank and was broke, or dead broke, as Mum said.

Chapter 42

Early the next day I received a phone call from China. It was Chairman Deng.

"Richard, my friend, how are you?"

My first thought was to hold onto my wallet.

"I'm fine, and I hope all your dragons have five toes."

"Thank you. I have called to let you know we are considering you for a serious honor."

"What is that?"

"We want to make you the Duke of Guangzhou."

"What!"

"Our ruling Communist Party has decided to revert to the imperial system. Of course, all party officers will have the new titles of nobility. We decided that you should be the one to have control of Guangzhou and its port. It needs wise leadership."

"What would a wise leader be leading, and what resources would they have?"

"The wise leader would own everything the state owned as their personal property. They could use it as they see fit. The wise leader would have control of local law and finances. The wise leader would invest in his property so that it would grow and give rich rewards."

As I thought, hang on to your wallet, oh wise leader.

"Tell me more about Guangzhou, I know nothing about the area."

"Guangzhou port is situated at the intersection of the three most important rivers of Dongjiang, Xijiang, and Beijing in South China. All three rivers have potential waterways, railways, expressways, and airlines intersecting here, thus a critical transportation hub can be formed here. It can be the main port of focus in the Pearl River Delta Region."

"The port's harbor area extends along the Pearl River coast and water areas in the cities of Guangzhou, Dongguan, Zhongshan, Shenzhen, and Zhuhai. The port is situated beyond the entrance of the Pearl River opening and can serve as a gateway for shipping activity for other harbor areas such as Nansha Harbor Area, Xinsha Harbor Area, Huangpu Harbor Area, and Inner Harbor Area."

"You are presenting the opportunities of the area but not the current reality."

"The current leadership of Guangzhou has failed miserably and the many yuan that were provided to make these things come to pass have disappeared along with the leader and his family. We will find them."

And Dad wanted to know what I was going to do with my windfall from yesterday.

"Will I be expected to live there?"

"That would be entirely up to you. Frankly, I wouldn't recommend it. Your life is so different from ours that while you are a good friend, you would be too exciting of a neighbor."

Maybe I should work on changing my reputation.

"I would have a free hand in investing in infrastructure and local manufacturing?"

"Completely. We are counting on it."

"Could I take local business partners and let them run the businesses up to the point that I'm a silent partner?"

"If you so desire, but why would you give up control and income?"

"I can only control so much. My immediate reaction is to set up a bank and make loans. Also, allow port authority bonds to be sold. That way I'm facilitating the operations but not tied to them on a routine basis."

"Maybe you are a wise leader."

"I don't know about that, but I have learned a few things with my ownership of Jackson Enterprises."

"Yes. We heard of your actions on the US stock market. You make a good friend and a terrible enemy."

"One tries."

"One other thing you should be aware of, there are some disputes about what areas are included in the various Noble Grants. There will be fighting. We don't expect any challenges from you, but you need to know of the possibility."

"So, I'm being made a duke with all power and responsibility for an area, and I will have to defend it."

"Possibly, the Imperial Army would be there at your need."

"What is your title going to be?"

"Prince of Beijing."

"Has a successor been named for Empress Ping?"

"Not at this time."

"It sounds to me like China is about to return to the level of fighting warlords."

"That is what we are trying to avert by raising the living standards of the people."

"The more I think about it, I'm going to decline the dukedom."

"You can't! We need the money you can bring in."

"I can still open a bank and back development bonds for Guangzhou, but having a title right now is the same as putting a target on your back."

"If you do that, China will forever be in your debt. We will have the yuan on the gold standard for international trade, but that does not cure our internal problems. If you jumpstart one of our major cities, it might prevent the violence we see coming."

"I have the money right now, so have your people get with Mr. Williamson to put a bank in place."

"What will you call it?"

"Is there a Bank of Guangzhou?"

"No."

"Then that is what we will call it."

We talked about some of the details that would need to be handled. It boiled down to them filling out forms for me, me signing them, and sending a bunch of money, dollars, or pound sterling.

I told him it would be in pound sterling as England was where my transactions had taken place. Well, they took place on Wall Street but as a British entity.

If this is Tuesday, it must be Belgium.

I called Jim and told him we would be opening a bank in China with my British funds.

"What did the Chinese offer?"

"A dukedom."

"What, did you take it?"

"No, it seems they are going to be jockeying for positions and unless I hired an army, I would be a prime target."

"Sounds dangerous, besides, you will probably end up as a British duke which has more prestige."

"How do you figure that?"

"The Brits always give a title or two to their highest taxpayers and you will probably have the highest tax bill in the country this year."

"That's true about the taxes. I know nothing about the titles."

My phone calls had taken most of the morning, so I goofed off until lunchtime. Mum was home so I told her about the offer from the Chinese to become a duke.

I must say that was one of the few times I saw Mum taken aback.

"What did you tell them?"

"I ended up declining as it appears they are heading for a spot of bother, and I don't want to be involved."

"I am making a significant investment in the city of Guangzhou to try to delay the problems."

"What sort of problems?"

"It seems all the communist leaders have decided they would rather have noble titles. They want to keep their power. I guess it would require a lot of new business cards.

"While they are rearranging the deck chairs some of them will try to grab an extra chair or two. I don't want to be there if they come for mine."

"Good thinking. What sort of investments?"

"A bank and support bonds issued for the water, rail, highway, and air infrastructure."

"How much?"

"Half a billion."

"I'm glad you aren't thinking small. You do realize that you are probably throwing good money after bad."

"Probably so, but if it turns out to be good money after good, then I stand to make some real money."

"Rick, you are already a billionaire. What do you want?"

"What comes after a billion?"

"The Yanks say a trillion which would be a thousand billion, but it is a million million."

"I guess I can forget that. There will never be a trillion dollars floating around."

"They almost managed it in Germany after the first war."

"True, but I'm talking about a normal economy."

"You are right about that, well, unless Mary gets involved."

We both laughed at that, but it was a laugh with reservations. Who knows what that girl will do when she grows up? According to her, that will be around twelve.

Speaking of the little devil, she came storming in from school. She was furious.

"That Patty is going to pay!"

"What has she done?"

"I saw her kiss Davy!"

"I thought he liked you?"

She wailed, "So did I! I'm ruined for life!"

At that point, I shut up. This was Mum's stuff.

"I'm late for golf practice, I had better go."

Mum gave me that look but I kept moving.

I rode George over to the practice area but neither John nor Sam was there. Some Park Rangers were using the driving range, but I didn't join them.

I had too many things going through my mind. Why on earth would the Chinese want to make me a duke? What would the reaction be at Augusta when it was revealed their greenskeeper was rigging the tournaments? Why did Don Carlo think golf was a game for gentlemen? Would I have to have the Kennedys assassinated to save myself?

The Kennedy question was the only one I could answer, I had always done my own dirty work, and I wasn't going to change now. I had to make peace with them. The question was, how?

Chapter 43

I didn't have much time to consider my relationship with the Kennedys. It was the start of Masters week at Augusta.

Practice rounds were to start on Monday, so John and I flew in on Sunday. My office had found a house to rent not that far from the golf course.

Renting out houses near the course was a common practice. There was a lot of money to be made and all those outsiders could be avoided. Hotels and restaurants would be jammed. It was a good time to spend a week at the beach. I didn't even ask what the house rental was.

Monday and Tuesday were practice days. Both days helped me to feel more comfortable with the course. It was interesting being grouped with professional golfers. They were polite but you could see they didn't take any amateur seriously.

Even though I had won a previous US Open, I was considered a flash in the pan not to be worried about. I had different thoughts on that.

Wednesday was a fun day. There is a 9-hole par-3 course on the edge of the main course. They have a par 3 contest where all the golfers participate, but it is a fun day. Many of the golfer's children were caddies that day.

Since I had no children, I asked Mary if she wanted the job. She said yes, even after she found out there would be no pay.

Now Mary is too small to carry a golf bag, so John carried it for her. She did wear a sign on her back that said, "Caddie in Chief." John had a sign reading, "Mary's Assistant Caddie." The crowd and TV people loved it.

We had a good time posing for pictures with the crowd as we went.

Now no one who has won the par 3 has ever won the Masters, so there is superstition involved.

Some of the pros who knew they had no chance at winning the Masters played all out on the par 3.

The winner would get a green jacket and a crystal bowl with the Masters' logo on it. I didn't even try. Deane Berman won at 5 under. He is a nice guy, and his family was thrilled at his win.

Mary took it in stride. I thought she might throw a fit if I didn't win but she had so much fun and attention I'm not even sure she knew a match was going on. Mum and Dad had been following us around in case things got out of hand.

Only once there was cause for concern. Reporters wanted to interview Mary, and not me. I wasn't concerned that I wasn't being interviewed but at what Mary might say.

The reporters were decent in their questions, keeping them about saving puppies, saving kittens, and saving ponies. Mary gave answers to everything.

To the question, "Why do you want to save puppies?" she replied, "Puppies are better than reporters who ask stupid questions."

When the laughter died down, she was asked if she was going to have a campaign to "Save the Whales."

"Do they need saving?"

"Yes, they do," replied the reporter. "What are you going to do about it?"

"I'm only seven years old. I can't save everything. What are you going to do about the poor whales?"

For some reason, the reporters lost interest in further questions.

I was asked, "How do you think you will do in the Masters?"

"I'm playing to win. So are many other fine golfers. Time will tell."

The house that we had rented was a nice one with a large patio. Mum and Dad had a cocktail party outside, catered by a local firm.

By invitation only, it was a civil event. The kids, Denny, Eddie, and Mary, made token appearances and went to the den to watch TV.

I was stuck doing a meet and greet with Mum and Dad. By this time all the financial papers and magazines had carried the story about the bank being taken down and that I had made a fortune.

This brought out all the people who had every good reason in the world that I should share, or just outright give them my new wealth.

It didn't take long, and I asked if I could use the microphone setup. I don't know why it was there as there wasn't anything scheduled.

"Ladies and gentlemen. As some of you are aware, I made a large sum of money on the stock market yesterday. I'm proud to announce all those funds have been used to create a new bank in China, the Bank of Guangzhou. We will welcome any investments you may care to make. This is not an official solicitation. It is just a notice that information can be obtained from the Chinese Embassy.

Have the Chinese even opened an embassy yet? No idea. At least this would get some of them off my back.

The women had also descended. Fortune hunters all. I didn't think it was possible to get tired of boobs being rubbed on my arm. I was wrong.

I left the party as soon as I could.

The next morning, Thursday, I was up early and got my run in. I was amazed that three die-hard women had just happened to run my route that morning. While two of them could out-sprint me, none had the stamina to do five miles. I did feel sorry for the one large-breasted girl who tried to run without a bra on.

Now those were some puppies that needed saving.

After a medium-sized breakfast, John and I headed for the course. I had drawn a 9:20 tee time. The higher ranked the golfer, the later their tee time.

All the time I had spent on the driving range and practice green paid off. At the end of day one, I led the field at 5 under. A prize was given to the low round each day. I now had a crystal vase with the Masters' logo engraved on it. It would go well in the trophy case set up in the Jackson House library.

I consented to be interviewed. Etiquette said that I would for the sake of the golf club. The questions were predictable and my answers more so.

Yes, I was happy to be the leader; no, I didn't think this would be an easy win. There were the world's best golfers here, and I would have to fight every inch of the way. And so it went.

On day two, Friday, things got serious. As the leader, I was in the final threesome. I was with Gary Player and Arnold Palmer, both gentlemen of the first water. Arnold picked up a stroke to be 7-under. Gary caught on fire and ended up tied at 7-under. I still led as I finished at 8-under.

My putting was devastating. I had three eagles that round so won four crystal goblets. At this rate, we would have to buy a cabinet for all the crystals I had won.

More silly questions, more answers; my answers were never silly, well maybe sarcastic, but not silly.

The one I liked best was whether would I turn pro on the last day if I won so I could collect the first-place money.

I couldn't resist it. "They have prize money?"

Saturday the field was narrowed down. The top fifty players including ties and anyone within 10 strokes of the leader moved on. I was still playing with the same group. At the end of the third round, Arnold lost a stroke and came in at 6-under. Gary caught fire and hit a blistering 10-under. It wasn't good enough to beat my 11-under. I wondered what we would do with all the crystal vases but decided that was Mum's problem.

Sunday was a terrible day. The rain started right after we teed off and didn't let up. When the lightning started, they called the match for the day. We would start over from scratch on Monday.

I felt bad for the ten players who had finished, especially for those who had moved up in the rankings. No one was threatening the leaders, but still, it would have improved their payday.

On Monday we played in twosomes. I was with Gary Player. As the leaders, we teed off last. We both felt the pressure and our games showed it. He lost 2 of his strokes to end up 8 under. I lost 2 strokes and ended up at 9-under to win the Masters National Golf Tournament. Gary laughed at his loss as he would still get the first-place money of twenty thousand dollars.

They must have a large closet full of green jackets because they had a forty-two long in stock. Even that could have used a little tailoring, but I didn't mention it. I was sure Harold could take care of it.

Besides the jacket, I received the Silver Cup which was for the low amateur score, and my name was engraved on the trophy which would be on display in the clubhouse.

In the post-round interview, a reporter asked why I didn't turn pro and take the money. I asked him if his newspaper had a financial page. They did. I suggested that he read it.

Chapter 44

There was a round of parties after the tournament ended. I was the guest of honor at each of them. It was funny that before the tournament, I was one of the many amateurs that had entered but didn't have a chance.

Now I had two major wins to my record, I was a new force to be reckoned with. I lost track of how many times I was asked if I was turning pro.

People couldn't get it through their heads that the golf circuit money didn't mean that much to me. Gary Player's first-place money was twenty thousand dollars. That was good money, ten thousand a year was considered an above-average living and he had won it in a week. That was two years' wages.

By that standard, I made 50,000 years' worth last week. I wasn't so crass as to say that. I kept referring people to *Forbes* or the *Wall Street Journal*. If they were too lazy to look it up it wasn't my problem.

Those who didn't ask me if I was turning pro wanted to know if I was after Bobby Jones' record of the only Grand Slam by an amateur golfer. That one I had to be more careful of because yes, I was. However, I didn't want to sound like a braggart or raise expectations. I would let my clubs speak for themselves.

Another realization that came as I attended these parties was that there were two types of people who gathered around me.

Some wanted to know the golfer, the movie actor, the hero, the inventor, the self-made person, or even the Boy Scout. What they had in common was they all wanted to be able to say they had some connection with me. To bask in my reflected glory if you will.

Then some wanted my money. This could be in the form of a gift, loan, or even theft. They considered what was mine as theirs.

I had been happily dealing with the first type with no problems. A handshake, a photo together, or even a publicity picture would satisfy their needs.

The second group could never be satisfied. They would be after my money all my life.

Would I end up a recluse as was reported of Howard Hughes? That didn't sound like living a life.

It did mean that I had to become less accessible to these people and plain hardened to their entreaties. That led to its own set of problems. I didn't want to become so hard and cynical that I wrote everything off, but at the same time, I had to protect myself.

I had to surround myself with people I trusted like Mum and Dad, Jim Williamson, Todd Pearson, and the rest of the business staff who helped me in the early days. Then there were John Wayne, Clint Easterly, Sam Monroe, Anna Romanov, and Dick Wyman to name a few.

For some reason, Nina came to mind, but I set her aside as one who had betrayed me. It still hurt every time I thought of her. I had been told that time would take care of that, in that I would think of her less often.

It was working. Instead of constant pain, it was now only hourly while I was awake.

She still wrote me letters which I read but never responded to. Her life was now miserable. From being the queen bee at her school she was now a social pariah. Those that she had dispensed largess to in the form of modeling jobs, or rides in my airplane, or even the Ferrari left her as soon as she couldn't provide them anymore. Also, they derided her for losing her meal ticket.

She kept trying to explain to me that she never considered me a meal ticket. The worthless prince had wooed her and played to her ego and in a moment of weakness, she fell for his line.

My problem was that it wasn't only one moment.

As for the prince himself, I had considered revenge in many a horrid form. In the end, I did nothing because he had done himself in.

Anything to do with me made all the tabloids. He and Nina made several weeks' stories. The prince had flown too high, and now all knew him for what he was. His social circle could forgive anything but making them all look foolish.

His invitations to the social events that counted among his kind went away. The last I heard he was working as a tour bus guide. If nothing else, he should know all the social dirt about the rich and famous whose houses he was showing to tourists.

After the last party, I took off my green jacket and flew to England. I had a lot of loose ends to tie up on the investment bank debacle.

The largest was to ensure that a holding company for Jackson Enterprises had been properly formed in England. Because of taxes the company now had to be outside of the United States.

It would also help protect it from the ire of the Kennedys. I still hadn't figured out how to make peace with them. My problems with them started when they came into the White House.

I think they had planned to be the ones who opened China to trade. This would create a strong legacy and destroy Dick Nixon's plan to be the one who opened them up.

What they didn't appreciate was that China had decided to open themselves up with the English being their main trading partner. I was merely a messenger when this all started. The die had been cast before JFK was elected.

Then there was the attempt to take over my company. All I can say is they started it. If anything, I should be plotting how to take them and the others involved down.

I saw no profit in that. It would lead to a series of feuds for the rest of my life. Even if I won the battles, the money wouldn't buy me peace with that crowd.

Currently, the only solution I saw was to put myself in an unassailable position. What form that would take I had no answer for.

As the Chinese would say, "I was living in interesting times."

When I got to England, I found out how interesting it could be. Mr. Norman had left messages everywhere for me. This included having me met at my aircraft by a uniformed member of the Coldstream Guards. I was to proceed directly to the palace.

I think that meant I was not to Pass Go or collect two hundred dollars.

I had a good night's sleep on the flight over, so I was ready for the day when we landed in London early in the morning.

I was driven to Buckingham Palace with a police escort, sirens, and all. I had no idea what all the fuss was about.

Usually, when I went to Buck House, it was for a meeting with Mr. Norman. This time I was taken directly to a conference room where the Queen, the Prime Minister, the Chancellor of the Exchequer, and several others who I didn't know awaited me.

I made a formal greeting to the queen and nodded to the rest. Until I knew what this was all about, I was saying nothing. They didn't have the Fifth Amendment in England, but I wasn't going to open my mouth and incriminate myself.

Elizabeth opened with, "Lord Blackhoof, thank you for your prompt attendance at our request."

I nodded in response. Nope, not going to incriminate myself.

"You have certainly set the ravens at the Tower in flight."

Oh great; the legend was that if the ravens remained at the Tower of London, England would stand. What have I done?

"This week the Bank of England received one thousand tons of gold for deposit and safekeeping from the Chinese. This alone has strengthened our country's economy."

"Then you moved production to our shores to provide desperately needed jobs. On top of that, you opened a European headquarters here, making our economy that much stronger."

"Then you made a series of trades in English pounds that made you a fortune which has now made you the highest taxed individual in English history. Again, strengthening the economy.

"We had made a promise to you that you would not have to pay taxes on English income. It is highly embarrassing that we must break that promise. You notice I have used 'We.' That is the royal 'We.'"

That one was easy.

"Your Majesty, before you break your royal promise, I would like to ask my taxes be the same as every other Englishman, that I will be given no special consideration."

The feelings of relief around the table were palpable.

"Countess Jackson predicted that would be your answer. We thank you."

Boy, while I slept the phone lines must have been burning up.

"Because of your actions, we have decided to offer you a dukedom."

Crikey, everyone wants me to be a duke.

"Your Majesty, I must decline. I recently declined that honor from the Chinese, and they would lose face if I accepted the British honor.

"Again, the countess is correct. Know this: You have a special place in the heart of England."

Interesting times indeed.

Chapter 45

After the meeting, I was invited to a ball on Saturday evening. It would be for the younger set of royals and their noble friends. Since I didn't have to be back in LA to work on the movie until Monday, I accepted.

At least this gave Harold something to do as it was in full dress, but no military. For me, that meant white tie and tails, with all my medals in miniature.

That was Saturday, I spent the next two days doing the mundane part of my work. I must have signed two thousand cards and letters to employees and friends. An autopen machine was sounding better all the time.

We used one for my general publicity work, but it looked like I would have to start using one more often. Only my most personal letters would be signed by me. I didn't like it, but it was one of the realities that I had to face.

Another was that I wouldn't be able to drive myself blithely around the countryside. Now it would be a limousine with a driver and bodyguard.

I checked up on how the establishment of the Bank of Guangzhou was going. Everything appeared to be in order. That made me suspicious. Nothing was ever in order when dealing with the Chinese. That is unless the powers that be wanted it to be.

Based on my suspicions I called Chairman or now Prince Deng. An aide told me to hold as my calls were to be referred to His Highness at once.

They were taking this change to a system of nobility seriously.

When he came on the line, I told him I was concerned about the new bank. There were no reported problems and on a project of this size and complication, there would be problems.

He agreed with my thinking and told me he would have it looked at. Heads would roll if someone were obstructing. I took that as a literal statement rather than a figurative one.

I didn't think that I wanted to spend too much time in China until things settled down. One could come down with a serious case of death for little reason.

Saturday I spent at the archery butts at the Tower. I hadn't practiced enough, and it was a use-it-or-lose-it operation. For me, it wasn't a sport but a tool of my trade. I'm not sure what my trade is but being able to place an arrow where I needed it had done well for me.

That evening, I arrived at the appointed time and place, this being the ballroom at the Plaza on the Strand. This was very convenient for me as it was only an elevator ride away and would make an escape if needed easy, to say the least.

I soon realized that I might need that escape route when I was announced. All eyes turned to me. As I entered the room, there was a flow of bodies toward me. Not a charge, which would be unseemly, more like a school of fish changing direction.

This school seemed to be made up of sharks.

The sharks, uh, guests were of two types, guys hunting for a loan and girls hunting for a husband. At least with the guys, you could give them the money and you could be certain you wouldn't see them again until they needed more.

The women would either stay with you your whole life or agree to go away as soon as you signed everything over.

There were probably some nice people in the room that I would like to get to know, but they avoided being near the sharks.

I talked to a couple of dozen as they welcomed me to England. I wonder if they knew I was born here. It didn't take long for my first impressions to be validated. There was no shame with this crowd as they openly asked for loans.

One guy at least invited me to play a few hands of cards with him and some friends. I knew how that would turn out, but at least he was willing to work for the money.

The girls were the worst. They let me know they were available and would be faithful, unlike that horrid Nina.

The comments about Nina nearly sent me into a rage, but I contained myself.

It was almost poetic that Lady Christine or better known as the Blonde Bitch was present. She of Mary-spilling-chocolate fame.

"Oh Richard, it is so nice to see you. I have missed your company."

"Do you still slap little girls like my sister?"

That stopped the show dead. The Scandinavian blonde blushed as I had never imagined anyone could blush. Almost a dozen people around her looked from her to me to see what would happen next.

What happened was I turned and left. There was nothing for me here.

We were wheels up early Sunday morning. What had been a pleasant trip had turned bad. I kept replaying my thoughts about Nina and my rage when other people talked badly about her. How did I feel about her?

I shrugged my gloomy thoughts off. I still had feelings for her, but I wasn't about to forgive her betrayal.

Instead, I got into a game of gin rummy with the hostesses and off-duty members of the flight crew. Talk about sharks. They took me for twenty dollars.

That was the highlight of the flight, losing a few bucks while laughing and joking with some nice people. The money meant nothing to any of us. It was the comradery that was important.

There is a lesson in this somewhere, I think.

I was back at Jackson House in time for dinner. Mum and Dad were fully aware of the events in England. They even knew about my leaving the ball early. I wondered who their spies were.

I knew that Mum had talked to the Queen so she knew the official portion of it, but how would she know about the ball?

I decided upon a unique approach. I asked her.

"Mum, how do you and Dad know about me leaving that ball early?"

Dad spoke up, "It came over the UPI wire. One of the paparazzi filed a story that was accepted."

I had forgotten that every move of that entire crowd was subject to scrutiny. I sincerely hoped that I wasn't considered one of that crowd.

Dad had a copy of the *Wall Street Journal*. They had run an op-ed by a concerned citizen. It took the position that Jackson Enterprises was too large and vital of a company to leave to a teenager. It went into detail about my recent public events, all interpreted as me being a petulant teenager with no sense of responsibility.

Too many people in America depended on Jackson Enterprises for their livelihood to leave it to a child. The company should be nationalized for the good of the employees and the nation. I shouldn't be allowed to take any of my operations offshore along with American jobs.

That last got to me. One thing Todd Goodson and I had made clear in a letter to all employees was that no jobs would be going overseas. These were all new jobs.

Pittsburgh couldn't support our worldwide needs, and if we were going into production elsewhere, it made sense to do it around the world.

Todd had canvassed many employees at all levels and reported back that there was a high degree of understanding and support of the company's needs.

I asked Dad if he could find out who wrote this piece. He said he would try but the *Journal* protected its sources.

Denny and Eddie didn't pay much attention to our conversation. They were arguing about who would win a fight, Batman or Superman.

Mary was listening intently. She didn't say anything, but you could see the wheels turning. I wondered what the outcome would be.

The next morning after my run and workout, I rode George over to the Forest Service Station. Sam and John were already there setting up the practice greens to reflect the south course greens at the Oakmont Country Club in Oakmont Pennsylvania. That would be the venue of the US Open in June.

Sam congratulated me on winning the Masters. I asked him why he didn't want to come to any of the tournaments.

"Too hard on my knees."

"We could get you a golf cart."

"Nah, always walked the course."

That West Virginian was certainly set in his ways.

I hit a round of balls at the driving range and called it a day.

I wanted to be at the movie lot on time. This was one of the few days that I would have real lines on a real set. Most of my scenes were in the saddle out on the range.

I was to pledge my undying love to Molly. The shooting sequence had me pledging my love. The next scene would see me getting shot down by a pretty Shawnee maiden. Ya gotta love Hollywood.

Chapter 46

The scene with the Shawnee maiden had Miss Shawnee of 1961. The 1962 pageant wouldn't be until later in the year. She only had three lines.

I had to wonder what the writers were thinking. I was supposed to fall in love with her and be ready to set Molly aside with such short contact.

That was in the movie. In real life, I was head over heels, and we had only exchanged names before our scene. Maybe the writers weren't so far off after all.

In the scene which was taking place in a general store owned and run by her parents, she was stocking a high shelf on a ladder when it tipped backward.

She was gorgeous. Tall, around five foot ten, light copper skin, coal-black hair, fine-featured with high cheekbones.

She was almost a stereotype of beauty. Her saving grace was a ready smile, which made her serious features light up.

Awendea told me to call her, "Wendy." She was brought in for two scenes. This was a reward over and above for being the beauty pageant winner.

I was there to catch her. We walked through the scene several times, and each time I ended up with an armful of a beautiful Indian girl. Maybe I was giving up on acting too soon.

It wasn't considered a dangerous stunt, so we did it ourselves. She was a good actress. She had the same wide-eyed look each time I caught her.

I would then set her down and ask her if she was okay. She would nod and turn away.

That was our introduction.

The next scene was me walking into the store and buying some stuff that I didn't need just as an excuse to talk to her. As she rang up

my order on the huge bronze cash register, I was visibly working up
the nerve to ask her to go for a walk that evening.

Then there would be a short scene where I found out her name.
While mailing a letter to my mother, I would casually ask at the post
office the name of the young lady at the general store. It is Awendea,
which means beautiful morning in Shawnee. The postmistress just
smiled when I asked.

I was shown walking back and forth in front of her store while I
finally worked up the nerve to go in the store to pop the question.

When I did, I was to be crushed by her reply.

"Why would I go walking with a no-account cowhand? I will
grant that you are good-looking. However, I leave tomorrow to go to
school in Edinburgh, Scotland."

I would then turn with shoulders slumped and walk away. What
I was not supposed to know at the time was Molly was watching and
listening one aisle over. This set up a breakup scene and fight which
would go on for half the movie until I won her back.

The reality of the scene being shot was that Sally was not even on
the set. Her shots were already in the can.

Back to real life, I asked Wendy if she had any dinner plans. She
didn't and accepted on her and her escort's behalf.

Dang! I was hoping to have a date alone.

It turned out Chief Redfoot was her escort. That made it easier,
or at least less awkward.

The chief had a twinkle in his eye when he told me that they
would accept my invitation. What I didn't know was that my parents
had extended an invitation to him and his charge for dinner at the
Brown Derby. I was welcome to join them.

Later that evening when we met at the restaurant I was surprised
by Wendy as she was wearing the proverbial little black dress. I don't
know what I was expecting, bead-encrusted buckskin?

She wore it well. Though I hadn't said anything or given myself away by my looks, I did chastise myself for stereotyping.

The chief wore a custom-made suit which set his rugged features off nicely. He also still wore his long dark hair in a headband. It was bright red.

Just to make small talk I mentioned I liked his headband. He replied that he wore it to meet the white man's stereotyping. My look of shock was met by a belly laugh.

"Oh, Rick, the look on your face was worth it. I always have worn headbands to keep my hair out of my food."

I blushed as red as his headband. I felt like I had just been paid back for my thoughts about Wendy.

Once past that, I held a chair for Wendy as the chief introduced her to my parents. He introduced her as his granddaughter.

I'm so glad I have kept my mouth closed. I just knew he had a tomahawk hidden somewhere under his suit coat.

It was a thin crowd at the Derby, so it wasn't a real surprise when the papa-rats-eyes closed in on us. They used their normal tactic of scouting the room out and then rushing the table with their chosen target.

They would be ejected immediately, but they still had time to get their pictures.

Mr. Cobb would apologize and give us a free dessert for the inconvenience. It had become a ritual that we all tolerated.

Since Wendy was sitting next to me, I could imagine tomorrow's headlines. I wondered what Nina would make of them.

Wendy and I got along well. I asked her what her plans were after the movie.

"I leave for Edinburgh Scotland to go to school once my scenes have been accepted by the editors."

I looked like a hooked fish as she explained.

"That is why the writers chose that line for me. They thought it would be a good inside joke and make it easy for me to remember my lines."

Chief Redfoot added to the conversation.

"She is going to study to be a doctor, just like Awendea my great-grandmother did at the University of Edinburgh."

That explained the epilogue which ultimately appeared at the end of the movie explaining that Awendea as portrayed by her great-great-great-granddaughter was the first female MD in the Shawnee Tribe.

Chief Redfoot never missed a trick in showing how the Shawnee had been civilized as long as or even longer than the white man.

The one thing that we all had a hard time getting in our heads was that the Indians had a thriving civilization going until the white man showed up with his new diseases which killed off ninety percent of their population and destroyed their nations.

The bottom line was that another budding romance was cut off. I wondered if Wendy even knew we had a budding romance. She was polite to me but never gave any indication that she might be interested in me.

We had a pleasant dinner, papa-rats-eyes aside. At the end of the evening, I told Wendy I would see her on the set. She told me she was looking forward to it. Hope springs eternal.

In the morning I rode over to the Forest Service station. Sam had the place set up to match Oakmont as much as he could. John and I talked about when we could go to Oakmont to play several practice rounds. It would have to be next week as I had to be on set every day this week.

After spending the morning hitting a little white ball around, I returned home and found a message waiting.

Would I please call Bobby Kennedy at the White House at my convenience?

"Please?"

"Bobby Kennedy."

"Convenience?"

Now those were words I never thought would be in the same sentence. I returned the call. I was put through directly to the attorney general.

"Rick, thanks for returning my call so promptly. JFK and I would like you to stop by the White House or even Hyannis Port when you get a chance. We need to talk things through and make peace with each other."

"I think that is a good idea. I have no desire to be at odds with you. I will be flying to Oakmont, Pennsylvania next week to practice at Oakmont. Why don't I continue to Hyannis Port and we meet on Saturday?"

"That would be great. We were planning to spend the weekend there anyway. Your name will be at the guard station."

"Thanks, I'm looking forward to this."

We hung up and I listened to the news on the radio while having lunch. The news out of China was confusing. It seemed several of the new nobles had died suddenly while attending a state dinner at the new empress's request.

It left the power structure in turmoil but troops loyal to the empress were preventing outright civil war from erupting.

Way to go Empress Ping! I wondered if Prince Deng kept his head.

I did have to make some phone calls to see what this was doing to the bank project. I was glad I wasn't in China to share their interesting times.

Chapter 47

I wondered what sort of person I had become that I was cheering the deaths of people I didn't even know. Granted, they were communists and had fought their way to the top on the bodies of others, but it still didn't seem right that I had cheered their deaths.

I knew Empress Ping and her actions had shown that she had the best interests of the Chinese people in her heart. It still didn't give me the right to be happy about the slaughter.

There was no doubt it was a slaughter, probably by poison. China was probably better off for it. Still, it didn't sit right that I was cheering the deaths.

I thought about calling the empress but didn't think she would appreciate the call if she took it. Beijing is fifteen hours ahead of us, so it was around 3 a.m. the next day there.

This was one of the few free afternoons that I had. The next day we would fly to Pennsylvania to play a couple of rounds at Oakmont to prepare for the US Open.

To celebrate my free time, I took my trusty T-bird on a ride. I had no destination; I was following my nose.

My nose took me out to the Ontario Airport where I looked up Mr. McGarry. He was there waiting for his next student, who wasn't due for an hour. We spent the time exchanging flying stories. Mine was about the 707-emergency landing and spotting Brigitte Bardot.

His were about the war and were much more exciting than mine.

He was just getting to the punchline of a story about being jumped by four Japanese Zeros when his student showed up. He told me he would finish it the next time I came to visit. He is a cruel man.

I drove back toward Hollywood and stopped at Warner Brothers. I was hoping to get in some sword work with the stuntmen, but they were all working.

I gave up and drove home. It was early enough that I saddled George and had an hour's ride around the public park. I didn't see any tigers or one of those fierce chipmunks.

Dinner was with my brothers and sister. The parents had gone to some charity dinner. I was glad that they didn't drag me along.

Denny was noticeably quiet during dinner so later I asked him if anything was bothering him.

"Rick, you caught Nina cheating on you. How did you get over her?"

So, my little brother has girl problems.

"I haven't. Part of me wants to fly to Europe and hug her and tell her all is forgiven. The rest of me says if she betrayed me once I would be insane to trust her again."

"You don't act like you are bothered."

"Remember, I'm an actor. Some days it hurts so bad I want to cry."

"So, it's okay if I'm all busted up and don't know what to do?"

"Welcome to the real world of men never understanding women and why they do what they do."

"I don't think I will date for a while."

"That's my plan."

"What about that beautiful Indian girl Awendea or Sally Fields?"

"Sally doesn't like my lifestyle plus she has a boyfriend and Awendea has left for Edinburgh to go to school. Don't believe everything you read in the papers."

"Thanks for listening and sharing Rick; this helps."

"I'm glad."

"Now if you want to share some of your money that would be nice."

"I will loan it to you if you use it to grow your business. Otherwise, earn it yourself."

"How much interest?"

"Two percent."

"That's better than Mary. She wanted four."

"Do you need it?"

"No, I just wanted to know what was available."

"Tell me. Mary wanted four percent. Was that per annum?"

"She didn't say."

"I would watch the little shark; she may have meant by the week."

"She would do that to family members?"

"Probably not; it would only be by the month."

At that, I heard a screech from behind the couch. Someone had been eavesdropping.

"Shame on you, Mary."

"I wouldn't charge my brother that much!"

"I know, dear. I knew you were there. I saw you crawl behind the couch when we came in."

"How else am I going to get good stories for my column?"

"Are you still doing that?"

"Not regularly, but I get one hundred dollars per special. The best part is Mum and Dad don't know I get paid in cash. I have over a thousand dollars hidden in my room."

"Then a trade—you don't report on this conversation, and Mum and Dad don't hear about your deal."

She whined a bit but made the deal. One thing about Mary was that she kept her word, well, except in Monopoly.

The next morning John and I took off for Pittsburgh to play several practice rounds at Oakmont. I was now prominent enough in the golfing world to be allowed to play almost any course.

That course is tough! The Donald Ross-designed course has earned its name, "The Monster."

While not dreading playing in the tournament, I knew it would be harder here than the Masters.

I managed to par the course on my first round. In the afternoon we went around again, and I only picked up 1 stroke.

I could only hope this course played this hard for everyone. According to John who had reviewed all the past tournaments, it would.

He also let me know that the two articles he was going to present had been sent off. The public one to *Golfweek*, the other to the chairman of Augusta.

I was received politely by the people at Oakmont but nothing over the top. It was more like we're glad you are here, along with all the other luminaries of the golfing world.

In a way, it was nice not to be picked out.

Friday's rounds weren't much better. The first round was 2-under and I thought I was getting the hang of it. I followed up with a 1-over-par. It was going to be an interesting tournament.

Friday evening, we flew to Boston, where we stayed at a hotel downtown. Saturday morning John went sightseeing while I took a limo to Hyannis Port.

I was let into the Kennedy compound without any trouble. Outside of the compound, there was a permanent camp of TV and radio broadcast trucks.

The windows on my limo were darkened so that people outside couldn't see in or take pictures.

While it hadn't been mentioned. I had guessed right as to what to wear at the compound. My California casual was perfect.

RFK and JFK were both waiting for me on the back veranda. There was a whole bunch of kids running around and having a good time playing touch football.

I was offered a lemonade as we watched the kids play. Once we were done, I was invited inside to an office.

The president had a stack of file folders over a foot high on his desk.

"Rick, we didn't know who we were dealing with. I asked the FBI to send over what they had. They sent this but told me there was more that they didn't have access to. I couldn't believe that someone would deny them information until they told me it was the KGB and East German Stasi.

"You have had an interesting time in the last several years. Starting with the Russian encroachment on the DEW line to your involvement with the Chinese.

"By the FBI's best estimate, you have killed five men and probably several more. They still are trying to figure out why your name was inside a bowling bag found in the trash from the Russian Embassy, one that was bloodstained.

"They suspect it is connected to some headless bodies found in a boxcar."

"Bobby and I knew you were a film actor and sometimes singer, but we knew nothing about your inventions.

"That explains how you were able to fend off the takeover attempt aimed at Jackson Enterprises. My God, man, you must be the richest person in the world right now."

"Then there are your high-level connections. Ike and the Queen we understand, they are an accident of your birth. Ex-President Hoover and the new empress of China are both surprises to us. All we know is that we have approached you all wrong."

Bobby spoke up, "I thought you were a kid who could be bullied; you aren't. If anything, you could do the bullying."

He continued, "Is it possible to start over with you?"

"Yes, it is, I'm not even sure what started us out on the wrong foot, but I would like a good relationship with both of you and the US government."

"Is it too late to ask you to keep all your operations in the US?'

"Yes, it is. Too many commitments have been made. At this point, if you tried to force the company to stay US-based you would have problems with Great Britain, West Germany, and the Empire of China."

"Speaking of China, can you tell us where it is heading?"

"I don't know, but I can tell you this, do not bet against Empress Ping."

Chapter 48

I spent the rest of the afternoon with the Kennedys. Mostly they wanted to hear more about my adventures. Bobby wanted to hear about the life-endangering moments, like riding a bull or jumping into a raging river.

John wanted to know about Bridget Bardot, Anna Romanov, and all the other women I had been seen with. The one name he didn't mention was Nina. He even wanted to know if Sharon Bronson, now Sharon Downing was happy in her marriage. There were rumors about him, and I began to believe them.

After what was a surprisingly pleasant afternoon, I returned to Boston to fly back to Pennsylvania. It was Saturday and the US Open started on Monday, so there was no sense in returning to California.

My parents had rented a house for our use during the week so that was taken care of. The flight crew would unload the Bentley for me, so I had my ride for the week.

By the time we got to Pittsburgh, unloaded, and got to the rental house it was time for bed.

In the morning Harold had set out my workout clothes as he knew I wouldn't skip my run.

I didn't know the area, so I stuck to the main roads. Not that they were divided highways. It was still early enough that the traffic was light.

The cars all had their headlights on, which didn't help as one driver swerved as they came up to me. I don't think they were trying to hit me, but I had to jump for my life.

Fortunately, my jump cleared a small ditch, and I was able to roll when I landed with no injuries. The car sped on down the road. I doubt if they even knew I was there.

Blue lights came on the vehicle behind the one that swerved. The Pennsylvania State Police pulled the driver over. They briefly talked to the driver of the car then backed the tenth of a mile or so back to me.

The officer wanted to know if I was okay or needed a ride to the hospital to be checked out. I told him that I was fine and that I had enough adrenaline to run to the hospital if needed.

He barked laughter at that and returned to the vehicle he had pulled over. As I ran past them, he was performing a field sobriety test on the driver. He had him place a finger on his nose and try to walk a straight line.

It wasn't going to happen. Six o'clock in the morning and this guy was drunk as a skunk. I was lucky to be alive.

I returned to the house and cleaned up for breakfast. The rest of the family wasn't due until later today. I had dispatched my plane to bring them from California.

My parents were still in line for a 707, but they kept selling their place in line. By this time, they would be getting the plane for free. Why should they buy a plane when they could borrow mine whenever they wanted?

It wasn't as though they flew that much. Most of their trips were short day trips on light aircraft. I thought they should investigate the Grumman Gulfstream G1 I had chartered to fly to Augusta.

The course wasn't open for practice rounds today. Those would start tomorrow. Today was for members only. I checked but I had nothing that reciprocated with them.

That left me at loose ends.

I was invited to a cookout for lunch at one of the member's houses and having nothing better to do, I accepted. The food was okay, and I would have had a good time if I hadn't had to spend it fending off his wife.

She was a second wife, what they called a trophy wife. I think she was looking to trade up. I left as soon as I could.

I had driven over, so I had the Bentley. I drove aimlessly around the area. There was a city park, so I pulled in and went for a walk. It was a circle trail and there were two cute girls I kept meeting up with as they walked the other direction from me.

First, we smiled at each other. Then we said, "Hi."

The third time around I asked if I could join them. They were fine with that. We introduced ourselves as Rick, Janet, and Barbara.

They had just graduated from high school and were both planning on attending Pennsylvania State. They wanted to know what grade I was in or was in college.

Not wanting to lie, I told them I was taking some time off from uni. They wanted to know what school, so I told them Oxford. I think they thought Oxford, Ohio. They told me I should think of attending a bigger school as I would have more opportunities.

When asked, I told them I was a junior. I finally got them talking about themselves. Both were working crowd control at the big tournament. They thought it would be fun.

When Barbara mentioned she was looking forward to seeing Ricky Jackson play, Janet stopped dead and looked at me.

"You're him, aren't you?"

"Guilty as charged."

"You dirty rat. You went to school in England at Oxford, not Oxford, Ohio,"

"You jumped to that conclusion. I didn't tell you that."

"No, but you didn't correct me."

"No, I didn't. It was enjoyable just being a guy for a little while."

That led to a long talk about the pitfalls of fame and fortune. I told them about the cookout I had been to earlier and how the wife kept hitting on me.

Janet whooped, "That was my evil stepmother! I can't wait to let her know that I know. Dad would drop her like a hot potato if he found out."

"Won't you tell him?"

"No, he is a jerk. He dropped my mother for a younger woman, so he deserves what he gets. I will blackmail Mommy Dearest for all I can get."

Barbara kept nodding her head, then said, "I bet you could take her for a T-bird convertible."

I suddenly wanted to be anywhere these two were not. Since we were near the parking lot, I told them I had to go get ready for a dinner engagement. Both pouted a little, but I made my escape.

I did have a dinner engagement of sorts. My family was unloading from two limos when I got back to the rental house. We had no specific plans other than eating out.

Dad managed to get a reservation at Hoffstot's Café Monaco which had been recommended by some local people. He had to use my name as a past champion in the US Open to get us in, but it worked.

I had to pay for the seating by having a picture taken with the owner, but it wasn't a big deal. I was used to this part of my life.

The table talk revolved around the flight out. It seemed Mum and Dad took a long nap on the flight and left the kids to their own devices. I wasn't about to question them on their nap.

The boys got a tour of the cockpit. Mary went through the entire aircraft accompanied by the head stewardess. They had a serious discussion on what changes Mary would make when she got her airplane.

No one doubted for a moment that she would get an aircraft of her own. She was using her clothing company's jet, but she wanted one for herself. She could afford it now, but Mum thought that she should graduate from a sixteen-inch bike to a twenty-four-inch first.

By the time she did that, I figured the bar would be raised to getting her driver's license. After that, she was on her own. Of course, in Mary's estimation that would make her too old to fly.

I was asked about my day. I let it all out, almost killed in the morning, hit on by a second wife, and meeting two avaricious girls.

As Dad said, "A normal day then."

That stopped me for a moment, "Yeah, pretty much."

People waited until we had finished eating and were getting up to leave before they approached us for autographs. The whole family was asked to sign various items. I had learned never to sign a t-shirt.

Mary always signed them and couldn't understand why I didn't. I was tempted to mention puppies, but with Mum standing there I didn't have a death wish; besides, I love my innocent, going on thirty Mary.

Eddie was the most excited about signing. I think most people wanted the complete family, so they asked him. It didn't matter as it was his first time.

Let him enjoy it. Writer's cramp would catch up with him sooner or later.

We returned to the rental house for a good night's sleep. Well, that is until our security guards made a racket capturing a couple of papa-rats-eyes trying to sneak into the house.

Mum and I were all for shooting them, but Dad just had them hauled to jail.

Chapter 49

Monday was the official start of the practice rounds. I had already been around the course multiple times, but this was one course you needed every edge you could get.

John had spent hours talking to every caddie he could about the course. He wanted to know things like whether there was a dangerous time of day for any winds. What was the grass like in the morning when wet, how did it dry out, and how long did it take to dry out?

He was trying to get ten years of experience on the course in three days. The more he could get the better. He was also cross-checking every piece of information. Just because someone told him that, it didn't make it so.

While he talked to people, I spent my time on the putting green. I did use the driving range to loosen up, but as they say, drive for show, putt for dough.

When describing Oakmont, on the surface you would think that it was an easy golf course designed for the weekend warrior. No water, no sharp doglegs.

Then when you added that it had over 175 deep bunkers, and oh yes, narrow fairways that weren't continuous to the green, and fast greens that slope away from the player, you have as nasty a golf course as you could imagine.

The greens were so steep and fast that Sam Snead was quoted as saying, "When I mark my ball, the coin even slides downhill."

This course was designed for a person who could hit a long ball accurately. That described my game.

I'm a strong hitter but John's talking to people paid off. At the time of day I would probably be playing as a past champion, there was a good chance there would be a light breeze in my face. That would take twenty to thirty yards off my drive.

So, we decided that I would play it safe no matter what the breeze appeared to be when I got to the tee. Mother Nature is not always your friend, and she could kick up a puff of air just as you complete your swing. I learned that one the hard way.

We also decided to make pars when possible by following Billy Casper's strategy in 1959 by laying up. This was not a course to challenge. If I could break even, I would be happy.

By laying up, I had a better chance of having the ball stick when it landed on the back-sloping fast greens.

Being able to see where the pin is and landing safely was worth the trade-off. Many a player would take extra strokes here. I would only go for it if I were behind and desperate.

The fairways were not a smooth continuous flow to the green. From the tees, you might have to carry two hundred yards of low rough, then have a small landing fairway, followed by more rough grass.

At least you could hit out of the rough between the fairways. The rough at the side of the fairways was ankle-deep and you could lose your ball if it rolled off more than two feet. Hitting it if you found it was a challenge.

This course demanded accuracy on its small narrow fairways.

Between the 4th and 5th fairways was the signature bunker named the Church Pews bunker. If your shot on either of those fairways drifted, you would end up in it.

There was the normal sand, but the sand was interrupted in the center by a row of grassed humps. There were half a dozen or so of these. Since they were lined up parallel to each other they looked like a row of church pews.

That was the type of deviltry built into this course.

All that thought and planning and I ended up 1-over for my Monday round. I had a bird on 2, a bogey on 5, and a bogey on 16.

That evening we had a small get-together at the rental house of Dad's business associates. I had to do the glad hand thing, but it was low-key, and I didn't get buttonholed by any men wanting a loan or investment, or any woman wanting me, for me, read wanting my money.

Tuesday's round was worse than Monday's. I ended up 2-over. I had done the same on everything but 16 where I had a double bogey. Not fun at all. By the muttering I heard from everyone else, I wasn't alone. This course lived up to its reputation of being the most difficult course in North America.

Mum, Dad, and I went to an official event where I was introduced as a past champion. I made the usual "Ah shucks" speech and left as soon as I could. My parents and I had driven separately for this very reason. They wanted to stay to schmooze a little.

Wednesday my golf looked up. I ended up 2-under. I managed to birdie 2, 11, and 18, with a par on 16. The only hole that gave me a problem was a bogey on 5. If I played like that in the tournament I would be on top of the leaderboard.

The night before the tournament I didn't go to any parties. I knew most of the players would be out, many of the amateurs having the time of their lives. The pros would be more circumspect but even some of those were known to get carried away, and I mean that literally.

On Thursday, round 1 started. I felt rather good about not disgracing myself. I also felt that I had a good chance to win. First, the only pressure I had was self-generated. I didn't need the money and I had proved that I could play golf.

With that attitude I was relaxed, that is until I came to the first tee; then every butterfly I ever had decided to get up and fly around my stomach.

I did manage to hit the ball straight and far out. How I don't know. Once I walked off the tee box things settled down. So much for cool, calm, and relaxed. I had to win this sucker for my self-respect.

I was 1-under for the day, 1 stroke behind Gene Littler. There was no drama in my play. I hit the fairways where needed and stuck the ball on the green. My putting held up on the lightning-fast greens.

The Stimpmeter had this course in mind when it was developed in the 1930s. It measured the speed of greens. This course was normally groomed to be a 14.0 on normal play. For tournament play, the greens were groomed to be a 13.5 or even a 13.0. This was killer fast.

Round 2 on Friday saw me tied at 3-under with Bobby Nichols and Arnold Palmer. We were followed by Billy Maxwell at 1-under. My nerves were settling down as I got more familiar with the course. As John put it, stay out of the rough and bunkers and 2-putt everything. It will be a cinch. Sure.

On Saturday we were scheduled for two rounds, so it would be a long day. I was glad I said no to any events while the tournament was on.

I ended the first round 2-under for the course and first place in the tournament. I had a 1-stroke lead over second-place ties Bobby Nichols and Arnold Palmer. I noticed Jack Nicklaus was now tied for fifth place. The Golden Bear was coming on strong.

The final round was the pressure round. Everything else was preparation for it. I followed the strategy that John and I had laid out in the first practice round. It gave me a par and the win.

The trick to the Oakmont was to realize you couldn't beat it, you could only break even.

Jack Nicklaus and Arnold Palmer were tied at 1-under. There would be a playoff on Sunday for the prize money.

Jack ended up winning the first place pro money of $17,500, and Arnold took home $10,500.

What occurred on the course from the crowd was disgraceful. Arnold Palmer was from nearby Latrobe, PA which made him a hometown favorite.

That was no reason for the ten thousand-plus spectators to heckle Jack as he played. He kept his cool. If anything, they were encouraging him. He was even for 18, while Palmer came in a plus-3. Arnold Palmer was always a gentleman and I think the crowd's antics bothered him more than it did Jack Nicklaus.

In the interviews after I accepted the trophy, I was once more asked if I was turning pro. I was a little arrogant when I stated that I couldn't afford the cut in pay to play golf full-time. I wasn't treated well in the golf magazines for my statement, but the businesspeople agreed.

The movie people loved it; any publicity is good publicity in their eyes. I didn't call the Queen or the empress to see what they thought. The Kennedys sent me a congratulatory telegram so I guess they had no problems.

When asked if I was going for a Grand Slam, my only comment was that I had entered those tournaments.

I did attend several parties Saturday night. It was an obligation of the winners. I spent a lot of time talking golf with Jack Nicklaus. I believe that he is a pro who is going to go places.

Sunday was a quiet flight home for the family. John was still talking a mile a minute. I think he was more thrilled with the win than I was.

All in all, an interesting trip.

Chapter 50

We were all exhausted when we got home from the trip. Dad carried Eddie to the car. I carried Mary, and Mum shepherded a dazed Denny. If someone had been able to carry me, I think I would have let them.

There were reporters lined up at the gate, but we didn't stop. I would have to talk to them but not that evening.

Between the golf and parties, it had been a hard week. Dad thought it was worth it from his point of view as he made several good contacts. Mum had twisted some arms for donations to her and Anna Romanov's charity.

I didn't ask, but I bet Mary even sold some dresses or something.

I was slow starting in the morning, but I did get my run in. I rode over to see Sam and John. They were both busy setting up the practice greens for the PGA and British Open tournaments. At least I would have almost a month to get ready for them.

In the meantime, we talked about the arrangements that had to be made for them to get to both courses in the next week. My plane was getting a workout, which was a good thing. An aircraft sitting idle will deteriorate quicker than one in service; at least that is what I had been taught.

Once we had the details hashed out, I headed back to the house for the part of the job I didn't care for, the press interview.

We had a wooden bleacher set up beside the house that we used for these events. When they were being set up, I asked for extra splinters to be installed. I never sat upon them to find out if it had been done.

There was a simple platform about two feet high at the front of the bleachers. A sound system had been brought out earlier and tested so I had to face the music.

Now there was a thought, maybe I could sing to them; that would keep it short. Nah, I'm not that mean.

I was expecting the usual questions about turning pro, going for a Grand Slam, and how did I feel about winning the US Open two times.

I was thrown for a loop when the first question was, "How do you feel about Nina getting back together with the prince?"

I felt like I had been drenched with a bucket of ice water. Then I realized who had asked the question.

"On what authority do you have that they are back together?"

He held up the front page of the latest issue of his rag. It showed Nina and the prince together. I had seen enough of these to know when pictures have been superimposed.

"So, your paper faked a picture. Now you are trying to get me to comment on the fake so you can stir up some controversy. I would like the gentlemen and ladies of the true press to excuse me for using the term paper when talking about this waste of pulpwood."

"People deserve to know how you feel about this," he shouted.

"I feel that you had better leave now."

"I have press credentials. I don't have to leave."

"Have it your way then. This press conference is over. You might want to run as your colleagues don't look happy."

"You just don't want to talk about the bitch!"

I managed to jump from the platform, go up three rows, and throw a right hook into his jaw before he got another word out.

This led to all sorts of complications, I knocked him unconscious, cameras were clicking like crazy, and questions were screamed at me.

Our security got control quickly. Smelling salts brought the jerk around.

He kept shouting, "Call the sheriff. He attacked me."

Dad had been watching from the sidelines.

He commented, "Good punch, Rick, but we have to call the sheriff."

Since we had a lot of witnesses and recordings of what happened, we made everyone stay.

Reporters were begging us to use our phones.

We were lucky in that a deputy sheriff arrived within ten minutes. After a quick talk with Dad, he took control of the situation. He had me go to the gate guardhouse and wait.

Later I was told he had all the reporters sit down on the bleachers. Then he called for backup.

The guy that I had knocked out came around and was screaming that I should be arrested and that he was going to sue.

I didn't hear any of this or I might have busted him again.

Dad told me the deputy had the guy show his ID for his report. Then the deputy came into the guard shack and made a phone call. I could hear his end.

He read off the information on the guy's driver's license. He made notes as something was read off to him.

He hung up the phone and told me, "Normally, Jackson, I would be putting the cuffs on you for assault and battery. You are the luckiest guy I know."

He didn't explain, but he went out and cuffed the guy and put him in the back of the cruiser. I could hear the yells outside, so I had to stick my head out.

I saw him close the backdoor of the cruiser and go up on the stage. To say there was a storm of questions would be to put it mildly.

The deputy held up his hands until it got relatively quiet.

"I just took into custody a man wanted for escaping from prison in Wyoming. We had a BOLO on him. Rick Jackson, a US Deputy Marshal, subdued him and held him for our arrival."

And I thought the newspapers made things up.

All he said was true but had nothing to do with the real story. I saw Dad talking to him while the reporters were going nuts again.

Since I didn't appear to be in trouble now, I walked up to the stage. I just thought they were yelling before. I held up my hands for silence. It took a couple of minutes, but they finally shut up.

"I would like to thank Deputy Fife for his fine work tonight. I thought I recognized the guy but wasn't sure until he kept talking. Then I subdued him. That is my story and I'm sticking to it. I'm also confused about how he got hired in the first place. Are all of you like that?"

This drove them mad. I went into the house. Other sheriff cruisers were showing up. Sheriff Burrell came rolling in. He, Dad, Mum, Deputy Fife, and I sat in the kitchen drinking coffee.

The sheriff told me, "By rights Rick, we should be hauling you away. Lucky for you he had several stories printed with his picture in them. The Wyoming State Police found out he would be out this way and put out the "Be On the Look Out" for him in this area."

"If they hadn't it would have taken us weeks to figure out who he was. You would be out on bail but would have the arrest on your record. As I said, you are lucky. I understand the real reason you punched him was that he called your girlfriend a bitch."

"She's not my girlfriend anymore, but I won't tolerate what he said."

Mum added, "Rick thinks she isn't his girlfriend. The way he has been mooning around, I don't think the issue is settled."

I don't know where she gets her ideas from.

The next day the newspapers and tabloids had a field day with the story. If you could think of a variation, it was printed.

I wondered what Nina would think of all this. I wasn't about to call her and ask. It was a shame we didn't have any mutual friends that would know how the other was doing.

I might be losing my mind.

The news on TV that evening was all about Vietnam, both
North and South. The government in the South had collapsed, and
currently, anarchy reigned. In the north, Ho Chi Minh had a heart
attack and died. That country was in turmoil, but there was no civil
war yet.

China had moved quickly and made an offer to the UN to send
peacekeeping troops to both North and South. Since they were
traditional enemies, that wouldn't play well with the Communists in
the North or whatever they now were in the South. This might even
unite the two.

I was thankful that I wasn't involved in that mess.

That lasted until the phone rang five minutes later. It was
Empress Ping for me.

"Rick, we need your help. We need someone to be a go-between
for North and South Vietnam. We know that if China goes in it will
be an all-out war. We only made the offer as a goodwill gesture to the
UN."

"You are in a unique position. You can sit down with the North
and talk about modernizing Haiphong Harbor. This will put
pressure on the North to have responsible leadership in place and
stop them from invading the disorganized South.

"The Australians with British backing are willing to occupy
Saigon to keep the peace there while you talk about modernizing
their series of ports.

"We hope that the warring factions will call a truce for the
opportunity to upgrade the ports."

"Who do you expect to pay for these ports?"

"China will arrange the loans as we hope to change our
relationship with our past enemies. We now know as the United
States has demonstrated, there is more than one way to influence a
country besides conquering it."

"So, you are going to loan my money to the Vietnamese to gain goodwill for China."

"I knew you were a smart one."

"Okay, if it will stave off two wars, I will try."

"You are a good boy, Rick."

Chapter 51

Hanoi didn't have an airport that would take my 707, so I had to fly into Hong Kong and then take a series of ever-smaller aircraft into Hanoi.

The last was a Cessna.

I was given a cool welcome into the country. They were not thrilled with me being an American or my British and Chinese connections.

What they were interested in was my money. So, what else is new?

I rode in a limo circa 1930. It had seen hard use. This was a poor country if this was the best the government could do; that, or they were sending me a message. From the looks of the few other vehicles on the road, I'm voting poor.

The hotel looked like it had been built by the French at the turn of the century. It looked the same as it did then. It would have helped if it had been maintained.

The conference room had a round table. I was told by my interpreter who had joined me in Hong Kong that this was because the various functionaries present couldn't agree on who would be the new leader of North Vietnam.

They were the most circumspect group I have ever dealt with. Nothing was said straight out because no one wanted to be the one to open the topic as they would be begging for Chinese help.

I decided that I had to break this log jam. Through my interpreter, I started.

"I have come to North Vietnam to ask for your help."

Now I was the beggar. Since I was a Westerner, I had no face to lose.

"My company is upgrading the ports of this region of Asia. Haiphong Harbor is one of those that we need in our trade network."

This was a bare-faced lie.

"I have arranged financing from the Chinese to do this. I would think that your country would be pleased to take the Chinese money, using your old enemy's money to attack them economically."

This phrase had been given to me by the empress's staff. The key idea here was, "old enemy," and "attack." This implied that China was no longer an enemy as in warfare, but if they wanted to have an economic war, game on.

This played to the two countries' history and changed the playing field.

"I have a request of my own that I would add. No war with the South. I need peace there so I can upgrade Saigon's Harbors. They will not compete with you as you are placed to ship to Japan, the Philippines, and China. They have the inferior markets of Australia, New Zealand, and Indonesia."

I had conveniently forgotten about India. Maybe I should go into bridge sales. This all led to a circular conversation until I realized that I had brought out nothing for their rice bowls. This was a polite way of saying bribes. How could I forget? I was in Asia.

"I will need to hire most of you as consultants to help my project along. I'm offering ten thousand dollars a year as a starting salary."

This was a bloody fortune to them.

No one immediately took me up on my offer. I didn't expect that. I did get a promise to set up a study group when the new leadership emerged. In other words, they wanted to fight it out to see who would run the country, then the winner would try to extract as much as they could from me.

That worked, while concentrating internally there would be no attack on the South. Also, with the prospect of millions from the

Chinese, they would be more interested in getting their differences settled peacefully rather than dying for the privilege of running this poor country.

Of course, I was later proved wrong. Some people would rather be the large frog in a small pond rather than a rich frog in a large pond. I no sooner left them to fly to Saigon than fighting broke out.

It came out in favor of a rich frog in a large pond, so it ended well from my point of view.

In the South, it was quite different. The Australian Army had joint exercises going with the South Vietnamese Army, so they were able to lockdown Saigon.

Arriving there was remarkably like my arrival in the North. I was bundled into a 1940s model Cadillac, a distinct improvement over my northern ride.

I was taken to a French-built hotel which looked better than the one up north, but not that much better.

Three groups were sitting at a rectangular table. I had an end to myself. At the other end was a man who I guessed was a schoolteacher. He was the representative of one of the factions. He was alone.

Oh, the two long sides of the table were the other factions, each on their side.

While one at the short end looked reputable, the others didn't. One group was dressed in a suit and tie, but they looked like they belonged in a gangster movie as the bad guys.

The others looked like highway bandits. None dressed alike. Their clothes were dirty and stained. I imagine the odor in the room emanated from them.

Standing behind me were the American ambassador and the Australian commander.

I made an opening statement through my interpreter that I was there to see if they could form a government that I could negotiate modernizing their port facilities with.

The American ambassador interjected, "There will have to be free and open elections first."

He no sooner got that out than one of the bandit types pulled a pistol and shot the leader in the business suit group.

I dove for the floor under the table as gunfire erupted around the room. When the gunfire ceased, with my weapon in hand, I crawled out from under the Australian commander and the American ambassador.

The commander was fine. The ambassador had taken a wound to his buttock as that was the last portion of him to go down.

The room was a shamble. There were dead and dying on both sides of the table. It didn't look like any of them survived.

At the other end of the table, the schoolteacher stood up. I looked around the room.

"It looks like the election has been held, and this gentleman is the winner."

It wasn't that simple. Both shot-up groups had other leaders who hadn't attended. The Australians sent messages to those who hadn't attended asking them to take the fallen leader's places.

As they showed up, they were taken into custody. Two of the major factions were now missing the top two layers of their command.

The guy who looked like a schoolteacher had been a schoolteacher. Trần Văn Hương had resisted both the French and the Communists who overthrew them. He was considered a moderate and was probably as good of a leader as we would get.

He and I adjourned to a separate office as the bodies were cleared under the Australian commander's direction. The American ambassador was carried out to a car where he was to be taken back to the embassy to be treated by an American doctor.

From the way the bullet skimmed his pants, I didn't think it went deep. The wound would be painful, and he wouldn't be able to sit. It would be nothing compared to the jokes and nicknames he would carry for the rest of his career. Or should I say the rest of his rear?

I decided to be blunt with Trần.

"China does not want war in Vietnam at this time. Not because they care about Vietnam. It is because a war here might bring the Americans in on the South's side.

"The Soviets want that to happen and are supporting the North because it will leave China in the middle.

"China has enough problems with its leadership currently. Empress Ping has asked me to help buy peace within the North and South, and between them. Once the Chinese leadership issues are settled, she doesn't care if this country tears itself up.

"I do because ultimately it is my money that is at risk in the development of your ports and even the aid money that will be available from China comes from me.

"What do we have to do to bring peace to South Vietnam without killing all the other faction's members?"

"Pay the army. The government is always behind in paying its soldiers. If you pay them, the army will be yours. I'm not talking about anyone above the level of colonel. They are all thieves. It is the junior officers and soldiers who are always hungry.

"This causes them to take from the villages. Pay them, and you will bring peace to the country."

"How much would this cost me every week?"

"The average pay for all ranks is ten American dollars a month. There are 100,000 soldiers."

"So, it would be a million dollars a month?"

"Yes."

"How would we ensure that the money goes to the ranks?"

"We would ask the Australians to distribute it."

We spent the next week ironing out details. Newly appointed President Trần announced that soldiers would be paid in American dollars and that they would receive two months back pay even though his government hadn't incurred the debt.

He had the entire South Vietnamese general staff arrested and their home and bank accounts seized. It netted enough to make the back pay payments.

I contacted my American bank and had pallets of one, five, ten, and twenty-dollar bills flown in.

Chapter 52

The Australians flew in a cadre of ranking officers to temporarily lead the South Vietnamese Army. I wondered how temporary it would be. That wasn't my worry. My worry was not to be identified as the leader of the army.

I was paying them and doing so better than anyone before me. If I wanted to take over the country I probably could. That was the last thing I needed. I would probably be assassinated the first week.

So, any suggestions I had were made through Trần, the civil authority to the army command. My thoughts were basic. Build infrastructure and train the army to be real soldiers.

A school system was needed. The French would have been ideal as they had set up the original system and it had worked. There was no way that the French would ever be invited back.

The British had a lot of experience in setting up colonial systems, so I suggested to Trần that he contact the British Ministry of Education for help on that front. He did and received an enthusiastic reception. It might have been because I suggested that he use the palace as an intermediary.

They needed several types of police forces. There were ones in place, but they were so corrupt they had to be disbanded and started over.

For their equivalent of the FBI, I suggested he go with either the FBI or MI5. For city police, I recommended the London police or NYPD. For sheriff's departments in the rural areas, I only knew George Burrell, so I recommended him.

Trần went with the MI5, the London police, and George.

To rebuild roads and bridges I had no idea who to contact. In a meeting that the American ambassador stood in on, he suggested South Vietnam put it out to bid. That worked well. The bids were on roads, sewage plants, clean water systems, and a telephone system.

Trân had his new Minister of Health, a doctor whose name I could never remember, contact the World Health Organization to do a survey to recommend what was needed to have a true healthcare system.

At the same time, they advertised internationally for doctors to come to South Vietnam to man government-run clinics. The same offer was made for nurses. The pay was good enough that they attracted a well-trained group. New doctors could earn enough in two years to start their practices.

All these efforts were publicized in the papers and on the radio. Trân took to making a weekly radio broadcast like FDR's fireside chats. The public loved him. They could see the physical results of his actions. He was working for them.

This all occurred over several months and was not as easy as I may have portrayed it. Trân and I would never be friends. The age and cultural differences ensured that. But we were colleagues in rebuilding a nation.

We gained a deep and abiding respect for each other. Once he realized that I expected nothing from South Vietnam, he was willing to listen and work with me.

I did truly little, almost none, of the real work. It was not all sweetness and light. The corruption in the country ran deep and had to be rooted out.

There were trials, but not like American trials, long technical affairs. This was more like ninety days, next case. Except it was more likely to be up against the wall, next case.

I had thought I was getting cynical. After this experience, I knew that I was still a babe in the woods.

Week three I received a summons. There was no other way to put it. Queen Elizabeth and Empress Ping had arranged to meet in Hong Kong, and I was to be present.

Flying to Hong Kong was my first chance to clear my head and try to process what had occurred in the last few weeks. I had been sent to the Vietnams to use my company's influence to build ports.

The ports were not the real objective. The real objective was to develop a set of conditions that would prevent a war between the North and South.

Not that the North and South particularly wanted a war. The Soviets were pushing the North into it, knowing that the United States would be forced into an unwinnable land war in Asia.

The Americans seemed to be oblivious to this fact and were taking no actions other than trying to support the previous governments which by their very nature were doomed to failure.

China was trying to prevent the war because they didn't want external distractions occurring as they settled their internal issues, the external distractions being the Soviets gaining more influence in the region while they concentrated on creating stability in China.

I didn't even want to think about what was going on in China. There would be no guilty finding in a trial, up against the wall. It would be up against the wall.

I thought about North Vietnam. All I had done there was broker a deal for peace in exchange for modernizing their harbor.

They would remain a communist government under the new leaders, however, that might shake out. All I could hope was that between the updated harbor and a stronger South Vietnamese Army, war wouldn't occur.

I wondered if the North's leaders were Communists or were frustrated capitalists like the Chinese. Maybe if they got a taste of the modern world and trade, they would shift away from the Communist Party's hardline and Soviet influence.

It certainly wasn't going to work out in the short term.

In Hong Kong, I was met at the airport and taken to the Peninsula Hotel to freshen up. My 707 with Harold and my clothes on board caught up with me so I was able to put on a good suit and tie. If I was meeting with a queen and an empress, I had better dress the part.

Another Rolls Royce ride and I was at Government House. The security was tight and obvious. In your face obvious.

I had to show my passport, my British diplomatic one, to get in. That was even after my name was found on the list.

I was escorted into the august presence of the royal and imperial ladies. Whoever said men held all the power had never met these two. Between them, they ruled most of the world's population. Granted, the Queen was head of a constitutional monarchy, but recent events had shown she had more power than they thought she did.

A good part of that was my fault. Parliament held sway over the Queen because they controlled the purse. I had been acting as Her Royal Majesty's purse for some time now.

Empress Ping was now for all purposes a god in China. She controlled everything.

With these thoughts in mind, I went to bended knee to the two ladies.

"Oh, Richard, give it up. You have earned the right to give a minor bow of the head," spoke Elizabeth.

Empress Ping came back with, "I don't know, I kind of like the bended knee; maybe we could have him do both?"

"Hmm, that is a possibility, or maybe we could have him crawl in on his belly."

You know that wonderful moment when you realize you have been had? This was mine.

"Have Your Whatever You Want to be Called Today summoned me for a reason other than to mock me?"

"Richard, mocking can be fun. There are so few times we can do that without creating an incident."

"Well then, mock away."

"We have a better idea," said Elizabeth.

Empress Ping continued, "You have done wonderful things for both our countries in the last few months. We both tried to award you with a dukedom. You refused us both. Now we will make you an offer that you can't refuse."

Why did I picture a decapitated horse's head in my bed? They waited for me to ask what it was, but I wasn't going to give them that pleasure.

Queen Elizabeth turned to the empress, "You win. I thought he would cave and ask. Here is your shilling."

She handed a coin over!

"Come with us."

We went into a much larger audience room left over from the heyday of the British Empire.

There was a crowd of people waiting, including my whole family.

Queen Elizabeth started it, "Richard Edward Jackson, I name you Duke of Hong Kong. It has neither land nor income attached, just the honor of the title and responsibility for the well-being of the people of Hong Kong."

The empress had her turn, "Richard Edward Jackson, I name you Duke of Hong Kong, it has neither land nor income attached, just the honor and the title and responsibility for the well-being of the people of Hong Kong.

"While at this time Hong Kong is under British rule, on July 1st, 1997, it will be turned over to China. Part of your responsibility will be to see that the turnover is such that the people of Hong Kong do not suffer."

Queen Elizabeth said, "Kneel, Duke Richard of Hong Kong."

I did and she tapped me on both shoulders with a sword that seemingly appeared from nowhere. She then handed the sword to the empress who did the same.

There was great applause in the background.

I bowed a full and deep bow to both ladies and backed out of the room. I was so proud I didn't turn and run like hell.

Mum, Dad, and my siblings joined me. They were excited for me; they knew what was happening. There were official photographers there to capture the event but thank goodness, no press.

Mum said, "There is one other person who would like to congratulate you."

She turned and a young lady was standing there. She looked worn, underweight, pale, and scared.

I noted all these in a heartbeat and must have teleported to her because she was in my arms.

It was Nina.

Finished for now.

Back Matter

The Richard Jackson Saga will continue in Book 12 Escape From Siberia.[1]

Visit my author page at enelsonauthor.com[2]

For information on hiring Janet E. Rupert to edit your fiction project, email:

janeteditorrupert@gmail.com

---

1. https://www.amazon.com/gp/product/B0979KN2WM
2. https://www.enelsonauthor.com/

Other books by Ed Nelson

The Richard Jackson Saga
Book 1 The Beginning
Book 2 Schooldays
Book 3 Hollywood
Book 4 In the Movies
Book 5 Star to Deckhand
Book 6 Surfing Dude
Book 7 Third Time is a Charm
Book 8 Oxford University
Book 9 Cold War
Book 10 Taking Care of Business
Book 11 Interesting Times
Book 12 Escape from Siberia
Book 13 Regicide
Book 14 What's Under, Down Under?
Book 15 The Lunar Kingdom
Book 16 First Steps
In the Richard Jackson World
Mary, Mary
Stand-Alone Story

Ever and Always

Cast in Time Series
Book 1: Baron
Book 2: Baron of the Middle Counties
Book 3: Count
Book 4: Earl
Book 5: Earl of the Marches